DEBAUCHED

Jennifer Dawson

Praise for Jennifer Dawson & The Undone Series

USA TODAY calls *Crave* a must-read romance

"*Crave* gets the balance between lust filled scenes and a meaningful plot just right. Neither takes from the other and together they just add up to a very satisfying and emotional read." —Between My Lines

"If you love Foster, Kaye and Dawson's *Something New* series you'll love *Crave* and the Undone series." —Caffeinated Book Reviewer.

"Every character in this book (*Sinful*) is amazingly written. " —Bookish Bevil

"You know why I love this author? She takes something absolutely mundane like a "Best Friend's Sister" romance and turns it into a masterpiece." —For the Love of Fictional Worlds

"*Crave* by Jennifer Dawson is a darkly erotic and deeply moving romance."-—Romance Novel News

"Jennifer Dawson's *Sinful* has amazing scenes that get my heart beating and calls for a cold shower, but the love story that is evolving between Leo and Jillian is amazing."—Courting Fiction

Step into *Debauched*
An Undone Novel

One night in a moment of sheer madness I confessed my secrets to him.

All my life I've been pretending. Pretending to be the woman I thought I should be instead of the woman I really am. I've been faking it and I am good. No one has ever guessed. Except him. He just looked at me and knew.

Chad Fellows is not the man I want, but he's fast becoming the man I need.

One night in a moment of sheer madness I held her in my arms and let her cry.

I did the right thing, letting her walk away, no matter how much she calls to the part of me that wants to rescue her. We are nothing alike, and she's a mess of complications in a life I'm trying to keep simple. But then I touched her and made her tremble and now I can't turn away.

Ruby Stiles is not the woman I want, but she's fast becoming the woman I need.

Other Books by Jennifer Dawson

Something New Series

Take A Chance on Me
The Winner Takes It All
The Name of the Game
As Good as New
She's My Kind of Girl (Coming September, 27th, 2016)

Undone Series

Crave
Sinful
Unraveled
Debauched

1.

Ruby

He's the first person I look for as I walk into the crowded room.

I don't want it to be true, but it is.

Chad Fellows. The cute, nice guy I'd deemed harmless and not my type when I first met him has turned into my biggest nightmare. And he's *still* not my type. At all.

I just can't stop thinking about him.

Chad is a responsible, employed IT manager, a stark contrast to my normal guy. I like my men with an edge. Artistic rocker types, with songs running through their heads, mattresses on their floor, and Peter Pan complexes.

Walking disasters are an acquired taste.

Since I was fifteen years old my preference has not deviated, much to my family's and friends' disgust, but that all changed eight weeks ago on Valentine's Day at our friend Brandon Townsend III's new club The Lair. Instinct warned me not to go that night, but I hadn't listened and now my perception of Chad had shifted around me and I'm not happy about it.

Thankfully, I haven't seen him since.

I don't want to see him tonight.

Only, I can't stop searching the crowded room for him.

While I've thought of him plenty, I've successfully avoided him since that night, when I'd made such a fool of myself. When I'd somehow ended up crying helplessly on his shoulder, distraught and emotional. When I'd let him see me as I never let anyone see me, vulnerable and lost. I cringe, remembering how I'd turned my face up to his, silently pleading to lose myself in him so I could avoid all that was wrong with me. I hadn't offered outright, but it had hung there in the air between us.

He'd sent me home in a cab. Untouched. Except for the imprint of his palm on my back.

The next morning I'd woken up hung over, humiliated, and thankful.

If I could avoid the evening's celebration I would, but I can't. It's my best friend Layla's engagement party. I'm her maid of honor. I'm duty bound, and I love Layla so much I wouldn't miss it for the world. She's been through hell and back and I will do anything in my power to help her build a road to happiness. I'm also compelled to make up for the petty jealousy I experienced, and kept hidden from her, on Valentine's night that started this whole mess.

My hope is Chad won't be here, but deep down I know that's a long shot. He'll be here. And my avoidance will be over.

After that disastrous night, the next day, he'd contacted me to make sure I was okay. Because that's the kind of man he is. There'd been something in the air, crackling over the line that hadn't been there in all the times I'd talked to him before. Something I didn't want to acknowledge. So I'd been polite, appreciative, but made it clear I didn't want him to contact me again.

He hadn't.

Supposedly he's a dominant. A trait that's become familiar to me watching Layla and her husband-to-be over the last year, and was on full display at the club that night. A trait I don't like but somehow can't stop being fascinated by. But there's not one thing bossy about Chad. In fact, he's exceedingly respectful of my wishes.

I can't figure out if I'm happy or disappointed about that.

All I want is for him to stop occupying my thoughts.

So I'd done the only thing I could think of and brought a date to the party. I'm hoping it ends my strange connection to Chad. Which is probably one-sided anyway. Since guys like him are supposed to go after what they want, and he's been radio silent.

I glance at my date standing next to me. Two months ago Tommy was my dream guy—wait—scratch that. He *is* my dream guy. A dark, scraggly haired man-child with moody chocolate eyes, a pouty mouth, and slim hips that move like the devil when he plays guitar. I was pining for him something fierce before but couldn't snag his attention.

In true bad-boy fashion, he'd asked me out once my infatuation moved elsewhere. We'd gone out a couple of times, usually after one of his shows where I've had a few drinks to convince myself I want him. After all, he's exactly my type. But I find I'm not able to get lost in the rocker boy angst of him like I normally would. I haven't slept with him—in fact, I've kind of avoided physical contact with him—and I have excuses for why that is.

Trying to believe it has nothing to do with my last conversation with Chad where I'd confessed the dirty little secrets I'd never planned on sharing with anyone.

Which is why I had to bring Tommy with me.

I need the illusion that I've forgotten all about what happened between Chad and me. That I've moved on. That I never told him anything important and private.

I'm good at illusion. It's my specialty. I'm convinced if I can make it through this night, my smile in place, my date by my side, it will be like Valentine's never happened.

Once he's out of my head, I can get back to the life where I belong. Singing in my bluesy club, hanging out with unemployed musicians, and making art for my favorite bands. Going to my day job to grind out a living before I can go slip into the night and get lost in lyrics and melodies.

Eventually I'll forget Chad knows things about me that nobody else does.

Tommy puts his hand on my hip, encased in a black pencil skirt that matches my black fitted top, with tiny white skulls where polka dots should be. I look very retro-glam. My dark hair is shiny and sleek, curling over my shoulders like Lauren Bacall. My eye makeup is a smoky cat eye that plays up the bright blue of my eyes. I've also slicked my lips with a crimson gloss that highlights my already naturally red lips.

I look good. Evidenced by the hungry appreciation in Tommy's gaze, but all I care about is it provides me with much needed armor against the man I don't want to see.

My best friend, and bride-to-be, Layla comes running over to me, a huge smile on her beautiful face. "You're finally here."

I hug her and lean back, giving her a long once over, before I whistle. "You look stunning."

She does. She's beaming with happiness, her dark chestnut hair a tumble around her shoulders, her blue eyes brilliant. She's wearing a white V-neck dress that ends demurely at her knees but hugs every one of her curves. She looks beautiful, sophisticated, and sexy.

"Thank you," she says, kissing me on the cheek. "So do you."

After a terrible tragedy that almost killed her, she's made her way back to life and has never been happier. I can't begrudge her that. Even if I experience unwelcome stabs of envy over the love she shares with her fiancé. Those are my problems, not hers. It's not her fault that, unlike me, she has excellent taste in men.

Her future husband, homicide detective Michael Banks slides up next to her, putting his big hand on her hip. Like Layla he's dark haired, but with unusual hazel eyes that stare right into you and make you want to fidget. He's also six-five and stunningly masculine. The kind of guy you can't help but look at on the street.

Together they make quite the pair.

Michael kisses me on the cheek and says, "Glad you could make it."

I beam at him, so wide my cheeks ache. "I wouldn't miss it. I'm the maid of honor."

"That you are," he says before holding out his hand to my date.

I quickly make introductions. "This is Tommy."

Tommy shakes Michael's hand. "Thanks for having me."

At least he's polite.

Michael nods. "Thanks for coming."

"Congrats." Tommy shakes Layla's hand too and nods at her appreciatively. "Nice job, man."

Never mind. I cringe and immediately hate him.

Layla gives me a little grimace. She's not a fan of my choice in men.

Michael's palm slides possessively over Layla's hip and he smiles. "I'm not sure I can take credit for her genetics."

Tommy laughs. "Killer place you've got here."

"It's my parents." Michael juts his head toward where the crowd is already growing. "Can we get you something to drink?"

"You got any Jack?" Tommy asks, rubbing his ridiculously flat stomach.

Why did I think this was a good idea? Tommy seems like a child in this crowd. Which, in fairness, he kind of is. Something that wouldn't have bothered me before, but now grates across my nerves like sandpaper. Before I would have liked that about him. It would have made him special in some twisted way.

At thirty-one, I've always been a free spirit and have no desire to settle down. I lived that life growing up and I can't go back. I'm a minister's daughter, raised in a loving but traditional family, that has never walked the wild side a day in their lives. Unlike my brother and sister who seemed to thrive in that environment, I was stifled by all that propriety. Every time I was required to go to another church event, shaking hands and smiling in my perfect preacher's daughter dress, I would swear this would never become me.

I left the second I had a chance and have never looked back. I want to be free. Free of mortgages and responsibilities and five-year plans. I don't want to change. But it seems like I am, despite my best intentions.

Layla grabs my wrist. "You guys go on, we'll be there soon."

Michael squeezes her hip, kisses her lips and murmurs something in Layla's ear that has her sucking in a little breath.

Michael is also of the dominant persuasion, as is his best friend and future brother-in-law, Leo Santoro, and their other friend, Brandon Townsend III. A persuasion I knew very little about before Layla started dating Michael and now can't seem to get away from.

I've been watching them for months. The way they all prowl around their women, possessive and commanding. I know that's what Layla and Jillian, Leo's fiancée, want, but I can't see the appeal. Which is yet another reason to stay away from Chad.

The two men walk away. Tommy looks like a stiff wind will blow him over he's so slight. Like a boy next to Michael's man.

Layla grins at me. "So that's the guy, right? The one you've been after?"

Had it only been two months since I was desperate for Tommy's attention?

A waiter passed with a tray of Champagne, and Layla stops him and grabs us two glasses.

I take a sip. "That's the one."

"He's cute." She lies.

While he's not her type, he *is* cute and girls go crazy for him. If you like musicians, Tommy's a catch. But I can't quite get excited about him anymore.

Unable to help myself I glance around the room but don't spot *him*.

I shrug. "He plays a mean bass."

"As long as he treats you the way you deserve, I'm happy." Layla waves at someone and takes a drink. "It's going to get crazy in a few, and I'm going to have to socialize, but I wanted to see how you were. I feel like we haven't talked since I got engaged."

We hadn't. I blame myself. She's been busy with her engagement but she's still made time to call me. I've been avoiding her.

I'm jealous, of what I'm not sure, because I don't want to get married and settle down, but it's been eating away at me. I hate myself for it and don't want her ever to guess while I'm desperately figuring out how to stop the feeling.

I bite my lip. "I'm sorry. It's my fault."

Layla's brow furrows. "You don't have to be sorry, but you seem like something is bothering you, and I don't know why you won't talk to me."

I don't want to bother her with my petty problems and hang-ups. Layla has been through so much and she's finally happy, I'm not willing to ruin that. I put on a bright smile. "I'm fine. I promise. Don't worry about me. You just concentrate on being happy, okay?"

Layla's blue eyes narrow on me and her suspicion is etched in the corners of her mouth. "Can we do dinner next week? Just the two of us?"

"Yes, let's do that." I hug her, distracting her away from studying my expression. "All we need is some girl time to cut through the crazy."

She laughs. "Probably. And it is crazy. So dinner."

"Dinner."

She steps back and squeezes my hand, before winking at me. "And, girl, you look hot as hell."

I laugh and shake my head. "Thanks."

"I have no idea how you pull off that look, but it's envy worthy."

I know she means it. I even know it's true. I'm just having a hard time feeling it right now. Somewhere along the way I have lost my mojo, and I don't know how to get it back.

So I fake it, like I fake everything else.

Layla sighs. "Duty calls. My future mother-in-law is signaling."

I give her a quick hug. "Go. We'll catch up later."

She takes off, leaving me alone.

And that's when I see him.

He's in the back corner of the room talking to Ashley, a friend we sometimes hang out with, who's been after him since the second she laid eyes on him. Ashley is everything I'm not. Blonde, cute, sexy, and a huge flirt. She adores men. But more important, she adores the chase.

She'd been chasing a guy named Trevor since college. Desperately in love with him, she'd let him use her for casual hookups whenever he'd been in the mood for easy sex. This summer, a week after Ashley went home with Trevor and convinced herself this was going to be the time she snared him for good, he'd met a "dancer", fallen instantly in love, and kicked Ashley to the curb forever.

Devastated, Ashley has been on the prowl for a replacement ever since, and every time she sees Chad she becomes like a dog in heat. Throwing herself at him mercilessly. Before Valentine's Day it had amused me. Now it doesn't.

Over her head, our eyes lock.

I can't really tell you what it is about Chad Fellows that has captured my undivided attention when he's everything I never wanted in a man. Yes, he's a good guy. He's stable, dependable, and compassionate. He's also gorgeous, if you like the all-American type, with high cheekbones, messy brown hair and direct blue eyes. He's tall and has a great body that defies his computer-geek status.

Sounds like a dream guy, right? He is.

He's just not *my* dream guy, including the fact that he's into the whole domination thing. A *thing* I definitely don't want anything to do with.

Gaze still intent on mine, he takes a drink out of a rocks

glass. He slowly lowers the beverage and even from across the room I can feel his slow once over as he takes me in.

Goose bumps break out over my skin. The hair along my neck prickles and a tingle races over my spine as the air crackles, connecting us from across the room.

As much as he's not my type, I'm not his either. Girls like Ashley are his type. But since Valentine's night there's something between us.

Something I need to break.

At that moment Tommy slides up next to me. "Hey, babe."

I want to kill him. Bash him over the head with his stupid guitar.

Chad cocks a brow then returns his attention to Ashley.

I've been dismissed. I grit my teeth. Well, good.

2.

Chad

I keep my eye on Ruby Stiles, even though I want to forget
that night where I'd held her in my arms while she cried. I have
a lot going on right now, work's crazy, I just got a promotion
and my competition for the job now works for, and hates, me.
I've got building development going on—a little side project I
started with one of my friends—that's now taken on a life of
its own. I'm putting everything I have into business right now
and Ruby is not something I want to distract me.

It's why I didn't press after I called her the day after
Valentine's and she gave me the brush off, even though I
wanted to. I'd hung up the phone and sighed in relief, because
when I'd called I'd been half afraid she'd want to follow up on
what had gone down between us the night before. Most guys
in my situation wouldn't have called Ruby at all, but I'm
unfailingly responsible, especially when it comes to women. I'd
done the right thing, ensured she was okay, and asked if she

needed to talk. She'd said no.

Responsibility absolved. That should have been the end of it.

Only, I haven't been able to get her out of my mind since that night. That strange, perception-altering night, where nothing played out as I'd been expecting. Before then, I'd always viewed Layla Hunter's best friend as a pretty rocker girl with whom I have nothing in common. She's beautiful and has a body that won't quit, but she didn't interest me that way I need a woman to interest me.

Then Valentine's happened and—I don't know— something changed between us.

I can still feel her quivering, trembling body in my arms. The stain of tears on her cheeks as she looked up at me with her blue, watery, desperate gaze. Still remember the sound of her voice as she spilled her secrets.

She is nothing I need in my life right now. And even though I don't want anything to do with the complications she presents, I can't take my eyes off her.

As Ashley drones on and on about a subject I can't even remember, I watch Ruby and that ridiculous excuse for a man she brought with her tonight. She might not be my type, but she looks gorgeous. Her code of dress seems to vacillate from retro rocker to pinup girl with an edge. Like a rebel Snow White.

She pulls it off very, very well.

Tonight she's decked out in an outfit right out of the nineteen forties, that slim-fitted skirt and black-and-white top hugging every curve to perfection. She's curled her shiny black, shoulder-length hair into sleek waves and even from across the room I can see the brilliance in her blue eyes. And then there's her mouth, full and ruby red, matching her name.

She looks different from every other woman in the room, and when her date slides a hand over her hip, I experience an inappropriate surge of possession.

As soon as he settles in next to her she darts a nervous glance in my direction. Our eyes lock, the air pulses, and she jerks her attention away from me. Right then I know her date is about me. That she's brought him as a diversion.

"So what do you think?" Ashley says, ripping me from my thoughts.

I stare down at the cute little blonde who, in theory, is exactly what I need right now. She's lush, pretty, and has a set of tits I could spend hours torturing. Best of all she's not mentally taxing. I'm pretty sure she's been discussing makeup for at least thirty minutes. She's the kind of girl you take to dinner and don't have to say a word because she talks a mile a minute.

I've clearly missed some sort of question. I give her my most winning smile. "I'm sorry, what did you ask?" I raise my hand to my ear and say in a too loud tone, "It's kind of loud in here."

She grins up at me, her expression brilliant and tinged around the very edges with desperateness. I've heard all about her trials and tribulations with the guy she used to hook up with. She's on the rebound and I'm her prey.

She hasn't seemed to cue into the fact that I'm not interested. What Ashley wants, I have no interest in giving her, and the truth is, I feel bad for her. She's been screwed over enough. Only I don't know her well enough to give her a much-needed lecture about men who don't treat her the way she deserves.

Her lashes flutter and bat up at me in an exaggerated way. "I said I have tickets to the Bulls from work and I was wondering if you wanted to go with me."

Oh hell. Now I'm going to have to hurt her feelings and I really don't want to do that. But my lack of attention is not getting through to her, so I'm forced to be direct. I put my hand on her arm and her skin is cold. "Thank you, that's very sweet, but I'm going to have to pass."

Her expression falls but I trudge on. Ashley doesn't realize this, but I'm doing her a favor by not wasting her time, and squashing any hope she might have for us. I want to give her the work excuse, but based off her history, that won't cut it.

I rub my hand over her arm and smile. "I'm not an option for you, Ashley. I'm sorry about that, but you deserve a guy that is going to give you the time and energy you deserve, and I'm not that guy."

She jerks a little under my touch. Her face twists for a moment before it surges with hope.

I repress my sigh.

She puts her hand on my waist and I immediately drop my hand from her. She shakes her head and laughs a little. "That's cute. But you've misunderstood; I'm not looking for anything serious. I'm not looking for commitment. I'm looking for fun. That's all."

All bullshit, but I'm more than happy to let her save face. She's looking for the loophole most guys would fall into, but I'm not that easily manipulated. Most women confuse good guy with push over, thinking that I am not wise to their games, but that couldn't be farther from the truth. I shrug. "I apologize if I misunderstood. But I'm not available."

Her attention drops to my mouth, turning hungry. Annoyed, I glance over her head and see Ruby talking to Jillian Banks and Leo Santoro, she laughs at something they say and then her gaze catches mine.

She frowns, and then it disappears almost as though she's caught herself. Which she probably has. I've noticed that about her. She filters everything. Reveals a glimpse of her true emotions before covering it up with what she believes she should feel.

"What about for fucking? Are you available for that?" Ashley's words rip me back to her. She's wearing a seductive expression and her hand has curled into the waistband of my pants. "We could go upstairs right now and I could blow your mind."

I resist the urge to express my exasperation with her. In her defense, this approach would work on ninety-eight percent of guys, so it's her misfortune I fall into the two percent. I contemplate my options. I could go stern, but she'd probably like that. I could continue being nice but assertive, but that doesn't seem to be working. I run through a couple other choices but decide on the truth.

I wrap my fingers around her wrist and forcibly pull her off me. Then I look deep into her eyes and say with complete sincerity. "I am not an option for you. We are friends and that's where you and I will stay."

Her expression falls again and her chin quivers the tiniest bit.

While I'm sympathetic, I don't relent. I release her hand and reach up to tuck a lock of hair behind her ear. "You've been hurt, Ashley. I'm sorry about that. But as a friend, let me tell you, this isn't the way to mend your broken heart. A man won't fix what's broken inside you. You have to do that all on your own."

Over her head I see Ruby climb the steps leading to the second floor.

I smile at Ashley. "I wish you luck. You deserve to be happy and I hope you find it. But I'm not your guy."

Her eyes brighten. "Okay."

I chuck Ashley under the chin. "You okay?"

She nods and points to a group of girls hovering around the kitchen island. "I should get back to my friends."

I smile at her. "Sounds like a good plan."

Ashley walks away, leaving me alone. I drain the rest of my drink and narrow my eyes on the stairs.

The last thing I should do is go upstairs.

I put my drink down on a small bar table.

But I'm going anyway.

Ruby

I am not jealous.

I stare at my reflection in the mirror in the upstairs bathroom of Michael's parents' house and repeat the words out loud. "I am not jealous."

I don't believe me.

There's a knot in the pit of my stomach that's been there ever since Chad's hand gripped Ashley's arm. A knot that grew when Ashley clung to the waistband of his pants and stared up at him in that way she had.

I was across the room, I couldn't hear what transpired, but I know Ashley. She's been using the same expression to proposition guys since college.

She's not the kind of girl men say no to when sex is on the table.

I swallow hard and flip on the faucet, letting the cool water trickle over my hot skin.

All right then, I've solved my problem.

I brought a date that will put Chad off any ideas my drunken confessions and clutching meant anything.

He followed it up by hooking up with Ashley.

Things can get back to normal now. We can go back to being friends and it will be like that whole night never happened.

Eventually I'll forget he knows my secrets.

I turn off the water and dry my hands before touching my fingertips to my cheeks to cool my skin.

I close my eyes.

Why did I tell him my secrets? I'm not like that. In fact, I play things too close to the chest. So why did I tell him something I have never told a living soul? I have no answer.

I just hate that he knows.

I blow out a breath. He'll never say anything. He's a good guy, unfailingly responsible. He'll know, but the secret will be safe with him. I'll pretend, and eventually it will disappear like it never happened.

I open the bathroom door; step out into the hallway, jerking back in surprise.

Chad's leaning against the wall, and while his stance is casual; his expression is intent and focused.

I gulp. On me.

I blink and manage to quell the gasp that rises to my lips. I need to be casual. To pretend he doesn't affect me. I give him a little wave of my fingers. "Hey, you scared me."

"Sorry." His voice sends a shiver down my spine.

I gesture to the bathroom. "It's all yours."

His blue eyes narrow. "I'm here for you."

Surprised pleasure bursts through me and I hate myself for it. I work to keep my expression completely neutral. I open my mouth to ask why that might be, but those aren't the words that come from my lips. "I feel duty bound to warn you Ashley's a bit clingy, so watch out."

No. Why? What is it about him that makes it impossible to hide my true feelings.

His expression flashes.

Tension tightening my muscles, I wait for him to call me out on my jealousy. He crosses his arms over his chest. "Since I have no intention of going home with Ashley, that's a moot point."

Instantly the knot in my stomach unravels. I'll think about why later, but now I need to remove myself from his presence before I give anything else away. I shrug. "It's not my business anyway."

He cocks a brow. "Don't pretend you're not relieved."

The tone of his voice makes my belly quiver. I tilt my head as the first stirrings of defensiveness rears its ugly head. "What you do, or don't do, has nothing to do with me."

"Maybe not." He straightens and closes the distance between us. "But you're still relieved."

He's close enough I can see the shards of white in his blue eyes, feel the heat of his body. The strange desire that swept through me that night when he'd held me surges. But this time I'm not safe. Unlike then, he's not in a comforting mood.

Heart a wild, untamed beat, I resist the urge to step back.

Chad is not the harmless guy I once thought he was. Underestimating him had been a mistake on my part, one I won't make again. Since I am apparently incapable of lying to him, I try diversion instead. "What can I help you with, Chad?"

His attention snags on my mouth before he meets my eyes. "I haven't been able to stop thinking about you since that night."

My breath kicks up as my pulse starts to pound. I mean to say it meant nothing, that we were drunk, that nothing happened between us, but those aren't the words that come. "You haven't?"

"No." His hand slides around my neck and I have to repress the urge to jerk at the contact. He puts his hand on my hip, and steps forward, forcing me to move back. He does it again, and then again until I'm pressed against the wall.

I'm not going to lie. It's thrilling. The kick of desire I feel is so strong it actually surprises me. It must be all the time I've spent thinking about him. Some sort of extended, silent foreplay.

He kicks my leg out, forcing my stance wider before he presses against me.

"What are you doing?" My voice is breathless.

He leans down and whispers in my ear, "Showing you."

The frantic beat of my heart sounds in my ears and when I speak, I tremble. "Showing me what?"

"That what you're feeling isn't one-sided." His fingers tangle in my hair, tugging until my head tilts and my jaw rises. I can feel his breath against my skin and I swallow the whimper.

I want him. More than I've wanted anyone ever. I've been infatuated over guys, angsty, giddy and longing, but this desire is new. Demanding. It terrifies me, because I know the truth. Which is bad enough, but he knows the truth too, which is worse.

I can't deliver on all this heat and tension between us.

When it comes down to it I'll freeze, which is what always happens. Chad knows I'm a fake. Pretending isn't an option. I put a hand on his stomach, intent on pushing him away, but don't. "That night was a mistake."

"Maybe so." He raises his head to look at me and when our gazes meet something electric crackles between us. "Tell me you haven't thought of me."

I want to deny, but I can't. "I have."

He grips my jaw, forcing me to maintain eye contact with him. "Have you slipped your fingers into your panties and come thinking about me?"

Say no. "Yes."

His fingers release my jaw and travel down the curve of my neck.

I'm hypnotized by him. Wanting to say no, to tell him to stop this madness, but the words never come.

He strokes over my collarbone. "There's one small step from thinking to doing. To it being my fingers. My cock."

I want so bad to believe in it, but I can't. I lick my lips and shake my head. "You know I can't."

I can't come with a guy. I'm defective that way. And no

matter how much I want him it won't work.

"I know that's what you believe. But it's not the truth."

It's Valentine's Day all over again. Like we've picked up exactly where we left off. "And you think you'll be the guy to change it?"

"Yeah, I do." There's no hesitation in his voice. Only utter surety.

Hope flutters in my chest and I hate it. There is no hope for me. "And why's that?"

"Because you can't hide from me." He runs his thumb over my bottom lip and my belly dips and heats. "But even more important, I won't let you."

This, right here, right now is why I need to stay away from him. Appropriate responses slide through my head, but I don't want to say any of them. All I want is to melt into him.

He makes me want to believe. And that's dangerous because it's not true.

He can't fix me.

I shake my head.

"I'm going to kiss you now."

"Okay." The word is a harsh whisper.

His lips brush mine, soft. Sweet even.

My breath catches and holds.

Another brush of his mouth over mine. Back and forth. He doesn't deliver the contact I desire. I stay motionless, barely breathing as he teases me, makes me want him even more desperately than I already do.

The tip of his tongue strokes across my lower lip and my nipples pull into hard, almost painful buds. I clutch at his shirt, fisting the material in my hands while I'm suspended in this time and space by the sensation of his mouth barely touching mine.

His teeth scrape over my flesh and I let out a gasp, bowing to force greater contact. In answer, he slides his hands down my arms and encircles my wrists, his fingers tightening around the fine bones, he raises them over my head.

Trapping me. Reminding me of his true nature and what

that means for me. The protest flits through my mind but evaporates as his mouth flirts over mine.

He's relentless. Brushing. Stroking. Nipping. Licking. Over and over, endlessly, until my whole body buzzes with him, all my senses consumed, my thoughts emptied.

He's not even kissing me. Not really.

He's playing with me. Like a cat toys with a mouse.

My nails dig into my palms as I clench my hands into frustrated fists, moaning helplessly when he captures my lower lip between his teeth and licks.

I arch, needing some sort of friction.

He inserts his thigh between my legs. My skirt is stretchy but it still doesn't accommodate. He grips my wrists in one hand, while the other skims down my body, before bunching my skirt high enough for his thigh to slide against my swollen center.

I have no idea how he's doing this but I don't ever want it to end.

Never has anyone taken this kind of time with me.

He presses his thigh where I need him the most, at the same time brushes over my mouth.

I whimper.

Against my lips he whispers, "I can feel the heat of your pussy through my pants."

His words only increase my arousal.

"Can feel your body straining against the desire to grind against me and relieve the ache."

My hips jerk in response and I'm practically panting.

"But I'm not going to deliver." The pressure between my thighs releases as he moves his leg. "I'm going to make you want it."

I shudder.

He bites my lip. "Beg."

I can't repress the sound that emerges from my throat.

His lips cover mine, hot and commanding, taking absolute control as his tongue plunges into my mouth.

I'm so crazy I lose myself immediately.

And then he's gone.

I chase him, but he releases my hands. For a second I'm free but then he grips me by the throat and holds me to the wall. Lust, so powerful my knees actually quake, storms away inside me. Instead of pushing him away, I clutch at his shirt and try and pull him closer.

He works his fingers under my skirt and into my panties.

Shock rolls through me and I freeze. But he doesn't seem thwarted by my sudden tensing. He slides over my skin, before circling my clit, featherlight.

Nothing more than a tease. And I want more. My god do I want.

He meets my gaze, which I'm sure looks like a deer in headlights. "I want you to remember this, how you feel right now, and know I haven't even started."

He releases his hold on my neck, and I sag against the wall. His fingers leave my clit and hook into the cotton of my underwear. Before I can process what's happening they are sliding down my legs. I can't think of anything but the fact that I'm limp against the wall, trembling with desire.

"Step out." His voice holds that edge I've heard in both Layla's and Jillian's fiancés.

I should say no, but I've somehow already stepped out. He rubs his thumb over the fabric and he slips them into his pocket.

All I can do is stand there, open mouthed, stunned, and more turned on than I've ever been in my life.

He smooths my skirt down my legs before straightening. "Ruby."

I blink. "Yes?"

"Lose the guy."

"Okay."

"Good girl."

I might hyperventilate.

He steps forward, cups my jaw and raises my chin. "And later, when you're in bed, remember who you're coming for."

And with that, he walks away, leaving me confused,

terrified and needy.

Chad

Walking away wasn't easy. But it needed to be done.

I slip out of the party and into the tail end of the Chicago winter, letting the cold night air work its magic.

Michael's parents live in the wealthy part of Evanston pressed up against the lakefront. The street is stately, filled with old neoclassic architecture and mature trees.

I walk down the block until I hit the lake, stopping to watch the waves crash onto the shore. Without a jacket the wind should be enough to cool me down, but with the imprint of Ruby's panties in my pocket, I'm struggling.

I reach for them, my thumb circling the damp center. She'd been so fucking wet when I touched her it had worked on every last ounce of my self-control. I could have dragged her into a bedroom and taken her right then and there, but that would have defeated my end game. While I'd flipped her switch, turned her on, and made damn sure she was desperate for me to touch her, she would have frozen as soon as I turned more serious.

Even that brief moment I'd played with her pussy every muscle in her body had tensed, and, despite her arousal, if I'd continued she would have started thinking.

I breathed in the lake air, listening to the waves in an effort to think about anything other than slamming my cock inside her.

Because I wasn't sure this was the smartest thing I'd ever done.

Pursuing Ruby will take work. Effort. Patience. And for what? We are not really compatible. We live different lives and have different goals.

But, Christ, I want to see her come. Want to be the one to make it happen for her.

Of course, the one thing we do have in common she won't even acknowledge.

I may not have been interested in her, but I'd kept an eye on her since I'd met her. After a blind date with Layla, Ruby's best friend, we'd parted ways only for me to run into her and Michael when I was out with a girl I'd been dating about six months ago. The girl didn't last, but to my surprise, my friendship with Layla and Michael had.

Ruby has intrigued me from the start—the lone innocent in her group of kinky friends. The exact opposite of my regular group, which is probably why I'd started hanging out with Michael, Leo and Brandon more and more. I still see my friends, guys I'd grown up with, but they no longer quite felt like my people.

As soon as I'd met Ruby I recognized the signs in her. Not that the other guys in the group, all dominants themselves, hadn't noticed too. We'd talked about it a few times, or mainly Layla had, with Michael telling her to leave it alone, but it had been a topic of discussion.

It's pretty clear if you know what to look for.

Despite her obvious tells, Ruby is hardcore insistent she wants nothing to do with being dominated, claiming to anyone who will listen she doesn't understand why anyone would want such a thing. But she can't quite hide her fascination, even though she believes every word she says with her whole heart.

I don't doubt Ruby believes it. I also don't doubt she doesn't understand why a woman would want to be dominated.

The problem is Ruby doesn't understand how submissive she really is. And the scene in the hallway only confirmed that. She's completely unaware she'd just submitted to my will. Sure, I hadn't pushed her, or made demands, because that would be unethical and wrong, but once I'd touched her she'd surrendered to what I wanted without protest.

I could see the struggle in her eyes. The inability to lie to me when I asked her a direct question. Her easy agreement when I told her to ditch the guy. The shudder of desire when

I'd called her a good girl.

I had zero doubts by the time that guy, her *date*, dropped her off he'd be gone. That even if sanity prevailed, and she processed she'd agreed to my demand without protest, she wouldn't be able to let him touch her. I was equally sure Ruby would come tonight and think about what happened between us in the hallway when she climaxed. And that when she was close and not filtering her emotions, she'd think of how I'd held her by the throat and squeezed while I rubbed her clit.

The tricky part came with what to do about it. Because these weren't things Ruby was remotely ready to hear. She has a laundry list of issues, and asking her to accept her submissive nature now was the equivalent of telling her she needed to go run a marathon tomorrow morning with no preparation.

But I can help her.

There's something between us. Something hot and tangible, and after eight weeks of going out on dates with girls I couldn't even remember and forgot the second they were out of sight, it's not going away.

I want Ruby and at some point she's going to be under me. Despite her protests and her disbelief, she will come for me. I've already started and there's no stopping us.

I just have to be very conscious of getting her consent on every single thing I do to her. So that when she comes face-to-face with her nature, with what she fears the most, I can remind her it had been her choice all along.

Ruby

I'm sitting across from Layla and Jillian in a crowded Sunday brunch spot in Lakeview. Layla called me this morning and asked me to come, and since I was about to jump out of my skin at my restlessness, I agreed.

Luckily, since they are both getting married, they are talking about wedding plans and I don't have to pay close attention. While Layla has just gotten engaged, Jillian's wedding is only a couple of months from now. She's going to be a classic June bride.

I love both of them—and over the months Jillian has become an actual friend to me instead of Michael's sister—but wedding mania is alive and well. Sometimes it bothers me, sometimes I feel jealous and petty, but today their preoccupation suits me quite well.

I have not stopped obsessing about Chad since our encounter in the hallway. All I can think about is how his mouth felt on mine, how my body had tingled, how much I wanted him, and how I wanted more.

Over the course of the evening, Chad had disproved any preconceived notions I had about him being a "nice" guy.

While we hadn't been alone for the rest of the night, he'd been like a magnet, drawing me to him over and over, preoccupying me. I'd wanted to be close to him. Wanted Tommy to be gone, which was bad enough, but I found myself wishing that I was *with* Chad.

He hadn't helped matters.

When we were together in a group, he'd catch my eye before putting his hand in his pocket where I knew my panties were. Then he'd stand there, a smirk on his face, making it clear to me he was touching my underwear, only to talk as if nothing out of the ordinary was happening. As though I wasn't bare under my skirt because of him.

It was like a train wreck, one I couldn't look away from. He'd held me captive. Breathless and wanting. I don't want it to be so, but I can't deny, it made me ridiculously wet. Like embarrassingly so. Every time I'd walk I'd be reminded of my slippery thighs and how swollen I was. There were a few times I was tempted to go into the bathroom and take care of the ache, but I convinced myself he'd somehow know and didn't want to risk it.

The whole thing was bizarre and strange. I've never been tempted like that, been so preoccupied with lust I contemplated taking the edge off. I barely knew what to do with it.

I have a complicated relationship with sex that, in my mind, bordered on dysfunctional. An unfortunate byproduct of growing up a minister's daughter. The sad thing is my parents are loving and affectionate and didn't push a negative agenda, but all that church sank into my brain and wouldn't leave. I want to be above it all, because I consider myself a modern, feminist woman, but my upbringing did a number on me I haven't figured out how to fix.

Somewhere along the way, in a quest for empowerment, I taught myself how to masturbate and give myself an orgasm; it was tension release versus being turned on. And, despite my best efforts, I have never been able to translate it to my relationships with men.

I've never experienced what I had last night, where it was literally all I could think about. Made all the worse by the friction of my enflamed flesh and press of my thighs. By my bare, slick skin. By Chad watching me in that way he had, knowing and confident.

I chose not to think about the fact that I'd done exactly what he'd asked of me and told Tommy it was over. I didn't even look back as he sped away. I'd already forgotten him.

I'd practically run to my apartment. I'd barely gotten in the door I'd been so crazy. I'd collapsed on my couch, and rubbed my fingers over my clit, thinking about Chad and the hallway, his words, the squeeze of his fingers on my throat. I came harder than I ever have, even arching a little and biting my lip. After, all I could think was I wanted more.

That it wasn't enough.

Just thinking about it now creates an unfamiliar kick of lust low in my belly. I blow out a long, slow breath and force myself to stop thinking about him and return to reality.

The din of the restaurant comes rushing back, suddenly too loud.

I look across the table and find Layla and Jillian staring at me, both wearing expressions that are a mixture of concern and speculation.

Layla raises a brow. "What exactly were you thinking about?"

Jillian grins. "And why are your cheeks so pink?"

My face heats even more and I pick up my mimosa. "Nothing."

"Did something happen last night?" Layla asks.

My mind fills with images of Chad, his teasing mouth and wicked words. I've never had a man talk to me like that. Most guys' idea of dirty talk is pretty cringe worthy, but Chad, the things he said—my skin flushes even deeper. I shake my head. "No, nothing happened."

Layla and Jillian look at each other.

"She's lying," Jillian says.

I want to tell them, because this is the kind of thing you tell your girlfriends, spend hours analyzing and dissecting, but I can't. One, what exactly was I supposed to tell them? Because what exactly happened? I have no idea. And two, which is the most important, they love Chad. I don't want them to get excited about something that will turn into nothing. How could it not? We are nothing alike.

So I put on my game face. "I'm not. Nothing happened."

"Did you sleep with the guitar guy?" Layla asks, the corners of her mouth turning down.

"No." I tuck a lock of hair behind my ear and take a sip of mimosa, letting the cool bubbling tang soothe my throat. "You'll be very proud of me. I broke up with him."

Layla blew out a sigh. "Whew. Good. I didn't know how to tell you I saw him making out with Shelly last night."

At the news, I feel absolutely nothing. Not even surprise. Guys like Tommy are invested in the rocker life fantasy, and fucking random girls while your date is occupied, goes with the territory. Besides, I wasn't exactly innocent. I'd let Chad touch me more in that hallway than I'd let Tommy in three dates. I shrug. "I wish her good luck dealing with his aggressive tongue in her mouth."

Layla and Jillian laugh.

Jillian wrinkles her nose. "God, I used to hate that."

"He was the worst." I make a jabbing motion with my finger. "Like hard, stabbing pokes."

"Yuck!" Layla exclaims.

I take another sip of my drink, downing the rest and putting it on the table, glancing around for our waiter to get a refill. "But rest assured, he's gone."

I wait for the conversation to turn away from my dating life, but Jillian narrows her eyes. "Something happened. You're preoccupied."

I bite my lip, looking for a satisfactory answer, but my phone rings, saving me. I open my purse and see Chad's name lighting up the screen.

My heart leaps in excitement, before starting a fast, steady pounding in my chest. I'd half expected last night to be a moment of insanity never to be spoken of again. I snatch the phone and say, "I've got to get this." Then I'm springing from the table and weaving my way through the people toward the door, the phone already to my ear.

"Hello." My tone is entirely too breathless.

"You sound like I caught you at a bad time."

At the sound of his voice, I fear I might hyperventilate. "No, it's okay. Just give me a second."

I push my way outside. The sun is bright, and while the air is still cold, it's going to be a nice day. I walk down a few shops before I stop. "Sorry, is that better?"

"Much. Where are you?"

"I'm at brunch with Layla and Jillian."

There's a quick pause on the line. I take the moment to calm my breathing and slow my galloping heart rate.

"Did you tell them about last night?" His tone is curious.

"No." I lick my lips and the cool air makes them sting.

"Why not?"

"What was I supposed to say?"

He laughs. "I fooled around with Chad last night while my date was downstairs."

I press my hand against the brick of the building. "Yeah, I don't think so. Although it turns out he was busy with one of my friends, so I don't think I was missed."

"Good, he wasn't ever going to give you what you need anyway."

I want to ask what Chad thinks I need, but I'm not sure I want to hear the answer. I clear my throat. "I didn't expect to hear from you."

When he speaks his voice is a low rumble. "Did you think I was going to leave you like that?"

I bite my lip; remember the sting of his teeth. "You walked away last night and didn't say anything, so yes."

"I walked away because you're not ready for me to fuck you

against a wall."

I sharply inhale at his words, all the heat from last night rushing back.

"I can hear how you like that idea, Ruby."

I press my hand against the brick even harder, using the scratch of the surface to focus, but don't say anything. Was this what phone sex was like?

Several beats pass before he speaks. "I didn't say anything because I wanted you to have time to think about what I'd done to you. About what I want to do to you. To give you a chance to decide what you want with a clear head."

I blink down at the sidewalk. "What do you want to do to me?"

"The list is endless." Another pause. "But dinner tonight is a good place to start."

"Dinner?" I squeak, trying not to think about how excited I am to see him. How these last eight weeks have been a constant state of longing.

"Yes. I'll be happy to take you someplace, but I'd rather cook you dinner at my place, if you'll let me."

"You cook?" I don't know why this astounds me. "I thought men who cooked were mythical beings. Like unicorns."

He laughs. "I cook. My mom taught me."

I think of my own mom, giving me lessons about a woman's place in the home and how to take care of a husband, like it was something to be proud of. "I don't want to inconvenience you."

"If I didn't want to, I wouldn't have offered. So seven tonight?"

I want to say yes so badly. I want to see him, but I can already feel myself getting tense at the prospect that he'll want sex. Most guys I've slept with had no idea I couldn't have orgasms. I'm a very good actress. But Chad knows. None of my normal distraction tricks are possible with him because I'd stupidly confessed all this to him in a drunken state of emotional upheaval on Valentine's Day.

I shake my head. "What about…" I trail off, unable to say the words.

"Coming?" he supplies for me.

"Yes," I whisper. "You know I can't."

There's silence for several long moments, before he says, "I know this is hard for you to understand, but you don't have to worry about that. Let *me* worry about that. We're going to talk about it, but we're a long way from orgasms even being on the table, okay?"

Something eases, but I am compelled to continue. He deserves something better. I clear my throat. "It's just that I'll be a disappointment that way. And I don't want that for you."

"It's not your decision to make, Ruby."

My heart gives a hard thump. "But—"

"This is a discussion best had tonight, curled up on my couch, instead of you alone on a street corner."

"Okay." My throat suddenly tightens. What is it about him that brings up all these hidden emotions? I hate it, but something inside me feels like it's exactly what I need.

"Ruby?" His voice drops.

"Yes?" My tone is husky and unsure.

"Did you come for me last night?"

"Yes." I don't know why I don't lie, or at least play coy.

"Good girl."

My knees actually quiver.

"I'll see you tonight at seven. Text me your address and I'll send you an Uber."

This is something the guys I date would never think of, they'd let me find my own way to their apartments. The consideration makes me…uncomfortable. "All right."

"And one more thing."

"Yes?"

"You and I are going to be seeing a lot of each other, so there's no reason to keep it a secret from Layla and Jillian. The decision is up to you, but don't hide on my account."

In a daze I hang up. Thirty seconds goes by where I stand on the street and watch the traffic, my mind a whirl. I finally manage to blink out of my stupor, text Chad my address, and slip my phone back into my pocket.

I walk back into the restaurant and sit down as my friends stare at me in anticipation.

Finally, Jillian asks, "Who was that?"

I look at her and then at Layla. I want to talk about this, at least to get some of it out there in the open. "Chad."

Their eyes go wide with surprise.

Layla leans forward. "Chad?"

I nod. "Last night, while Tommy was kissing Shelly, I was kissing Chad. Or rather, Chad was kissing me."

"Oh. My. God." Layla plants her hands on the table. "Tell us everything."

Jillian nods. "Don't leave anything out."

And I don't. Well, that's not true. I tell them the basics, of talking on Valentine's Day, the hallway, about dinner tonight.

But how he makes me feel, I'm not ready to even to think about that, let alone talk about it.

Layla and I are sitting on my couch that doubles as my bed, in my tiny studio apartment. I could get a bigger place if I wanted a roommate, but I like living alone, being completely independent of anyone else. If I want to leave dirty dishes in the sink I can, and don't have to worry about inconveniencing anyone.

The place is small, the size of a large hotel room. But I have room for my desk, computer and a place to sleep. I don't need much and I don't like being attached to things.

Jillian left us at the restaurant to go study at the library, and Layla had come home with me to help me figure out what I wanted to wear. We'd settled on a pair of skinny jeans and an off-the-shoulder Ramone's T-shirt.

Layla looks at me, bites her lip, and looks away.

She's got something on her mind but isn't sure if she

should say anything. She's been giving me Layla clues all afternoon.

I raise my brow. "What is it?"

She frowns. "I'm not supposed to say anything."

My chest squeezes. I experience a moment of dread as I contemplate what she's hiding. "If you didn't want to say, you wouldn't have said anything at all, so spill."

"Michael told me to leave it alone, but I feel duty bound as your best friend to tell you."

I roll my eyes. "I'm not going to tell Michael on you."

"Oh, I'm not worried about that." She grins, and shrugs a shoulder.

There was a time where I thought I'd never see Layla smile again, that her eyes wouldn't be anything but flat, cold and distant. But she's outdone herself. She's happy. She radiates a health and vibrancy that makes her absolutely gorgeous.

I'd forgotten, in those dark times, how beautiful she was. She's older, all traces of girlhood long gone, and she's magnetic. The kind of woman men follow with their eyes as she crosses a room.

I'm thrilled for her—and a tiny bit jealous. Not because of her looks, but because she's managed to fight for her happiness and win, while I'm still struggling to find my way.

"I assume this is about Chad?" Does he have a secret girlfriend? I frown, no, that can't be it. He's too upstanding for that.

"I don't want to scare you." She tucks a lock of dark chestnut hair behind her ears.

"I'm a big girl, I can take it."

"It is about Chad."

The tension curls tight in my sternum. "If he's a serial killer, it might be best if you tell me now."

She laughs. "God no, nothing like that." She clears her throat. "You know he's dominant, right?"

Oh, that. I blow out a deep breath and nod. "I know. He told me on Valentine's."

Her brow furrows. "Are you're okay with that? You've told

me often enough that's not your scene."

An image of Chad's hands around my throat flits through my mind, the imprint of his fingers, tight around the cords a sharp memory. "It's not, but he hasn't been like that to me."

Her brows draw even deeper. "He hasn't?"

I think of him holding me against the wall. A flash of heat spikes in my blood and I shake it away. I don't want to think about his tendencies. Besides, it's not like he made me kneel on the floor or anything like I've seen Michael make Layla do. I shake my head. "No. Besides, it's a date. One date that probably won't go anywhere. We're nothing alike so it's not like we're going to end up together."

Layla's expression turns speculative. She tilts her head. "So why are you going? If there's no future?"

This is where Layla and I are different. She's goal orientated, she likes order and plans, she likes things to have purpose.

I can't deny her the point. The truth is, I don't know why I'm doing this. Other than Chad seems to touch some part of me that's remained untouched all my life, and something in me needs to know what lurks there, even though it terrifies me. I can't deny Chad feels like the key to…something. I just don't know what the something is or how to define it. Those are too complicated to discuss though, to explain to her what I can't explain to myself. I shrug. "Why does there need to be a future? Can't we have fun without worrying about where it's going to lead?"

I wish I believed this. It's not *just* fun. I'm not sure it's fun at all.

Layla nibbles on her bottom lip before nodding. "You're right, but Chad's a part of our group now, I don't want things to be awkward if someone gets hurt."

"It's dinner, Laylay." I smile as reassurance, wanting off this topic. "You went to dinner with him and now you're friends. It's possible."

Right after Layla met Michael, Chad and Layla went on a blind date set up by her sister and while it didn't lead to love, it had led to friendship.

"He didn't kiss me." Layla's frown is back.

"Only because he had to compete with two men." My counter argument. When they'd gone out, Layla had been using Chad to avoid Michael, and had been in deep mourning over the death of her fiancé, John. He didn't stand a chance with her, and Chad is a smart, intuitive guy, he surely picked up on it.

"That's a point."

It is, but the idea of them back on that date long ago gives me pause. Layla is much more Chad's type than I'd ever be. If she hadn't met Michael first, would she be with Chad? Would they be a couple? Getting married? I can see them together, crystal clear in my mind. Or at least, I can see Chad with someone like Layla. They'd be one of those perfect couples everyone loves to hate.

It's further confirmation we're fundamentally incompatible.

But I'm still going to his house tonight. Because there's something between us, and I need to find out what it is so I can exercise him from my mind.

Chad

I open the door to find Ruby standing there, a bottle of wine in her hand. She's wearing a leather jacket, skinny jeans and is shivering.

I smile and usher her in. "It's cold."

She shudders. "It is."

Her hair is pulled back into a high ponytail and her blue eyes are stunning, her lips red. She looks adorable, although I won't tell her that. In my experience, telling a woman she looks cute isn't taken as the compliment intended.

She blinks at me, and scrapes her teeth over her lower lip.

"Nervous?" I ask, even though I already know she is.

"Yes." She hands me the wine, glancing around. "I don't know why we're doing this."

I put the bottle on the table in the foyer, before walking over to her. Sometimes you have to let the anticipation build, but this isn't one of those times. I slide my hand around her waist, tangle another in her hair, and kiss her.

Other than a gasp of surprise, she freezes, but I don't let that stop me.

I coax her pretty mouth, that's been driving me crazy for the last two months, into a response. I stroke my thumb over her rigid jaw, before applying pressure.

She opens to me. Her muscles uncoil, and her lips part, as her body melts into mine. Last night I hadn't allowed myself the luxury of deepening into the kiss, but I do now.

I slant my head, stroking into her mouth with my tongue. She shivers against me, but this time, it's not from the cold. She presses into me, rising up to fit her body against mine. Her fingers crawl up my shoulders to my neck, before her grip tightens.

Everything between us turns hot. A bit desperate.

My natural instincts take over and my mouth turns harder, more aggressive, more demanding.

She moans, and plasters herself to me, like she can't get close enough.

And as things are about to spiral completely out of control, I pull away.

She chases my mouth, but I grip her ponytail, holding her still, making it clear I'm calling the shots here.

Breath fast, she blinks up at me, her gaze glassy.

I brush lips over hers, nip at her, before licking with my tongue. "Does that answer your question?"

She nods and says in a panting voice, "It does." Her expression clouds over. "But…I can't…"

She'll never relax until I make her believe I won't push her on this. That I won't get carried away and try for the sake of my own ego. It tells me everything I need to know about Ruby's relationship with men. That she's always allowed them to put their needs above her own. Until I show her, my word will have to do. I grip her jaw, give her my most serious look, and repeat a variation of what I said to her before. "This isn't your concern, let me worry about making you come."

"But…" she tries again, her voice shaky and unsure.

The best thing I can do for her right now is to put the

worry off the table. She's far from ready for me even to try and, and I won't until it's all she can think about. I tighten my hold on her jaw. "When you're with me, it's not your responsibility anymore. Understood?"

"No." She laughs a little, but her anxious expression relaxes a bit, and I understand, even if she doesn't, that my words soothe something inside her.

She's been carrying around this deep dark secret of hers for years, faking her way through every single sexual encounter she's had, and she's scared because she knows that's not possible with me.

I can only continue to reassure her. I stroke my thumb over her jaw. "Tonight all I'm going to do is kiss you, all right? Nothing more. Nothing less."

Her brows furrow but she nods. "Okay."

I smile down at her. "We're going to eat, drink, talk and make out like a couple of teenagers. Do you think you can manage that?"

"That I can manage." Her expression clears and she beams up at me.

For an instant I'm dazzled, because I think it's the first genuine smile she's given me, and it's fucking breathtaking. I brush over her lower lip. "You are so gorgeous."

The frown returns and she shakes her head. "Don't say that."

I lean down and kiss her again, claiming her mouth for a fraction of a second before pulling away. "You'll learn soon enough that I always mean what I say." I put my hands on her shoulders. "Now let's get you out of this jacket."

Ruby

The kiss has shaken me, and I'm beyond nervous, but I shrug out of my coat. He walks over to the hook and hangs up my belongings, and I just kind of stare, stunned at the breadth of his shoulders, the taper of his waist, and lean cut of his hips. The way he fills out a pair of jeans.

He turns around, flashing me that smile, and he's so damn good looking I barely know what to do with my attraction. How is it possible I hung out with him for all these months without thinking much about him, and now I can't get him out of my head?

And that kiss. I can barely think.

He grabs the bottle of wine I brought before taking my hand. "Come on in."

Chad lives in a townhouse, but I had been so anxious, so consumed by him, I hadn't paid any attention to what I walked into. For the first time I absorb the place.

I suck in my breath. "Wow."

It might be the coolest place I've seen. It's got a loft, industrial feel to it, and the back of the house is almost floor-to-ceiling windows, looking out onto a spectacular view of the skyline. The floors are driftwood gray and wide planked. Everything is in shades of grays and white but instead of looking cold, it's inviting. The kitchen is sleek and modern with industrial appliances.

The place also smells delicious, like Italian food, but that was the least of my awe.

I drop his hand and walk into the huge room, spinning around to take in how fantastic it all is. I look up at the ceilings that seem to go on forever. "How tall are these?"

"Twenty-five feet." His voice is filled with pleasure. "Do you want the tour?"

"I'd love one. This place is unbelievable." I've never really thought much about what an IT person made, but a townhome like this had to cost a fortune. I wanted to ask, but didn't know him well enough. Software must be more lucrative than I'd imagined.

I grin at him. "I think this is the coolest place I've ever been in."

He laughs. "I did everything myself, so I'm going to take that as a compliment."

Surprised, I raise a brow. "You did it yourself?"

I find I want to know all about him. It's so odd. So strange. There's nothing about us that goes together, but I suddenly find him the most fascinating person.

He shoves his hands into his pockets. "I bought the building during the real estate crash. The neighborhood was still up and coming, and the place was in foreclosure so it ended up being a steal. Previously an abandoned factory, I had it rezoned and divided. One of my friends is a contractor so we decided to try out our hand at real estate. When we were done I kept the house I liked the best, and we sold the other ones."

My mouth falls open and before I can censor myself I spit out, "Didn't that cost a fortune?"

He shrugs. "We didn't do it all at once. The building sat for a couple of years. We did lots of stuff ourselves in pieces. It was a gamble that paid off."

I'm impressed. "I love it, it's gorgeous."

"Thanks." He laughs, a little chagrin. "It's my pride and joy. And I found I liked doing it. My friend and I have bought buildings and gutted them, and sold them off a few times now. It's a hobby of mine."

I know enough about Chicago real estate to know that if this place is any indication, it was a lucrative hobby. I gaze at him, my eyes narrow. "Are you saying you're a secret real estate mogul?"

He laughs. "Hardly. It's just something I like to do in my spare time."

"Some hobby." In continued awe, I walk to the back of the house where a dining room table sits and is already set for dinner. For us. The table is heavy, with thick distressed wood, stately high-backed benches on the sides, and high-backed leather chairs on either end.

It looks almost medieval. I run my hand over the wood and stare at the place settings. He used real plates. White and crisp, like out of a magazine.

It sounds silly, but it touches me, and scares me all at the same time. Nobody has ever cooked me dinner before, or gone through any sort of trouble for me. The last guy I dated for any length of time lived in a hovel with a mattress on the floor. I don't think he even owned plates. We used to sit on the floor and eat Chinese takeout of the box with chopsticks.

As strange as it sounds, I'm more comfortable with that. The lack of expectation makes me relax.

This makes me nervous.

Chad comes up behind me and puts his hands on my hips before leaning down to whisper in my ear, "Come on, I'll show you the rest."

His voice sends tingles down my spine, and I try not to think of how much I want him.

He takes me down a hallway with lower ceilings, showing me a half bath and a spacious room he's set up as an office. It's the messiest room I've seen, filled with computer equipment and three huge computer monitors. Piled with books. It makes me happy. Makes him seem more human.

He walks me up a spiral staircase and shows me two spare bedrooms, another bathroom and his master suite.

I try not to gasp as I enter the room. Try not to blush at the sight of the massive bed, or wonder if I'll be lying in it. The headboard is wood with thick posts and it looks like dynamite wouldn't move it.

The covers are thick, charcoal gray and inviting.

I have an image of tumbling across it, hot and restless. I tense.

I can't live up to the expectation of that bed.

Chad comes behind me and circles my waist, pressing his back against mine. "You're thinking about being in this bed, aren't you?"

My body grows even more ridged. "How do you know that?"

I don't know why I ask the question, why I continue to be surprised he can read me.

"It's written in your face, in the tension of your body." He leans down and kisses me, open mouth on the neck, his tongue pressing against my skin. A part of me wants to lean into him but I can't. His teeth scrape along my earlobe. "I'm going to take you to bed, but not before you're ready to be there."

I draw in a stuttering breath. "I don't think I'll ever be ready."

"Time will tell." He straightens, his lips leaving a distracting path along my neck. "I need to show you one more thing. My favorite part of the house." He goes to the closet and by the glimpse I get, it's huge. He comes back and holds out a zip-up sweatshirt. "Put this on."

I stare him. Wasn't he just talking about taking me to bed? I take the coat and put it on. Then he leads me out of the bedroom and down the hall to another staircase. We walk up and he opens a door, and we step out onto a huge rooftop.

I stop in wonder. "Holy shit."

He has a three hundred and sixty panoramic view of the city. Fifty people could stand out here and not be crowded. I shiver against the cold, but walk over to the railing, gazing out over the city.

He comes to stand next to me. "Crazy, huh?"

"It's fucking spectacular." Because there is no other way to describe it.

He laughs.

Before I can process what I'm saying, I blurt out, "Can I come live with you?"

He laughs again and winks. "I don't know, what are you going to give me in return?"

The question makes me ache in unexpected ways I don't like. Because the truth is, I have absolutely nothing to offer a man like Chad. He's got his whole life together. He's a thriving member of society.

I look back out over the city.

Who am I? I don't even know. I'm just drifting along, with no plan and no purpose. Something that never bothered me before, that now doesn't seem like enough.

From the corner of my eye, I glance at him.

He makes me want more.

I'm sitting at the table, on the high-back bench, trying not to fidget. Chad works in his kitchen, putting the last touches on the dinner he's made for me. The politeness I was raised with makes me want to help, but he'd said no. Insisting I sit and relax. As though relaxation is possible. I run my finger over the tine of the silverware. The table already has warm bread, salad and red wine, poured into huge goblets.

He places a plate of pasta in front of me, with marinara sauce and meatballs, before putting his hand on my neck and rubbing. "I thought this would be pretty safe."

"Thank you, it's perfect." I put my napkin on my lap and try and process that I'm in Chad's house, that he's kissed me, that I kissed him back, and now he's made me dinner.

He returns to the kitchen for his own plate, sitting down at the table, in the chair next to me.

It's silly, but nerves dance in my stomach. If you would have told me six months ago, when I'd first met Chad, he'd make me more nervous than any man I've ever met, I would have said you were crazy. But here I sit, unable to calm my anxiousness.

I look up to find him watching me with that expression he has.

I suck in a breath and say, "I don't know what I'm doing here."

He smiles, grabs his wine and juts his chin at my glass. "Have some wine. It will relax you."

With trembling fingers I raise the goblet and take a sip.

His fingers play over the stem and he narrows his gaze on me. "I think you know exactly what you're doing here, and it scares you."

The guys I'm used to are filled with subterfuge. Filled with games. I'm not used to Chad's directness. With anyone else I'd play it off, laugh at the notion that I'm scared, but I can't help feeling Chad sees right through me. That lying to him is futile.

And, for some odd reason I can't articulate or understand, something deep inside me wants to be brutally honest with him. It's a luxury I want to give myself. To shrug off the pretense and lay myself bare.

As scared as I am, I trust him implicitly. It's like everything about him calls to me, insisting I tell him my deepest, most closely held secrets. I pick up my fork, but make no move to eat. "I am scared."

He nods. "Tell me why."

The words come to my lips, and I don't repress them even though my nature is insisting on it. "Because you know the truth about me, and I don't like it."

He puts down his glass and leans his elbows on the table. "I don't know the truth about you. I know one small thing, and your ability to have, or not have an orgasm, does not define you as a woman."

My brows knit and I'm glad I'm not eating because my stomach turns to lead. Of course, I know that. But this failure of mine is how I've defined my relationships with men for so long I can no longer separate it. I shrug. I don't know what to say.

His gaze pulls at me and I can't help but respond.

When I meet his eyes he says, "I will know you though."

"To what purpose?" My voice is more strained than I want. "I'm hardly your type."

He chuckles. "And I'm hardly yours, but here we are."

I clear my throat. "We have nothing in common."

"True," he agrees.

It's weird how he doesn't try and deny it, doesn't try and talk me into why this is a good idea. I raise my brow. "So?"

He scrubs a hand over his jaw, as though he's contemplating. After several moments of silence, he says, "After that night, I was happy when you relieved me of any responsibility. I wanted to walk away."

I blink. Well, that's honest. My grip on my wine tightens and I take a big gulp, letting it warm my empty stomach.

He continues on, only giving my large sip a passing glance. "It wasn't personal. I have a lot going on right now, I was recently promoted at work, and I have two buildings I'm trying to get ready to sell. I want easy and uncomplicated." He gives me a smile. "You're neither. So I was as eager as you were to walk away, willing to dismiss what happened between us as a one off."

"I can still walk away." It would take care of this, put it to bed, and that can only be a good thing.

"You can, but you won't, and neither will I." He meets my eyes with a direct, steady gaze. "That was decided as soon as I touched you last night."

"Why?" Heat rises to my cheeks, I clear my throat. "Did you touch me then?"

"Because I meant what I said, I haven't been able to stop thinking about you." His eyes skim over my face, lingering on my lips. "I went out with three girls since Valentine's, and I didn't want any of them."

This fills me with such pleasure I'm almost embarrassed. A smile I want to hide tugs at my lips. I look down at my plate.

He laughs. "You can be happy about it, Ruby."

The smile grows and I shrug. "Sorry."

"Don't be. I'm sure as fuck happy that guy you brought

didn't touch you." He points to my plate. "We should eat."

I pick up my fork again and spear a bite of pasta. "I only brought Tommy because of you."

"I know."

I'm beginning to wonder if there's anything Chad Fellows doesn't know. I almost take a bite but then I pause, and ask, "Did Ashley offer to sleep with you?"

"Yes." The word is direct, without any hesitation.

I raise my eyes to his. "I'm still afraid."

I don't know why I say this, but I do. I want to admit it.

"That's okay." Chad reaches for my hand and squeezes my fingers. "All you need to do is trust that I've got you."

With those words, something inside me eases, because I believe him.

Chad

I kept the rest of dinner a light affair. I made sure Ruby had plenty of wine, and I steered the discussion to casual first-date conversation. We discussed our favorite books, movies, and music. I discovered we had more in common than I thought. How we both liked foreign art films that nobody else wants to see. That we both liked to think looking at the lake, and both hated the same best seller everyone else loved.

It had taken a while, but she'd finally unwound and now she sat on my couch, tucked into the corner, a glass of wine in her hand. We were well into our third bottle and everything had become easy between us, except for the sexual tension that hummed like an electric wire.

She took another sip and settled into the cushions. "I can't believe you know how to cook."

I put my hand on the back of the couch, taking a long look at her body. She's built lean, almost slight, but she has a full chest that's out of proportion to the rest of her body. On another girl I'd suspect they were fake, but Ruby wasn't a boob-job type. Sitting there, her black hair pulled back, her blue eyes glassy but happy; I have to work not to think of all the things I want to do to her.

All things that will have to wait. I never break my promise and I'm not about to start with this fragile, scared girl.

I smile at her. "Why's that?"

She shakes her head and her ponytail swings. "In my house, that's women's work."

I know Ruby grew up in a small town in Southern Indiana where her mom and dad, brother and sister and their families still live, but that's as much as she's told me. "Women's work, huh?"

She laughs, rolling her eyes. "When I go home to visit it's like I've stepped back into another era. The women cook and clean and take care of their men. The men sit around with their feet up."

Another piece of the Ruby puzzle clicks into place. But I'm not going to call attention to how growing up like that colors her perception of domination. Those conversations are for much farther down the line. "Well, in my house, my mom was a diehard feminist. My dad is more traditional, but she put the kibosh on that—as she says—five minutes into the marriage. I have two brothers, one older, one younger. As the only female in the house she was determined to make sure we knew how to treat women." I smile, thinking of my fierce mother. "She refused to raise helpless men."

Ruby's expression is sheer delight. "She sounds like someone I'd like."

"You would, and my mom would love you." I laugh and take another sip of wine, a pleasant, leisurely buzz sliding gently through my bloodstream. "I think my dad is continuously confused how he ended up married to her."

"Do they have a good marriage?"

I nod. "They do. As my mom says, he'd go mad with a normal woman."

Ruby chuckles, cocking her head to the side. "I thought you'd said on Valentine's they were a family of doctors and you were a disappointment."

I rub my hand on the back of my neck. "You remember that, huh?"

"I do." She bites her lower lip. "It's how I felt in my house growing up."

I want to follow the thread, but know it's smart to be open with her to get the answers I desire. "My mom is a neurosurgeon, my dad and oldest brother are heart surgeons, and my youngest brother is an orthopedic surgeon resident." I smile. "And then there's me."

"Does it bother you?"

I answer honestly. "I try not to let it, but sometimes it does. I have their same work ethic and drive, but coding software doesn't quite live up to saving lives."

Her expression softens. "It does if saving lives doesn't make you happy."

"Good point. Growing up I thought being a doctor was the only profession available. I had no idea people did other things." I laugh, as I continue the story, remembering. "I used to sneak off into my room and take computers apart as stress relief. When I went to college I tried, I majored in premed, like I was supposed to. I hated it, but kept trying to ignore how much I hated it. On break my mom decided it would be fun to let me watch a surgery, hoping to inspire me to follow in her footsteps."

I shake my head, thinking back to the embarrassment.

Ruby's eyes are wide. "What happened?"

I blow out a breath, prepared to humiliate myself for her benefit. "I fainted."

Ruby bursts out laughing and covers her mouth. "I'm sorry."

I squeeze her foot and she tenses under me. I grin. "Brat."

"Then what happened?" She's still giggling and it makes me happy. Makes it worth it.

"My mom figured out this probably wasn't a good sign for my medical career. She sat me down and I confessed my dirty little secret: that I hated all things medicine, couldn't stand the sight of blood, and I was miserable." I drink down the rest of my wine, picking up the bottle and pouring the rest into our glasses. "She broke the news to my dad and I changed my major to computer science after the break. He's forgiven me, and tries not to be too disappointed that he doesn't have the trifecta of surgeon sons." I have a decent relationship with my dad but he doesn't quite understand me. My mom is the nucleolus of our family and everything revolves around her. "I tend not to have a lot to contribute at family dinners."

"I can relate to that," Ruby says, her voice soft.

"Tell me." I keep the demand out of my voice.

She takes in a deep breath and blows it out. "I'm a minister's daughter."

And another piece of the Ruby puzzle falls into place.

7.

Ruby

Surprise flashes across Chad's features before the light of understanding dawns in his eyes. As though everything about me suddenly makes sense. And I suppose that's not far from the truth. I normally don't talk about my family, especially with guys, but Chad makes me want to tell him things.

I don't know why, maybe because he's so forthcoming, but I want to tell him all the things that makes me, me. All the things I keep hidden. I feel safe, because there's no coyness about Chad, he has no artistic sensibilities that make the guys I'm usually with so invested in being tortured.

I blow out a long breath. "They're great people and I had a normal, loving childhood. They're not fire-and-brimstone types, preaching hell and damnation. They are just deeply religious and conservative. My dad is the minister in our small town. My mom's a stay-at-home wife. We went to the Christian school, church on Sunday, choir on Mondays, bible study on Wednesdays, and church socials on Friday."

He wraps his long fingers around my ankle and I jump a little, repressing my desire to jerk away. It's not that I don't want his hands on me, because the truth is, I've thought of little else since he kissed me in the foyer. It's the strength of my desire that scares me, that makes me want to distance myself.

He doesn't say anything about my sudden tension, instead he nods. "That's a lot of church."

"It is. My brother and sister are eight and six years older than me. They live in the same town we grew up in, within two miles of my parents' house, and are just as devout. I've never asked, but I think I was a surprise baby."

He smiles and squeezes me a little. "In more ways than one, I'm sure."

The wine has gone to my head and I hold out my hands. "This is what you get for not using birth control."

He laughs, a rich hearty sound. He tilts his head. "So we're both rebels." His fingers work under my jeans leg.

I rest my head on my open palm. "Can a software developer be a rebel?"

"Oh yes." He strokes over my skin and heat sears up my leg.

Our eyes meet and I blurt, "I guess you think that explains my sex problems."

He cocks a brow. "Do you think it explains your sex problems?"

I break the contact to stare into my glass, the dark red liquid a gentle sway. "I don't think it helps. All that godliness, even though I'm not like that, seeped into my brain."

"I can understand that."

I frown; the alcohol has made my tongue loose. "It's not like they even said sex was bad, but I was required to be upstanding, a proper minister's daughter. They preached abstinence in school, and the dangers of sin. I didn't buy a word of it, but somehow it made its way into my subconscious."

"So is there a part of you that thinks sex is bad?" His voice is gentle when he speaks, his words followed by another stroke of his fingers over my ankle.

I swallow, thinking about the question. "Not exactly." I bite my lip. "I don't know what it is. I can't relax."

He shifts on the couch, puts his glass on the table, and then takes mine and puts it down as well. I watch him with wary eyes, unsure of what he's going to do and on guard.

"Do you feel relaxed with me?" He moves and pats my hip. "Scooch over."

I slide to the edge of the couch, that's deeper than most I've been on, and he squeezes in next to me, putting his hand on my stomach.

I suck in my breath. "Sometimes?"

A smile twitches at the corners of his lips. "I know you're not now."

"I'm not."

"Why?" His thumb traces over my ribs and I barely breathe.

"I don't know what you're going to do."

His hand skims up my body, trailing between the valley of my breasts before he cups my jaw. "We're going to talk. I'm going to kiss you. And at some point I'll send you home."

I don't want to go home. The notion surprises me. I've always reveled in my own space. But there's something about Chad's home that invites me in and makes me want to stay. I nod. "Okay."

"I promise I won't take it any further." He brushes his lips over mine, before scraping his teeth over my lower lip.

The gasp that escapes is involuntary.

He does it again before saying against my mouth, "I like when you make that hot, needy little sound."

Pleasure races through my bloodstream at his words, mixing with the alcohol and making me dizzy. When his mouth passes over mine again, I catch his lips, wanting him to stay. He deepens the kiss, sucking me under. There's no slowness, no lazy pull. No, it's instantly hot.

His tongue touches mine. Our lips tangle, slide together,

part only to reclaim.

His fingers wrap around my throat.

The feel of his hands pushes my body into overdrive. Another whimper escapes my throat. I clutch his arm as I cling to his lips with mine.

He slants his head, deepening the connection between us, his leg slides over me, parts my thighs. I shift, turning toward him to feel the pressure of his body against mine.

I don't know if it's because I trust him, believe his promise, or I just want him, but it's like I'm on fire. I begin to squirm against him, my mouth turning frantic and desperate.

He flips me over, rolling on top of me, sliding between my legs. I arch up, gripping his hips with my thighs.

The kiss transforms into something consuming. His mouth becomes demanding and ruthless. And it sucks me completely under. I'm lost. I rock against him again, his hard cock presses against my soft center.

Our breathing kicks up.

The air turns hot and humid.

And it goes on and on and on. Dragging me deeper. Lighting me up.

Making me want and need and lust.

As erotic as our kiss has become, he makes no move to take it further and—I don't know—it frees something deep inside me. The worry, the pressure that I'll fail dissipates and I sink into the kiss.

Into him.

Chad

I haven't made out with a girl in forever.

I've been kissing Ruby for over an hour and she's driving me right out of my fucking mind. The more she trusts I'm not going to demand more, the hotter and more needy she becomes.

It's addictive.

She arches into my cock, her body now demanding, insistent. I ignore all my instincts to grip her hips and surge against her. To unleash on her.

She wants it, she's practically begging for it, but if I do, she'll freeze.

This is the only way to build her trust.

I finally pull away from her. Smoothing my hand over her stomach, I move to her side, attempting to catch my breath. I've forgotten how erotic just kissing can be. The intoxication of letting the anticipation grow and build, knowing you can't go any farther. I can't remember the last time I've even wanted. The last time my willpower tested.

I rest my head on my open palm and she blinks up at me, her breasts a rapid rise and fall. Somewhere, over the course of our rolling around on the couch, her hair has come out of her ponytail.

Her blue eyes are glassy, her hair a wild mess, fanned out over the couch, her mouth swollen, red, and wet. She's a fucking work of art right now, and lust rushes through me, but I push it away.

I rub my thumb over her lower lip. "Someday this mouth of yours is going to be wrapped around my cock, and that is going to be a very pretty sight."

She sucks in her breath and holds.

I continue my slow stroke. "Is that a good sound or a bad sound?" I already know, but I want her to admit it. I want her to begin to associate her arousal with me.

"Good." Her voice is husky and a bit lost.

I let my attention fall to her lips. "Do you like the sound of my cock in your mouth, sliding in and out of your lips, over your tongue."

"Yes." The word is sweet, filled with longing.

I love her expression right now, so open and trusting, as though she can't even fathom lying to me. "Why?"

She scrapes her teeth over her lip, glances away.

I grip her chin and force her back to me, putting a hint of

demand in my voice. "Tell me why."

She gulps and averts her gaze. "It's something I can give you."

I have to bite back my moan. It's such a beautifully submissive thing to say. Even if in her mind she thinks that it's because of her other issues. I brush a kiss over her mouth. "Do you want to please me?"

"Yes." Not even the slightest hesitation.

Christ. What am I going to do with her?

Well, I have plenty of ideas, but I'm going to need to take my time. But I can't deny she's doing something to me. Something more than sex and desire. Something more than my need to help her. Something I haven't felt in a long time, maybe not ever.

I take the first step in binding her to me. "I want you to do something for me."

She stares up at me with those trusting, vulnerable eyes. "What?"

"When you come for me, I want you to call me after and tell me."

Her whole body tenses, but I was prepared for that. I trace a path over her ribs and make no comment on her tension.

She shakes her head.

"Yes. It's something you can give me."

She sucks in a breath. "I can't."

I expected her resistance too and I'm prepared. "Ruby, how many times since Valentine's have you come thinking about me?"

"I don't know."

She starts to squirm and I put my leg over hers so she stills "You've already admitted you have."

A flush splashes on her cheeks. "I have."

I kiss her, letting my mouth linger, letting her get sucked under before I pull away. "Since that night have you come thinking of anyone else?"

She shakes her head.

I lean down and whisper in her ear, "I already know your

secrets. Already know I'm the man you're thinking about. Already know you're too turned on to go to sleep tonight without touching yourself. I know *all of this*. All I'm asking is that you call me and confirm what I already know."

She blanches, looking horrified, which is perfect because I'm twisted and like her distress. I trace her collarbone. "Let's make it easier. Tell me what you've thought about so far."

Stark dismay plays over her features before she rolls into me to bury her face into my chest, shaking her head.

I laugh. God, she's so adorable and innocent and there's something addictive about it. Maybe it's because she's such a surprise. She's nothing like the girl I thought she'd be when I first met her. "You have to tell me now."

Her head shakes viciously again and she says into my neck, "I can't."

I stroke down her spine and kiss her temple. "And why's that?"

"It's embarrassing."

I smile. "You know there's not much you can say that will shock me." I feign a shudder. "Unless it involves needles and blood. Then you're on your own."

She laughs and the sound vibrates against my throat. "No! It's nothing like that."

If I want to know, I'm going to have to take her options away. I work my hand under her chin and force her to look at me. I meet her gaze and say in a tone that broaches no argument, "Tell me."

Her pupils dilate and she can't quite disguise the tiny tremor. She licks her lips. "It's humiliating."

"And why is it humiliating?"

She blinks. "I'm afraid you're going to laugh."

My heart gives a hard kick against my ribs. Reassuring her isn't enough. She'll need an example. I run my thumb over her lower lip. "Once, I dated this girl that liked to be a pet. One day I threw a ball to her and she crawled after it like she was a little puppy for an entire afternoon. I didn't laugh once. And I promise you I won't laugh at whatever you tell me."

Instead of her expression lightening as I'd expected, it grows more worried. When her chin trembles I say, "What's wrong? I promise whatever it is, whatever you want to say, will be okay. That it sounds worse stuck in your head than it will to me."

My reassurance doesn't clear the tension in her features, but I can't back down. I'll need to push her, break down all her walls and barriers. As much as it frightens her, it's what she needs.

She opens her mouth, but whatever words she's about to say stalls on her lips. "I can't."

"You can and you will." I tighten my hold on her jaw. "You want to tell me, it's your brain that stops you."

She squirms and I release my hold on her. She rolls to her back and stares up at the ceiling and huffs. "I don't know why I want to tell you things."

I know why, but she's not ready to hear those reasons. I place my open palm on her stomach. "Does it matter?"

She swallows and I see the cords of her neck work. "I want to make up a story. To pretend."

I say nothing; just let her work through her thoughts.

She blows out a breath and runs her hand through her hair. "I can't seem to lie to you. No matter how much I want to."

"Is that a bad thing?"

She nods. "I don't want you to know the truth. I want you to want me."

I'm missing something key here, but I don't know what, and won't until she tells me what she's thinking. But I can assure her of my desire. I curl my fingers around her ribs. "I do want you."

Still staring up at the ceiling, her brow furrows. "You belong with a woman like Layla."

I don't doubt that the knowledge that Layla and I went out on a date once upon a time makes Ruby curious, I also don't doubt she believes the statement, but it's also a diversion. And evasions don't fly with me. "You're stalling."

Her frown deepens. "I am."

"It's not going to work. Sooner or later I will find out what you're thinking." I inject that dominance into my voice, knowing the secret part of her will respond. "Sooner is better."

"Why does it matter?"

I lean down and whisper in her ear, "I want to know what makes your cunt greedy."

She gasps, and her body arches, before she settles.

"Now tell me."

Attention still intent on the ceiling, she bites her lip. "That's the problem."

"What's the problem?"

"You have it wrong." She turns and buries her face in my neck again.

I wrap my arms around her and let her hide, wishing I could tell her how much it pleases me that she turns to me in her distress. "Then set me straight."

"I'm not thinking of anything kinky or interesting." She presses in closer to me. "What I think about is boring."

Ah. Now things are starting to add up. I recognize my mistake, the inadvertent pressure I put on her. Her fantasies are innocent, because she has no real experience with depravity. Has no frame of reference, or sexual experience, that drove her crazy. I tilt her chin and kiss her ruby-red lips. "My only expectation is you tell me the truth. All I want is to know what you're thinking in that complicated brain of yours."

When her expression starts to clear I know I'm on the right path and continue. "This isn't about giving me a story to jerk off to, this is about learning you. Understanding what makes you tick. Nothing more, nothing less."

She trembles a little. "Do you promise you won't laugh?"

I brush my thumb over her lower lip. "I promise."

"Okay." She hides her face again. "All I thought about was you standing over me."

The concept is innocent, but the implications are not, and she has no idea what that kind of image does to a guy like me, but now's not the time to clue her in. I prompt her further. "Am I watching you touch yourself?"

She nods.

"Good. I like that idea." I kiss her temple and her muscles loosen. I rub a thumb over the line of her jaw. "I'll tell you a secret."

She tilts her face to look at me. "Okay."

"Men are simple, visual creatures." I kiss her, licking my tongue along flesh made swollen from my mouth. "A girl so turned on she can't help but touch herself while you watch, is probably on most guys' top five sexual fantasies list."

Her whole expression transforms and she gives me a heart-wrenching smile. "Are you saying that to make me feel better?"

I take her hand and press it to my lips before moving it to my cock, straining against the zipper of my jeans. "Does this feel like I'm faking?"

She shakes her head.

I release her hand and it travels back to the safety of my chest.

She sucks in a little breath. "Thank you for not laughing."

I grip her neck and give her my most serious, most intent look. "Sweet or dirty, innocent or depraved I want to know it all."

"I'll try."

I smile down at her. "That wasn't so terrible, now was it?"

"Yes it was."

I laugh. "But later, you'll call me and tell me, won't you?"

She starts to tremble and she clutches my shirt. "All right."

I stroke down her spine. "You're a good girl, Ruby."

She shudders. Sucks in a stuttery gasp, gripping me tighter.

I fist her hair and tug so her face tilts. I lick her, and then scrape my teeth over her jaw. "You're *my* good girl."

She melts into me, and our mouths once again fuse together.

This girl is mine. She will come for me.

It's just a matter of time and patience.

Ruby

I'm lying in bed, staring at my ceiling, panting for breath. I tried so hard to resist, not wanting to make the call I'd promised Chad, but in the end I hadn't been able to deny the ache.

That's never happened to me. I can always resist.

It's two in the morning, I'm exhausted, and when I'd agreed to call him I'd convinced myself I'd go home and go to bed. That I'd have nothing to report.

The darkness enveloping me, I'd lain in bed, replaying the night over and over again until I burned with lust. It was such a strange experience, because it was nothing I'd ever felt. Before Chad infiltrated my thoughts orgasms had been functional, a once in a while occurrence to relieve stress, not neediness. Something I should do because it seemed the only thing I had available to prove I wasn't sexually dead.

But tonight, I felt turned on. Hot. Wet. And swollen.

I don't understand what Chad is doing to me. Or how he's

making me respond when no one else has.

The way he kissed, it was better than sex. Way better.

He kissed like I was the only woman in the world. That he'd never tasted anything so good in his life. Like he couldn't get enough, but he'd been true to his word, and never gone further.

It had given me a freedom that was foreign to me.

I hadn't had to think or plan what I was going to do. I didn't have to think about what kind of guy he might be, what kind of sex he was into so I could play my part. I didn't have to fake *anything* because he expected nothing from me. For the first time I let myself feel, surprised to find I could.

I glance at my phone, lying on the table next to me. I'd promised.

He'd made me a promise earlier tonight and kept to it. Now I had to do the same.

My cheeks flushed. I picked up my phone and pressed his number.

"Hello, Ruby." His voice is sleepy.

I clear my throat. "Did I wake you?"

"You did, but I don't mind."

I bite my lip. "Should I have waited until morning?"

"No," he says, his tone filled with that steady surety that soothes me. "If I'd wanted you to wait, I would have said so."

A distant part recognizes what I'm doing and wants to stop me, but I'm too tired for that. I close my eyes. "All right. Thank you for a lovely evening."

"You're welcome. Are you busy after work?"

My heart leaps with excitement. "No."

"Do you want to go see a movie?"

"Yes." I'm almost embarrassed to admit to myself, that I would have said yes to almost anything to be with him. Oh god, I'm turning into one of those girls. I'm not sure I can handle it.

"Good."

"All right then…" I clear my throat again. "Good night."

Just as I think I've gotten off scot-free he says, "Aren't you forgetting something, girl?"

A lightning bolt of need shoots straight through me. How many times have I witnessed Michael call Layla "girl" with an envy I can barely admit? My face heats. "Um… No?"

He chuckles low and lazy. "So you are not calling to tell me you fucked yourself with your fingers and came?"

He makes it sound so good. So delicious and wicked.

"Oh, that." I try and make my voice light. "That too."

"Tell me." His voice lowers. "Say the words, I came thinking about you."

I lick my lips, going hot all over again. "I came thinking about you."

"Did you think about tonight?"

"Yes." It's so much easier when he asks me questions.

"Did you think about me standing over you?"

"Yes." I had, I pictured him staring down at me, his blue eyes hot, his gaze intent. And the more I thought of it, the hotter I got.

"Did you play with your nipples?"

I don't understand how he does it. My belly turns heavy with lust. "Yes."

"And I watched you?"

"Yes." My breathing kicks up.

"Are they hard and begging for attention right now?"

At the words, my nipples pull impossibly tight. I croak out, "Yes."

"You're going to touch them and listen to me talk. Your nipples are all I want you to touch, understand?"

"Okay." I can't believe I'm doing this. The part of me that always rears up tries to stop me, whispering this is wrong, that I shouldn't, but I don't let her win. Chad is accomplishing something no other man ever has, and I don't want to stop.

"What are you wearing?"

"A tank top and underwear." My tone is filled with breathless excitement.

"Lose the tank top."

I work it over my head and toss it to the floor.

"I want you to sleep like that tonight, picture me behind you, playing with your breasts, my hard cock settling into the curve of your ass."

The image is sharp and crystal clear, and I want it to be reality. "All right."

"Are you lying on your back?"

"Yes."

"Close your eyes, and think of me standing over you, and circle your nipples."

My lashes flutter closed, my breath kicks up, and I drag my fingers over the puckered skin. I gasp, arching a little. I see him like he was tonight. His arms crossed, looking down at me.

"You do know at some point I'm going to be standing over you, watching you do this, don't you, Ruby?"

The thought terrifies me and fills me with a needy anticipation. I want to protest it will never work, but don't. Instead a needy whimper leaves my lips.

His voice grows lower, more intimate. "Do you like it soft, or hard?"

"Both." My fingers move insistent over my nipples.

"Is soft more of a tease?"

"Yes."

"I'm looking forward to having my mouth on them."

I moan, and roll my nipple between my thumb and forefinger.

"Just keep it soft until I tell you otherwise, okay?"

I slow my pace. I can't help it. I don't know why. I just find his instructions so reassuring. They relax me. I don't have to think about anything but the sensations racing over my skin, heating places I thought didn't exist. "Okay."

"You have the most fantastic breasts, at some point very soon I'm going to play with them for hours." He laughs, low and wicked. "And I do mean *hours*."

I gasp, fingers tightening.

"I'm going to lick and suck and bite."

"Chad." His name is uttered in a voice I've never used before, full of throaty rasp.

"What do you need, Ruby?"

"I-I don't know." All I know is I want something only he can give me.

"You can picture it right now, me bending down, my mouth sucking, can't you?"

"Yes."

"Have you ever tried to lick your own nipples?"

His words shock me, sending a jolt of electricity through me. "No!"

That's completely depraved.

"Your breasts are large enough to let your tongue play over them."

"I'd never…" I trail off on a startled gasp as my fingers grip my nipple and tug.

"Remember, soft, Ruby. Gentle."

I slow, my body breaking out in a sheen.

"Do me a favor, dip those fingers between your legs and tell me how wet you are."

Yes. I want that. I slide my fingers into my panties to find myself wetter than I've ever been.

"Are you wet, Ruby?"

"Yes."

"Good, now circle your nipples with your wet fingers."

I can't explain it, how he's making me burn, or even *why* he's making me burn. I've play acted before, stroking my nipples for some guy because he liked to watch, pretending I'm some porn star to get him off, but this is different.

It's the dirtiest act I've ever engaged in.

It feels wrong, and right, and everything in between.

I gather my wetness and then paint it over my nipple, sucking in a breath.

"Again."

I don't even hesitate.

"Again."

"Chad." My voice is almost unrecognizable.

"Am I standing over you?"

"Yes."

64

"What do you want me to do? Just watch you? Or lick your nipples?"

"Lick me." I'd kill to have his mouth on my breasts right now.

"I'd lick your skin clean. Then start all over again."

"Oh please."

"I will, Ruby, I promise you that. Until then, lift your breast and do it for me."

"I don't think I can." That's too wicked. But even as I protest I want it, to pretend it's him.

"We'll see. Won't we?"

"I…" I trail off.

"Here's what we're going to do."

"Okay."

"We're going to get off the phone and when we do, you're going to come hard for me. I want you to let it all go, okay? Don't think about anything. You're by yourself. You don't even have to tell me what you did. I only have three requirements. Okay?"

"I'm listening." I want to come so bad I'm about to explode.

"I want you to think of me, standing over you, my tongue sliding over your nipples. I want you to be completely abandoned. And lastly, I want you to do whatever comes naturally. I don't want you to censor yourself at all. Does that sound fair?"

I nod and realize he can't see me. "Yes. I'll try."

"Good girl. In return, I won't even ask. Won't even hint. You won't have to tell me anything you did or thought. Unless you want to, of course."

"Never," I gasp out.

He laughs. "Entirely your choice, girl. Come hard. I'll see you tomorrow."

And with that, he's gone.

I put the phone down. Thinking about the heat that laces all our conversations. The ways he makes me burn with something I don't even have a name for. I close my eyes and think of him, exactly the way he described, as he instructed. I shudder.

I pull and tease my nipples as I've never done before. I promised him abandoned and even though he's not here and he'll never know, I give it to him. Here, by myself, with no one to worry about, I can be free.

I throw my head back, and tug on the hard buds, plucking them over and over again as I moan. My hips rise of their own volition. I call out his name into the darkness, feeling silly and hot all at the same time.

And finally, when I can stand it no more, I raise my breast; tilt my head and lick, my tongue brushing the very tip of my nipple. It throws me off a cliff I've never let myself experience, and I shove my hand between my legs, rubbing my clit as my tongue flicks over my nipple and I envision Chad watching me. Alternating between my lips and his.

I come in an explosion, crying out in abandon as the orgasm rocks through me. Reeling through a climax that goes on and on, barreling over me in endless, violent, mind-numbing waves.

When I finally settle, I curl up on my side and wish he was behind me, keeping me warm. My last thought before I drift into a dreamless sleep was I want him to know, simply so he can understand his power over me.

9.

My phone rings at nine-o-one the following morning, about four minutes after I sit down at my desk. I work for a small specialty ad agency as a graphic designer. It's a job, and at least it's kind of creative, and I don't have to sit around looking at numbers and spreadsheets all day.

It's not my dream or anything. It pays the bills.

I'm not sure I know what my dreams are these days.

Before I can turn introspective, a trend it seems, I pick up my cell. "I'm impressed you waited this long."

Layla's laugh fills the line. There was a time I thought I'd never hear her laugh again and the sound is still music to my ears. That period of time, when Layla's fiancé John had died, was the darkest time in my life, although it was much worse for Layla. He'd been my friend, and I'd grown up sheltered in this small, perfect town, bad things happened to other people.

But when Layla speaks, her voice is happy. "Michael insisted I wait until at least nine before I hound you."

A small smile flits over my lips, tight and a touch swollen from my night with Chad. I run a finger over my mouth. True to his word, we'd made out like a couple of teenagers, yet there was something erotic and dirty about the way Chad kissed. Something addictive no sixteen-year-old boy could ever manage.

"I have nothing to report. We had dinner at his house and talked." I clear my throat and lie. "It was the most innocent date I've had in ages."

On the surface, it had been innocent. And so much more. I can barely admit it to myself, but some secret part of me was starting to believe Chad might be able to help me. That if I let him in, he can fix that broken part of me.

I didn't like the thought. It's not a man's job to fix me, it's my responsibility, not his. After two nights I already felt this crazy, girlish giddiness, and it worries me. He is not my savior. I'm supposed to be my savior.

And I don't want to feel this way about him. I don't want to feel this way about anyone. Over the years I've grown dependent on my lack of response, it keeps me safe, and a part of me wants to stay safe. What's the point in opening myself up to someone so ill-suited for me? It can only end badly. The thought pops into my head—I should cancel. End this.

I envision getting off the phone with Layla, calling Chad and saying the words that will end this madness between us. And realize… I don't want to.

He holds the key to something I didn't know I was looking for.

"Really now?" Layla's voice rips me from my thoughts. "That doesn't sound like Chad. Or you, for that matter."

Layla knows me better than anyone, in all things but sex. When it comes to sex, she only knows the pretend Ruby. The Ruby I present to the outside world. Sexually confident and independent. A woman strong in her beliefs of empowerment, liberation and choice.

It's not a lie; I do *believe* all those things. I just can't execute them. I sleep with guys, because I didn't want the shackles of conservativeness weighing me down, but I don't know how to free myself of the invisible binds that tether me. I don't know how to turn off my brain and let the pleasure in. Don't know how to lose myself.

My mind scrambles through what I should tell Layla and settles on a loose version of the truth. "We are taking things slow. It's important we stay friends, so when it ends, nobody gets hurt."

My chest squeezes. I'm afraid it's already too late for that.

Layla is silent and I know she wants to question the whys with her planner's brain and is contemplating if she should push. Finally, she says, "Did you have fun?"

"I did." Was it fun? Or was it discovery? I didn't know.

"Are you going to see him again?"

"Yes, we're going to a movie tonight."

Layla giggles. "I want to grill you so hard right now."

My mood lightens, and I laugh. "Thank you for restraining yourself."

"There's something you're not telling me. You're never this secretive."

I wasn't. Normally I told her every detail of my night. What we did, how the guy played me his guitar, or sang me his latest song, or read me his poetry. I'd tell her if I had sex, telling her how good it was, and how he might be the one I stayed with for more than a couple months. Both of us knowing it would never last.

The truth is, Chad is the most stable, most conservative guy I've ever gone out with. Chad is a relationship guy, the guy you bring home to your mom. God, if I brought Chad home, my mom would fall to her knees and praise Jesus her baby had finally found her way.

He's everything I've never wanted in a man. And I've never wanted a man more.

I have no idea what to make of it, or what to do about it, let alone what to say to my best friend, who knows something is different about me. I try again to throw her off the trail. "I'm not being secretive, there's nothing to tell. We had dinner, we talked about our childhood and all the normal first date stuff you already know about him anyway, and that was pretty much it."

"You didn't have sex?" Trying to figure out if that's what I'm not saying.

"I'm sorry to disappoint you, but no we did not. All he did was kiss me." For hours, while he made my body come alive, frustrated with need and desire for perhaps the first time.

"There's something."

I roll my eyes. "Isn't that enough? Is Chad the kind of guy you've been hoping I'd find my way to? Someone dependable and stable that won't bum money from me, or sleep on a futon and cheat on me with other girls?"

"Well, yes...but only if it makes you happy."

"You're getting your wish." I play with the mouse on my computer. "I don't have a lot of experience with nice guys, but maybe they take things slow."

"I guess that's what's confusing me."

"What?"

"Chad isn't a regular nice guy."

And then I understand what she really wants to know. If Chad is being dominant, trying to control me. I frown? Was he? I didn't think so. That's not how it felt. He wasn't pushing me the way I've seen Michael push Layla. He wasn't making demands on me. I think of our conversation last night, his whispered instructions hot in my ear. There'd been no demand there. He was only allowing me to relax so I didn't have to think. That can't be the same thing.

I shake my head. "He's been nothing but respectable to me."

There was a moment of silence before she says, "Good. You deserve someone who will treat you right."

"Let's not get ahead of ourselves. It's a few dates."

"I know, but I can't help it. I'm sorry."

"You're entitled as my best friend." I glance at the clock on my desktop. "I've got to get to work."

"Me too. There's one last thing." She clears her throat. "On the sixteenth we're supposed to go to dinner at Gwen's, it will be Michael and me, Leo and Jillian, Brandon and...one of the three girls he's dating and decides to bring. Do you and Chad want to come?"

My throat grows tight. I'd been on couples nights before—but my date and Chad's were other people—going together, with everyone knowing we were together, wondering why we were together, I'm not sure I'm ready for that. "That's in a couple of weeks. We might not even be together then."

"Or maybe you will."

I try another excuse. "He might be busy."

"Why don't you ask him and let me know."

I nod. "Okay."

"Talk soon."

She hangs up and I stare into space. I'll worry about it later. Worry about Chad, and what he's doing to me, how he's changing me, later.

Now I'll immerse myself in work and not think about anything else.

As soon as I buzz Chad up to my apartment I grow frazzled. A million thoughts race through my brain at warped speed. How my studio apartment will look to him. My place is like a dorm room next to his grown up adult house.

But more than that, I worry he'll take one look at me and know what I did last night thinking about him. I still can't believe I'd been that crazy, so lost in my own lust I'd actually done…that.

I bite my bottom lip. The only thing that makes me feel better is I know he won't ask. Because he promised he wouldn't and I believe him. The only way he'll ever find out is if I confess to him, which of course, I won't.

There's a knock on my door.

I open to find him standing there, looking like an ad for some sort of all-American dream magazine. He's wearing a white button-down rolled up to the elbows, and flat front, light gray pants. His hair is expertly tousled; his blue eyes bright, his smile devilish.

We couldn't be more mismatched. I'm dressed in black skinny jeans, a strategically ripped black T-shirt and black biker jacket. My hair is haphazard, my eyes smoky.

He grins at me. "I hope you plan on living up to that bad-girl outfit you got on."

I flush and wave a hand at him. "I thought we were going casual."

He steps into my apartment. He looks all wrong, he belongs in his house, not mine. "I got held up at work and didn't have time to change."

He steps toward me and my heart leaps and bounds against my ribs. Nerves make me skittish and I blurt, "We don't go together."

My agitation doesn't seem to faze him. He walks up to me, and grasps me by the neck, and without another word, his mouth covers mine.

It's a hard, aggressive, assertive kiss. There's no tentative exploration. He kisses me like he has every right to do so, like it's not even a question. With possession.

I shudder against him, melting into his body.

As I'm about to lose myself completely he pulls away. His tongue licks over my lower lip. "Our bodies disagree."

I clutch at his shirt and pant out, "I'm not your type."

"And I'm not yours." His hand settles on my hip and it's like a brand against my skin, hot and heavy even through the fabric of my jeans. "But I still want you and you still want me."

He brushes his mouth against mine. "And let's be honest, our normal types haven't been working out too well, have they?"

I blink at him, my fingers tightening on the fabric of his shirt. "What are you saying?"

His grasp squeezes on my neck. "I'm saying my normal type hasn't held any interest for me since Valentine's Day. And neither has yours."

I meet his eyes. "Are you always so honest?"

"Yes." The word is simple and straightforward. There's no guesswork with him, no trying to figure out what he's thinking, and I like that about him, no matter how uncomfortable it makes me.

He releases me, only to take my hand, which he raises to his lips. The action, for god knows what reason, makes a flush break out on my face.

"That's a pretty pink." He nips at my knuckles and I feel it all the way down to my toes. "How far should we go tonight?"

"W-what?" My heart is pounding so hard I can hear it in my ears.

"Should we only kiss again?" He licks across my skin. "Or can I play with those fantastic breasts of yours?"

"You're asking?" My words stutter and tumble from my mouth.

His eyes darken, turning hot. "Would you rather I decide?"

He's been here five minutes and I already feel like I'm going to burn up. I nod. "Yes."

He pulls me close and whispers in my ear, "I'm going to enjoy licking your nipples. Rolling them against my tongue, sucking them until they turn as red and swollen as your mouth."

I whimper, my legs quivering. I clutch at him as though I'm scared if I let him go, he'll be gone.

"I'm going to make you beg for my fingers between your legs, stroking over your wet clit, but I'm going to deny you." His teeth scrape the flesh along my earlobe. "I'm not going to stop playing with you until you're rubbing your hot little cunt against me and pleading. And I'm not going to deliver. That's as far as I'm going to go. All you're going to be able to think about is how long you're going to have to wait until I touch your needy pussy like I did in that hallway the other night."

He raises his head and meets my gaze, which has to be glassy, matching the lust streaming like heroin through my blood. "Sound good?"

I nod.

"Good. Time to go."

Chad

Ruby doesn't say much of anything as we drive to the movie theater in the slow stop-and-go traffic that clogs Chicago streets this time of night. She's lost in her thoughts and I let her be, dragging her along by the hand as we walk to the theater and I pay for our tickets to the indie art film we both wanted to see.

It's a Monday night, and I expect the theater will be near deserted. Which is perfect for my plans. I've already figured out Ruby needs to have things spelled out for her. That knowing what to expect, and what she doesn't have to worry about, relaxes her. That the freedom not to worry helps clear her mind and allows her to focus on the desires of her body.

I don't understand this by magic like she probably believes. I know these things because I have years of experience with submissive girls, and this is a very common trait. Not that I can explain that to her, because she's not ready to hear it. Despite the needy readiness of her body, she's not ready to come for me. If I tried now, it would be a disaster, and she'd end up feeling like a failure, and I can't have that.

She doesn't understand what I'm doing, or how I'm making her want to fuck so desperately, and she doesn't need to for it to be effective. All I care about is every time I tell her what to do, and she does it successfully, I'm building her confidence.

When she called me in the dead of night to confess, that's a success. She doesn't see it that way, because she only defines success by being able to come on my hand or my cock, but every time she comes thinking about me, because I tell her to, even though I'm not there, I'm building up the connection in her mind.

It's why I didn't need to ask her about last night, because I already know she did exactly what I told her to do, because that's how she's designed. And even though she doesn't understand or want to acknowledge it, the end result will be the same. Her confidence will grow, her limits will stretch and her boundaries will expand. She thinks it won't work, but I know better. She's at a disadvantage, because I know how she's wired a thousand times better than she does.

I'll use the power only for good. To empower her, and allow her to become the woman she's meant to be, and not the woman she's pretending she is.

I buy popcorn and pop, somehow pleased when she wants regular Coke instead of diet. She casts furtive glances at me as we walk to the theater.

When we walk into the darkened room she goes to walk down the steps, but I stop her and nod. "Back row."

Her eyes widen and flash with a mixture of fear and excitement.

The exact type of expression I get off on, which would probably terrify her. I jut my chin toward the row and when we sit down in the middle, I say, "In case I get the urge to lick your nipples during the movie."

She sucks in a breath and her cheeks heat.

It hasn't escaped my notice that Ruby's arousal increases in direct proportion to how dirty I talk to her. Nor am I above using it to my advantage.

By the time I fuck Ruby she's going to be able to think of nothing but my cock sliding into her willing cunt twenty-four hours a day, seven days a week. The only real question is how long that will take. But it doesn't matter, because I'm nothing if not patient.

My attention falls to her lips. Right now we're the only people in the small theater. "Have you ever let anyone play with you in the movies?"

She shakes her head.

"We'll have to change that, now won't we?"

Her gaze darts around the theater.

I push the bag of popcorn into her hand. "Have some popcorn."

She takes it but makes no move to eat. The theater darkens

and the pre-trailer commercials come on. I put my hand on her thigh and she jumps.

I lean over and whisper, "Remember I'm only going to kiss your lips, and your breasts, nothing else. No matter what."

She nods.

Another couple comes into the theater and she tenses.

I chuckle and squeeze her leg. "They won't save you."

She licks her lips and darts her gaze to mine. "I don't think I want to be saved."

My chest squeezes. She kills me when she says things like that. I work my hand up her leg, high on her thigh and kiss her. Her mouth clings to mine. I want to take her, defile her. I want to ruin her. But I can't do any of that.

I pull back, work my hand between us, swiping my thumb over her hard nipple.

She makes that needy little gasp in the back of her throat.

A loud action movie trailer comes on the screen and I whisper, "That sound makes me so fucking hard."

She makes it again and clutches my shirt.

I stroke the distended bud. "Later tonight, I'm going to have you stretched out over my bed, naked from the waist up and I'm going to make a feast out of you."

She makes a needy sound.

"What, Ruby? Tell me what you're thinking."

She looks at me, and even in the darkness I can see the desire in her eyes. "I want it now."

"I know." That's the whole point, to give her a chance to want. To need.

Even if it's torture.

10.

Ruby

I'm exactly where Chad told me I'd end up.

Stretched across his fantastic bed, naked from the waist up, my body on fire. His tongue plays over my nipple, before he sucks deep and my hips rise from the bed with a needy jerk. I cry out, desperate for him to provide some sort of friction, but he doesn't deliver.

Like he said he wouldn't. Like he promised.

I have never felt anything like this.

I'm not sure if I love it or hate it.

He's just so…relentless.

I don't remember one thing about the movie tonight. All I remember is the feel of his palm hot on my thigh, the stroke of his tongue over my lips. The pull, straight to my core, as he slid over my breasts.

His teeth scrape over my flesh and I gasp out, "Chad."

He raises his head. "Have you had enough?"

Have I? "I…" I trail off and lick my lips. "I don't know."

77

"You let me know when you figure it out." His mouth returns to my breasts.

How is he doing this? His fingers roll the distended bud and it makes my clit pulse like it has its own heartbeat. I want him to touch me so bad, but I'm so scared. Terrified as soon as he does I'll freeze, and lose all this heat and desire. It's like being on a roller coaster. Elation and fear all rolling together, combusting through my system, confusing me.

"Please..." I don't even know what I'm asking for. What I want?

He raises his head again, stares intently at my face. He must not like what he sees there because he moves to the side and props his head on his open palm. His free hand plays over my ribs, before lazily circling my nipple. "Tell me what's on your mind."

I shake my head. I don't even know. Nothing is wrong.

"Are you overwhelmed?" His mouth is full from all the time we spent kissing, his hair bed rumpled.

Why is he doing this? Taking this much time with me? Why is he doing this when there are so many better options out there? I suddenly need to know. "Are you frustrated yet?"

He frowns. "No."

"How can you not be?"

"It's been two dates."

It's true, but I know these aren't typical dates for him. The desire to ask him about the dominance he must be repressing for my benefit tangles in my throat. I don't want to ask. Because I don't want to hear the answer. I'm not ready to deal with the part of him that will be our undoing. Layla once told me that for people like them, it's as much a part of their makeup as hair color. It's only a matter of time before keeping it locked away starts to weigh on him.

I can't start to need him. There are too many differences between us.

But I can't say any of those things because I want to ignore it. For at least a little while. Is that so wrong? I settle on part of my worry, the easier part. "You can't say this isn't the tamest date you've been on."

He shrugs. "It's also the hottest."

"You don't have to say that."

Like lightning, his hand leaves my breast and grips my jaw, forcing my face to his. "I always mean what I say. Always."

I gulp.

There's an edge to his tone as he continues. "You've fucked guys, maybe even after the first or second date, but tell me, Ruby, did you feel like this? Even when their cocks were inside you?"

I shake my head. "But that's different."

"Why?"

"Because I'm dead below the waist."

He laughs.

I push my head back against the fluffy pillow to glare at him. "You're laughing?"

He grins, and with his rumpled hair and the color high on his cheeks, he looks devilishly boyish and disarming. It's what I believed about him since I first met him, but I know it's a lie now. The only thing true about him is that he's the devil. He puts his hand on the curve of my hip. "Is that why you tried to get me to rub your pussy for the last hour? Because you're dead below the waist?"

A flush of heat rolls across my chest. I bite my lip. "That's not normal."

He gives me a little squeeze. "There's a difference between being dead between the waist and your brain getting in the way of relaxing enough to have an orgasm with someone else in the room."

Is there? My brow furrows. "And you think you'll be able to get me to relax?"

He strokes over my stomach, making slow circles over my belly, ribs, and the curve of my waist. I get lost in the movement, the hypnotic dance of his golden skin against my paleness.

Finally he says, "I'm not sure relax is the word I'd use. But, yes, I'm going to make you come."

The knowledge that I've always been a failure at sex, wars with hope. I want to believe him, but I can't. "I have years of experience that say otherwise."

He meets my gaze. "Has anyone really tried? You've been faking your reactions for so long you've never given any guy a chance to test you."

He's right, and that he sees this so clearly makes me feel small and vulnerable. "Can I have my shirt?"

"No." The word is simple and straightforward.

We stare at each other for endless moments, and his gaze is so direct and unwavering, I end up dropping my gaze.

He starts his lazy path over my skin again. "I know this is hard for you, I know you want to control and manage your way out of this. But you're not going to be able to do that with me, Ruby. You're going to have to trust that I know what I'm doing."

All this focus and attention, it makes me uncomfortable. It's part of my unease. I blink, my throat tight. "What about you?"

"What about me?"

I bite my lip and heat infuses my cheeks. "Can I at least do something for you so I don't have to worry."

His expression turns perplexed. "Worry about what?"

"I don't like the idea that you're suffering because of my issues." Embarrassed, I clear my throat. "Not that I'm saying I'm so irresistible you have to struggle. It's just if I could take care of you, it would make me feel less guilty about all the attention you're paying me while you're forced to deal with my problem."

He stares at me for several long moments before he shakes his head. "What am I going to do with you?"

"Umm…" I shrug. "I don't know. I'm sorry I'm such a pain."

"Ruby." He waits until I meet his eyes. "You are *not* a pain. I'm not doing you a favor."

I frown. "I don't want you to suffer because of me, especially when I know you can go find another, less difficult woman whenever you want. I feel guilty you're wasting so much time on me when you have other, more attractive options."

Maybe if I take care of him, take the focus off me, this heaviness in my stomach would go away. "Can I please take care of you?"

He looks at me for a long, long time, then shakes his head. "No, you may not."

Something flutters through my belly, but I don't know what it is. All I know is it makes me wary. My throat grows tight, there's a suspicious stinging in my eyes, and when I speak, my voice trembles. "You don't want me?"

Chad

Christ. Ruby has no idea how much she's testing me right now. How sweet and addictive her vulnerability is to me. It's not her innocence that's tying me up in knots; it's her trust, her ability to lay herself bare for me.

People underestimate the truth. Underestimate how hard it is to be brave and speak it, even when they are scared. That Ruby does this with me so quickly, and so fucking completely, is one of the most gorgeous things I've ever seen.

She has no idea how rare it is. Or how strong and powerful it makes me feel that she's chosen me as the person to tell her secrets. Dominance and submission is not about rules and orders and scenes, but this, right here, is submission.

Laying yourself bare and trusting the other person won't break you.

And I will not break Ruby.

There's so much tangled up in what she's saying I have to think through what to address first. I take her simplest and last question first. "Ruby, we are just starting to know and learn each other, so I understand you don't trust this about me yet. But I don't do things I don't want to do. Don't say things I don't mean. And I do want you. If I didn't, I wouldn't be here. I have a lot going on right now—I'm learning a new job at work, I've got more buildings under renovation than ever before. My partner is getting married, so things he normally deals with are left to me. The truth is, a simple, uncomplicated girl is exactly what makes sense right now."

Ruby tenses under my palm and I know this notion doesn't sit well with her. But I continue, because being honest with her, not feeding her some bullshit line, is the only way she'll believe what I say.

I cup her jaw and force her attention to me. "You are not easy. I'm not going to pretend you are. Yes, you're right, there are girls I could call that would come over without question, do whatever I want, and have orgasms without me even breaking a sweat."

She tenses again, steeling herself with her invisible armor against her perceived failings, but I don't even break stride. "You don't make sense. You take time and patience and understanding. You're right; I have lots of options to choose from. And I choose you. It's that simple. In the sea of options you're the one I want. You're the one that keeps me up at night, the one that preoccupies me at work, and makes me so fucking hard I think I might go crazy. I want you more than I've wanted anyone in a long time, and you're worth the effort to me."

Under my fingers her throat works and her chin trembles as she struggles not to cry. She turns toward me; pulls from my grasp. I let her go, only to wrap her back up again as she buries her head in my neck to hide. I wonder if she understands how sweet it is, that even in her emotional distress, she turns to me instead of away.

I kiss her temple. "Your value and worth to me is not if you come or if you make me come. It does not define you, and orgasms are not the only checkmark of a positive sexual experience. Until you realize that, I'll have to wait to have your lips around my cock. Do we understand each other?"

She shivers in my arms and nods before mumbling against

my neck, "But I'd feel better."

I lean back and tilt her chin until she looks at me. Then I brush my mouth over her full lips. "Ruby, I want the same thing you do, and that's what you don't understand."

"I don't know what you mean." Her voice is shaky and full of emotions she's probably been repressing since she was old enough to know what sex was.

"I want you to suck my cock because you want to, not because you want me to get off to relieve your guilt. Because you think it buys you time."

Her eyes grow wide and huge with understanding, before she shakes her head. "No—"

I cut her off with a ruthless kiss. "When you beg for it, I'll consider it, but not a second before."

She shudders, her expression turning confused, and lust filled, before flashing with shame.

She sees these desires of hers—to please and obey and give up control—as a weakness. But she'll learn soon enough that they'll lead to her power, and when that day comes it will be a sight to behold.

I'm going to be the man that witnesses the transformation.

I lean down to the shell of her ear. "Ruby?"

"Yes." Her breath is hot against my skin.

"I want you to spend the night."

She melts into me. "Okay."

11.

Ruby

"Ruby. Ruby!" A voice rips me from my wandering thoughts and I jerk in my office chair to look at my friend and coworker, Ryan Kemp. He flashes me a boyish grin. "What are you thinking about? I've been calling your name for a minute."

"Nothing, nothing at all." I will my cheeks not to heat.

I'm doing it again. Staring off into space and thinking about Chad. After two weeks of his constant torture, I'm a mixture of exhausted and manic, running on my hundredth wind, mooning over a guy I hadn't given a second's thought to three months ago.

Ryan slaps his hands on my desk and leans forward in excitement. "Is this about a guy? Did you finally score the bass player?"

Ryan works with me in the graphics department and looks like he should be a surfer in Southern California, instead of suffering through Chicago weather. He's blond, with light golden-brown eyes, and a tall, lanky build. He has the most charming smile and is unbelievably good looking. He's also gay. Two years ago, we bonded in the break room over a love of music and the musicians that break our hearts. He's my best work friend.

I have said nothing about Chad. I still don't know what to say.

No matter how I try, I can't stop the heat crawling up my neck. I don't know why I am so nervous and skittish to talk about Chad, but I am. Everything we're doing feels so incredibly intimate, so unbearably private. It's like a part of me believes that anyone who sees me will instantly guess what we are doing together. How much he's coming to mean to me.

In my vast history of dating, nobody has ever attempted to learn me the way Chad has, and he's fast becoming an addiction. But like any addict, I want to hide him away so nobody can guess the havoc he's causing in my life.

I shake my head. "Nope. The bass player is off my radar."

Ryan narrows his eyes, peering at me intently. "Then who is it?"

"Nobody." I tsk and roll my eyes. "Not everything has to do with guys."

Ryan waves a finger over me in a big circle. "There's only one thing that puts that look on your face. A hot musician. So spill."

Hot musicians seem so simple now. "Don't you have work to do?"

"Yes."

My text buzzes and my stomach leaps when I see Chad's name on the screen.

Ryan leans over the wall of my cubical. "Is that him?"

"No!" I bite the inside of my cheek to keep from grinning.

"Chad, huh?" Ryan waggles his eyebrows. "Sounds preppy."

"You can go now." I point in the direction of his cube, two down from me. We used to sit right next to each other, but we got moved around and separated when the new girl came. We try not to hold it against her.

Ryan raises a brow. "Is he preppy?"

He's not going to give up and he knows me too well. I sigh. "Yes."

"What instrument does he play?"

I smile and tilt my head to the side. "SQL."

Ryan's expression widens in surprise. "He's not a musician?"

I shake my head, feeling like I'm betraying some sort of secret, unspoken code by dating a grown up. I lower my voice and whisper as though I'm saying something obscene, "He's an IT guy."

Ryan bursts out laughing. "When can I meet him?"

"Never," I hiss, before waving him away. "Now go."

My phone beeps again and it's Layla. I pick up my phone. "I have to get this."

"Don't want to leave Chad waiting, huh?" Ryan grins at me. "Don't forget to play hard to get."

Brow furrowing, I stare down at my screen and realize with a sudden strangeness that I don't have to play those kinds of games with Chad. That I don't have to play *any* games. In the brief time I've been with him I always know exactly what to expect. There is no guesswork. Even more strange, I like it.

I break all my rules for him. Every single one of them. I'm emotional and vulnerable. I make confessions like they are going out of style. I've learned over the past two weeks that I can be completely honest with someone. For the first time in my life, I feel authentic. Every time I admit that I'm scared, or insecure, I gain a tiny bit of freedom.

Before Chad, I believed I'd be bored to tears without any sort of angst and drama. That nice, stable guys weren't my cup of tea. My experience has always been that if a guy is too into me, I somehow lost interest in him. But I don't feel like that at all with Chad. If anything, I am more infatuated than I've been in forever.

Why don't I feel like that though? Shouldn't his utter conviction and commitment to spending time with me be a turn off?

For the millionth time I wonder what he's doing to me. How he's doing it.

I swipe the screen and look at his text. *I'll miss seeing you tonight. Sing pretty.*

I sing at The Whisky tonight and won't be seeing him. I text back, *I'll miss you too.*

It's not a lie. I will miss him. Miss talking to him. Miss the way he kisses me. Touches me. The way I squirm as I silently urge him to take things further, even though I know he won't. I've never been preoccupied by sex before. It's strange, disconcerting and intoxicating. It's like he's an itch right under my skin.

A buzz on my phone. *If you come tonight, I insist you call me and tell me about it.*

A strange urge creeps over my skin. The urge to test. To see what he does. I don't know what I'm hoping for but I don't resist. *And if I don't?*

I hold my breath, waiting for his response, not sure what I want him to say. His dominance lurks in the back of my mind, like a monster in a closet I don't want to open but keep turning back toward, over and over again. In the time I've spent with him he's never pushed me the way I have seen Michael and Leo push. Has never overtly ordered me to do something.

But there is…something…and part of me is waiting. I don't want to deal with it because I'm certain it will be our undoing. I'm not like Layla and Jillian and never will be. Someday, I'll have to confront it, but I don't want it to be today.

Yet, here I am, testing to see what he'll do.

While I wait, I look at Layla's text, asking me if Chad and I are coming to dinner tomorrow.

My stomach flutters and I study my computer screen displaying the graphics for the ad campaign I'm working on. I've been avoiding. I swirl my mouse, and feign like I'm going to do some actual work, but really I'm waiting for the sound of my phone.

It comes five minutes later, and I about jump out of my chair before lunging for my phone.

Your orgasms belong to me now.

I stare at the words, reading them over and over until they blur together. Excitement and panic bounce across my skin, making me hot. How am I supposed to respond to that? And why do I like the way that sounds?

Chad has a way of describing things, of talking, that sends the type of lust I thought people made up, flooding through my system. Between his wicked tongue, skilled hands, talented mouth, and a patience that continues to shock me, my body is coming alive for the first time.

It makes me hope. And dread that day where he finally tries and I fail.

He repeats over and over again that doesn't define me as a woman. While I appreciate the words, I don't believe them. The truth is I want what everyone else has. I'm not saying it's everything, but it is important. It's something I can't give him, no matter how hot he makes me. No matter how he makes me believe.

I read his words again. I have no idea how to respond so that's what I text. *What am I supposed to say to that?*

His response comes a minute later. *All you need to say is yes, Chad, I will call you.*

I try and imagine what Layla might say, or Jillian, but I have no idea, and as much as part of me wants to test I'm not ready to confront that topic that sits between us. I type back. *Okay.*

Good girl.

I shiver and my stomach heats. The first time I heard Michael call Layla that I'd been appalled, the words were ones you said to a dog or a child in a cooing voice. But I can't deny when Chad calls me that it morphs into the best two words to ever grace my ears.

Thinking of Layla, I turn back to her text. She wants to know about dinner. I haven't said anything to Chad. I bite my lip. I'm not ready yet. They are a tough group to be around, and I am not ready to watch the way they are with each other, knowing Chad's ignoring that part of himself for me. I tell her we can't because he has to work.

There's nothing wrong with avoiding it for a little while. It's too new and I feel too exposed.

I need to stay in this bubble where it's just him and me. Where I can pretend all this other stuff doesn't exist.

Chad

With Ruby working, I meet Michael and Leo at Brandon's new club, The Lair, for a few drinks. When I'd gone out with Layla on a blind date over a year ago I'd never expected to see her again. I'd never thought I'd end up becoming friends with her fiancé and his friends.

But life is funny, and things have a way of working out in ways you least expect.

The guy who introduced me to the scene back in college was way more hardcore than I'll ever be and his crowd liked the extreme. They hung out at leather clubs, participated in slave auctions, and were into heavy degradation. While I was immediately attracted to dominance, I've never had any desire to treat women like objects meant exclusively for my pleasure.

We quickly lost touch.

My long-term, childhood friends are regular guys. Not that there's anything wrong with that, but there's parts of me I don't discuss with them. Begging their girlfriends for blowjobs are problems I just can't relate to.

On the other hand, Michael, Leo and Brandon are the first guys I've met like me and are fun to hang around with. They operate the same way I do. Their girls don't call them sir or master. They aren't into a lot of rituals or anything hardcore, nor do they refer to themselves in the third person. They are into the mental game of dominance. They are guys I can have a beer with, and casually mention I tied a naked girl to my coffee table for a couple of hours while the Bulls played just to watch her squirm.

I slide into the booth in the corner Brandon reserves for us anytime he knows we're coming in. Leo and Michael give me identical, sly grins.

"Hey." I ignore the looks and signal the waitress, a submissive girl named Mandy that took a liking to me Valentine's Day, despite no encouragement from me. Her expression brightens when she spots me, and she hurries over, eagerness in the bounce of her step. She's got on a short, tight, show-stopping black dress that highlights every attribute she has. She comes to stand in front of me and purrs, "Can I get you the usual, Sir?"

Technically, Mandy is exactly my type. She's beautiful, with her long brown hair and doe eyes. She's also uncomplicated. She's submissive, likes to play and doesn't seem interested in commitment. For my busy life, she's perfect, and wouldn't make any emotional demands on me. Her one fault is that she thinks she's in control, but I could disabuse her of that notion pretty quickly. On Valentine's I thought about it for about half a second, before I dismissed her in favor of talking to the complicated, conflicted girl who sat next to me.

To think, that night I'd only wanted to be Ruby's anchor in an overwhelming situation, to soothe her and make her feel safe. To be her friend and ease her distress.

Now I can't get her out of my fucking head for two seconds.

I smile at Mandy. "I'll take Knob Creak, neat."

She trails a finger down my forearm. "A man after my own heart."

She turns and saunters away, her gait seductive and coy, fully expecting me to watch her retreating form. I swing back to Leo and Michael who are still grinning at me.

I nod. "What's up?"

Michael wraps his fingers around his glass and gives me a sly look. "Layla is looking for intel."

I shrug. "She's not going to get it from me."

Leo scrubs a hand over his jaw. "So, Ruby, huh? That's interesting."

"Is it?" I keep my voice level.

"Yeah," Leo says, his expression amused. "We haven't had this much excitement in a dog's age."

"That's sad." Laughing, I point at Michael. "He got engaged."

"Everyone knew that was going to happen." Leo shrugs a shoulder, before eyeing me with interest. "But *this,* nobody saw this coming."

"Except Brandon." Michael points and I follow his gaze and spot Brandon Townsend the third heading in our direction.

Brandon is old Chicago money and it shows. He's got an aristocratic air about him with blond hair, blue eyes and high cheekbones. He's tall, lanky and attracts women like he's the Pied Piper of submissive girls.

He owns the Underground club where Layla and Michael met, this club, the building where construction for offices is underway, an old, historic Chicago mansion in the Gold Coast, and god only knew what else.

From what I understand he inherited a shitload of money but also has the Midas touch. *Everything* Brandon touches turns to gold. Jillian, Leo's fiancée, found an unknown artist, Gaston Lamar, and Brandon has turned him into the talk of Chicago. In a few weeks, they are hosting a private art show for the guy, and made it so exclusive congressmen were begging for tickets.

That's how Brandon was. What he did. The two of us talked a few times about going in on a development, maybe condos, because he liked how I did things, but we'd yet to find the right project, and neither one of us was impatient. I knew we'd find something though, and when we did, I had no doubt they'd be sold before we even started construction and we'd make money hand over fist.

Brandon came to stand in front of the table a smile on his lips. He held out a palm. "You both owe me twenty bucks."

Leo and Michael both sigh and dig money out of their pockets, tossing it on the table.

I furrow my brow. "What did I miss?"

Brandon grins at me. "On Valentine's Day I called you

hooking up with Ruby, they said I was crazy. We wagered. They lost."

I shake my head. "You're betting on my love life?"

Michael shrugged. "He was being a real prick about it."

"We thought it would shut him up," Leo says.

Brandon slid into the booth next to me. "Thanks for proving me right." He scoops up the money. "This will buy a round of drinks tomorrow night."

Confused, I ask, "What's tomorrow night?"

Before anyone can answer, Mandy comes back with my drink, and slides it in front of me. She glances at Brandon, before her gaze darts away. She clears her throat. "Is there anything else, Sir?"

We shake our heads and, timid as a mouse, with none of her customary flirt, she walks away.

"What's that about?" I ask.

Brandon's expression twists in annoyance. "She fucked my manager, in my office no less. She's lucky I didn't fire her."

I laugh. Obviously, Mandy wasn't too hung up on me.

From my experience there's not much that Brandon is not up for, and sex seems to be his vice of choice, but he doesn't tolerate subordinates fucking around with his management.

Brandon frowns. "Laugh if you will, but now I need a new manager. Maybe I'll go female this time around. Someone who won't take shit from anyone and believes in rules."

"You fired the guy?" Michael asks. "You're a hard ass."

"Of course I fired him. I have more tolerance for Mandy, who can't help she likes attention from men in power, but he was supposed to be in charge, and no fucking the staff is one of my only requirements. I'm not about to get stuck with a sexual harassment suit because he can't keep his dick in his pants for five minutes." Brandon still looks irritated by the whole situation. "I walked right in on them. Idiots didn't think to lock the door. How can I have someone that stupid working for me and handling money?"

Leo scrubs a hand over his jaw. "On your couch?"

Brandon scoffs. "Yes, on the couch."

Leo shrugs a shoulder. "In fairness, it's kind of entrapment, that couch begs to be fucked on."

"I know," Brandon says, shaking his head. "I bought it so *I* could fuck on it, not my employees."

Both Leo's and Michael's faces turn smug. I laugh, jutting my chin on them. "I think it's made the rounds."

Brandon zeros in on Michael, his expression full of cunning. "Your sister doesn't surprise me, she's such a depraved little girl and I do enjoy when Leo makes her squirm in front of me. But sweet, innocent Layla?"

Leo rolls his eyes. "Be nice."

Michael blanches and narrows his gaze. "You're an asshole."

But the three of them laugh, because it's all in good fun. They seem to make the best of the fact that Michael's sister is marrying his best friend and that calls for some awkward situations.

Brandon sighs, the corners of his mouth dipping. "Well, that little Mandy is skating on thin ice, so she'd better quake before me if she wants to keep working here."

Not willing to allow another tangent, I return to the round of drinks Brandon mentioned. "What's going on tomorrow?"

Michael squints, scrubbing a hand over his jaw. "We're going to dinner. Layla said she asked Ruby."

"I see." Ruby never said a word. And wasn't that interesting? Learning Ruby is a challenge but there are a few things I understand about her. While she might sing in front of a room of strangers, she prefers to stay in the background. And going to dinner with everyone would put the spotlight on her. So she's avoiding.

"She told Layla you had to work," Michael says.

"Nope." I shake my head.

Leo cocks a brow. "So you'll be there?"

Now I have an excuse to go to The Whisky tonight and confront her, which suits me just fine. I've been thinking about her all day and I want to see her. Besides lying, even by omission, doesn't sit well with me and she will explain herself.

"We will be."

I slip into the back of the bar about fifteen minutes before her set is ending. I don't know what I expect to find, but what I see stops me dead in my tracks. She looks right out of a forties nightclub with a current, edgy vibe mixed in.

I lean against the back wall and soak her in. My cock turns to granite at the very sight of her. Up there on the stage she looks exotic and mysterious, with her black hair, smoky eyes and lips slicked with crimson. She's wearing a red dress that's painted on, has a square neckline, three-quarter sleeves, and ends at her knees.

I figured she had a good voice if she was hired to sing, but she's even better than I expected. It's full and rich and the low rasp of it shoots straight through me. She's singing "Iris" by the Goo Goo Dolls. About not wanting the world to see her, and it's so authentic, so true to what I know she's feeling, I tumble deeper into infatuation.

The song ends, and there's whistles and claps. She smiles, turns to her band, and the melody to a song I don't recognize comes on and she starts to sing. I watch her, captivated, until she finally leaves the stage.

When she walks off, a guy in skinny jeans, a tight T-shirt and shaggy hair, not dissimilar to the one she brought to the engagement party saunters up to her. I bristle, my instincts going on high alert. I know this guy is her type. I can picture him with a guitar in hand, full of rocker boy angst, spouting bad song lyrics to express emotions he doesn't actually feel.

I don't like it.

Possession thrums in my blood, hot, thick and irrational. I straighten from my position against the wall.

The guy puts his hand on her hip, and squeezes, giving her a long once over.

I grit my teeth. *She's mine.* The words pound in my head, over and over again.

Christ. I'm fucking jealous. I *never* get jealous. Jealousy is for weak-minded, insecure men. With clenched hands, I fight back the base, foreign emotion.

She beams up at him and it's like a punch in the gut. Just as I'm about to fly off the handle and do some sort of crazy, caveman shit, she swivels, pushes his hand away, and shakes her head.

Where is this coming from? I saw her with another guy at the engagement party and didn't view it as anything but a minor annoyance.

He grabs her wrist, but to my relief, she shakes her head again, pulls away and walks down a hallway.

I spring forward, following quickly as not to lose her.

Okay, I'm running to catch up to her.

As she's about to disappear through double doors, I call out, "Ruby!"

She whips around and surprise widens her features. "Chad. What are you doing here?"

I take her hand, pull her into a deserted corridor, push her up against the wall, and claim her mouth. She tenses for a fraction of a second then melds into me.

Our mouths fuse.

My tongue slides against hers.

I grip her hips, the hips that guy dared to touch, and tug her closer.

My head slants, deepening the kiss.

She throws her arms around me, pressing her body full against my length.

Every time I touch her I've been slow, careful and calculated. Holding myself back not to overwhelm her, but I can't do that right now. It's imperative she understand how much I fucking want her even though I can't sink into her hot cunt yet.

The kiss turns hotter. Wetter and more desperate.

With one hand planted on those hips that belong to me, I wrap the other around her throat and squeeze. My mouth is possessive, claiming and demanding, and she responds to me just like she's meant to, with needy urgency.

Our breathing turns fast, the air humid.

And when I can stand it no more, I rip away and as she pants against my skin, I whisper in her ear, "If we weren't taking this slow, there's not a thing in this world that would stop me from shredding your panties and fucking you against this wall."

She jerks and whimpers, rubbing her hips against my cock.

I nip my teeth along her jaw, and thrust against her, hard. Letting her get a taste of the full force of my hunger for her. "You're mine. I'm going to own every inch of your body and mind."

She moans and clutches my shoulders, her nails digging into the fabric of my shirt.

"Do you want that, Ruby?" I have to know.

Another needy whimper. "Yes."

I lift my head to look at her. Her lipstick is smeared, and I'm sure it covers me as well as her. I swipe my thumb over her lower lip. "I've marked you."

Like a good little submissive girl her pupils dilate, and she sucks in a breath at the words.

I slide my fingers over the nape of her neck and ask, "Why did you tell Layla I was working and we couldn't go to dinner?"

Her body tightens and her expression immediately turns guilty. Emotions pass over her features before she straightens her shoulders. "I didn't want to go."

"Why?"

She swallows. "I'm not ready to be around them."

"Why?"

"They're all so…" She waves her hand. "You know."

"Kinky?"

She nods. "You won't go past second base and I feel like an eighth grader."

She's adorable. I meet her gaze and take away her choices in this matter, unsure what the consequences will be. "We're going to dinner."

She blinks. "I don't want to."

I could let her argue her way out of this, and while I understand her trepidation, letting her prolong the inevitable will only increase her stress. This is where her not being willing to entertain her submissive nature becomes tricky. Because the truth is, if I demand it, she'll resist but ultimately give in to my desires. The question is if I coax.

I decide to demand and see what she does. "We're going."

Her brow furrows. "Why?"

"Because it's better to get it out of the way so it can stop being weird for you."

"Is it weird for you?"

"No."

"How can it not be weird when they're so…" She gestures with her hand again, unable to bring herself to say the words.

I press my thumb against her pounding pulse. "If we're fucking or not has nothing to do with dinner."

Her gaze turns wary.

I know the real reason she doesn't want to go and in my mind it's not a good one. Right now, locked away just the two of us, she can pretend my being dominant doesn't exist, and at dinner she won't be able to do that. Even under the most normal of circumstances, if you know what you're looking at, the power dynamics between the couples is clear. On a night where everyone knows, like on Valentine's or tomorrow at dinner, they aren't at all shy. Ruby doesn't want to be confronted with what's sitting between us, unspoken.

I have no intention of pushing her on that, because she's not even close to ready, but I'm not going to let her skate out either. The longer she avoids her friends, the more it will grow in her head, and I can't have that.

I stroke down the curve of her neck. "All that matters is you and me. Nothing more, nothing less. There is no competition between them and us. Michael, Leo and Brandon are going to do what's right for their girls. I am going to do what's right for *my* girl, understand?"

A giddy excitement rushes over her face for a split second before it's gone, hidden away. She nods.

"We're going to dinner."

"Okay." She licks her lips. "Does it bother you?"

"Does what bother me?"

Wide blue eyes look up at me and the longing flashes, making them pool liquid for a fraction of second before they become guarded again. "That I'm so far behind where I should be?"

I narrow my eyes and it dawns on me, Ruby, with all her nonconformity, "I don't want to live a regular life" talk, is a closet perfectionist. An overachiever. Maybe it's not manifested in her career, but it is there, hidden under the layers of her outer shell. She's put so much pressure on herself to live, and be a certain way, she can't remember what it's like not to compare herself and come up lacking. I'm the first person she's ever let see this side of her, that she's ever told the truth to, and she's waiting for me to reject her at every turn.

"This isn't a race." I shift my attention to her mouth and then back to her wide, stunned blue eyes. Words won't make her believe, but actions will. "I saw that guy touch you."

Her brow furrows. "What guy?"

That she doesn't remember fills me with a primal satisfaction I don't want to think about. "When you got offstage, a guy came up to you and put his hands on your hips."

"Oh. That."

"I didn't like it." My fingers curl around her neck and squeeze.

A smile lifts the corners of her lips.

I smile back. "Do you like that? Me being jealous?"

"Yes." She blinks up at me, but this time her expression is sly and coy. Mischievous. "Should I not?"

I laugh, shaking my head.

"What?"

"What are you doing to me, Ruby?"

"What do you mean?" She sounds genuinely confused.

I grin down at her. "You can't even begin to comprehend the fucked-up thoughts in my head when I saw him touch you."

"Like what?"

I lean down and kiss her before pulling back to say against her lips, "Possessive things."

She shivers, tilting her hips into me.

I skim my lips over her jaw. "Like how you'd better not let him touch you again."

She giggles and the sound is like music to my ears, all her previously coiled tight muscles unwind. "That is possessive."

"Not that I'd ever say anything so ridiculous."

"No, never." Her voice is amused and filled with happiness.

When I get to her earlobe I tug on it with my teeth. She jerks against me. "Don't pretend it doesn't flip your switch though."

Her fingers tighten on my shoulders and she sucks in her breath. "It does."

"And why do you think that is?" Curious as to what her answer might be.

For the first time since we started this madness she initiates touching me. Her mouth presses against the line of my jaw and then her tongue flutters, sending a spike of electricity over my skin. Then she whispers sweetly, "I want you to want me."

"I do. More than you know." I smile against her neck. "Don't let him touch you again, Ruby."

"I won't."

Of course she won't. Because she's a good girl and her body already knows exactly whom it belongs to.

Me.

12.

Ruby

So here I am, at dinner.

I don't know how I let Chad talk me into this, but I'm fast learning the man is very convincing.

Out of the corner of my eye, I shoot a sideways glance at him. His arm is resting on the back of my chair, and there's no stress in his body at all. Tonight, he's wearing a black shirt, a pullover that's tight across his broad shoulders and flat stomach, and a pair of jeans. His hair is strategically messy, his expression open and easy.

I want to lick him. Bad.

It's such an odd, foreign thought. So unlike me. But it's true.

I think of last night, the guy that touched me when I'd come offstage. Typical of guys like him, Slade—who's real name is Harry—sensed my sudden disinterest in him thus making me immediately attractive. Because with guys like him it's always about the game. The chase. He'd been someone I'd lusted after and thought was unattainable. But when he'd asked me to come back to his house to party, a previously coveted invitation, I had wanted nothing to do with it. I hadn't expected to see Chad, the night had been free to do with what I wanted, but going with Slade, sounded like the least fun I could possibly have. I'd rather have slept.

I didn't know what Chad was doing to me, but he was like a drug, flooding my system and I couldn't get enough. And I'm not going to lie—although I'd never admit it to my feminist sisters—when he'd told me not to let Slade touch me again, even though it had been half a joke, it had made me so hot, so turned on, I wanted to attack him.

Chad insisted we get a good night's sleep, so he took me home, and after we made out for forty-five minutes and I was panting and desperate and crazy, he left.

Of course, I had to call him five minutes after he'd gone to tell him I'd come. He'd laughed, teased me about it not taking long, and then said good night.

Yes, he'd teased, but it was true. The more time that passed the easier it became. It was like I was constantly on fire and orgasms were becoming ridiculously easy, and the results ridiculously explosive. The strange thing was, I found myself wishing it was him. I wanted to feel his hands, not mine. In my fantasies, he'd moved from witness to participant. And instead of him standing over me, distant and removed, I envisioned him moving inside me, desperate to feel the weight of his body over mine.

I've never desired sex before. I've desired touch. Kissing. Roaming. But desiring sex was something new to me. I beg him to touch me. Take me. Beg for things I don't even understand. When I was with him, all I could think about was him pounding into me. What I want hovers just out of my reach, full of shadows. I'm not quite able to articulate this need, this driving hunger for…something, but I know Chad will give it to me.

He catches me watching him and winks.

I promptly blush and look down at my plate.

We're at Gwen Johnson's restaurant, a trendy hot spot with a six-month waiting list, but since Jillian and Gwen are best friends we get a table whenever we want it. Jillian, a former waitress here, has already arranged what we're going to be eating, drinks have been ordered and now we're waiting.

To my relief, nobody made any comment about Chad and I being together, and for that I was thankful. My guess is Chad said something, because Layla and Jillian look ready to burst with questions, but remain suspiciously silent.

This is one of the things I adore the most about Chad, he thinks of everything, even the little things most men are prone to forget. While not being grilled is a relief, I'm still on edge.

Brandon also has a date with him, the red-headed designer he mentioned spanking on Valentine's Day. The woman is stunningly beautiful, which seems to be Brandon's type, but she seems rather bored with us all.

Although in fairness, maybe she feels as awkward as I do, being the lone stranger in our group of well-acquainted friends.

I smooth my napkin over my lap. I dressed carefully, wanting to be casual, but still in line with what I knew Layla and Jillian would wear. I'd fretted for an hour and finally picked a super short black pleated skirt, black over-the-knee tights that left a strip of thigh bare, black boots and a tight black T-shirt that hugged every curve.

Chad had taken one look at me and said, "That outfit is going to be trouble."

I'd chosen right. I felt good, less like an imposter and more like myself.

Chad was changing me—but instead of this being bad like I would have believed—it's somehow empowering. I'd spent so much time pretending, playing a role; I'd underestimated the freedom in being true. Chad made me feel safe, he knew my secrets, and instead of it making me weak, my confidence grew by the day. He allowed me to be scared or worried or nervous, and the oddest thing happened. The more I let myself admit all these things that plagued me, the less I felt them. One by one, they were unraveling inside me, losing their power and I felt myself emerging from a shell I'd been in for so long I hadn't realized I even wore it.

The waitress came back and gave us all drinks, some magical cocktail Layla swore was heaven in a glass.

Brandon raised his glass. "I think we should have a toast."

Everyone picked up his or her glass.

He smiled. "To debauchery."

I laughed, along with everyone else, because it was so Brandon.

We all clinked in a toast and drank.

Brandon caught my eye, gave me his wicked grin, and my stomach tightened. "Since we're all such good friends here, and the lovely Ruby has finally found her way to Chad where she belongs, I think we should make dinner a little more interesting."

I immediately stiffened. This was exactly what I'd been afraid of. I cannot participate in their games. I can't.

Chad puts his hand on my bare thigh and squeezes. I know he means it to be reassuring, but it doesn't help my stress level that is now off the charts.

Michael raises a brow, shaking his head. "Jillian is still my sister so you need to behave yourself."

My galloping heart slows fractionally, as this might be my saving grace. I bite my lip and barely breathe as I wait.

Brandon nodded. "I've taken that into account."

Michael sighed. "Why do I not want to hear this?"

"Where's your sense of adventure?" Brandon's voice is full of sly amusement.

Michael rolls his eyes. "Why do your adventures always include my sister?"

"Hey! I'm not that bad!" Jillian exclaims, her smile huge.

Leo grins. "She's actually very fun."

Brandon shrugs at Michael. "It's not my fault your best friend is marrying your sister." Brandon gestures around the table. "Do you expect the rest of us not to have any fun because you're related?"

"Yeah," Michael says, with a sharp nod, but his hazel eyes

sparkle with mirth. "That's exactly what I expect."

Layla covers her smile with her hand.

Brandon puts his hand on his date's neck and strokes his fingers over the supple lines. "Stephanie needs to be put in her place publicly on a regular basis or she gets out of line, don't you, darling?"

For the first time the redhead looks human because her cheeks flush bright pink and she straightens out of her perceived boredom so fast it borders on comical. She shakes her head. "No!"

Brandon laughs. "Who knows better? Me? Or you?"

Distress flashes over her beautiful features and I soften to her. She clears her throat and looks down at her plate. "You."

"Exactly." Brandon leans over and kisses her neck. "And you went over budget again, didn't you?"

She nods.

He trails a thumb over her jugular. "Since those spankings I keep giving you have turned into quite the incentive to spend my money, I think it's time to come up with something a bit more creative to take care of this problem."

"Please no." She shakes her head and turns pleading eyes to him. "I'll be good."

Brandon gives her a smile so evil, I'm shaking for her. "After I'm done, of course you will be."

I drain my glass in one gulp, it's as delicious as Layla promised, but right now I need it to go to my head to lessen my anxiety.

Thankfully, Gwen, another gorgeous, supermodel redhead comes up to the table a smile on her face. Dressed in a black T-shirt emblazoned with her restaurant's logo, she's tall, thin and has those light blue eyes natural gingers often have. She's like, stop-in-your-tracks stunning. "How's everyone doing tonight?"

"Everything is awesome, Gwenie," Jillian says, looking at her friend.

Gwen glances in my direction and beams at Chad. "This is fun and new."

Chad shrugs as if it's no big deal.

I feign a casualness I don't feel.

Gwen points at my empty drink. "Can I get you another?"

"Yes, please, that'd be great." I want to ask for her to bring me two instead of one, but I keep my mouth shut. I don't want anyone realizing how distressed I am.

This is exactly why I didn't want to come to dinner tonight, what I'd been dreading.

I don't want to be involved in this.

Gwen starts talking about new menu items she's preparing for us, but I can't pay attention because my mind is spinning with all the possibilities.

Chad squeezes my leg again, harder and more insistent this time, and I jump, jerking my attention toward him. He narrows his eyes, studying me intently. His hand leaves my leg, grips my elbow, and says to the table, "Excuse us for a minute."

I stand on shaky legs and follow him, not sure where we're going, just thankful to be away from the table so I can breathe for a minute. Grateful he silently understood I needed to get away. He pulls me down some stairs to where the bathrooms are, and while it's crowded here, the din of the restaurant isn't blaring too loud in my ears.

He tucks me into a corner and shields me with his body, wrapping his fingers around my neck. "Take a deep breath, and relax."

I suck air into my lungs.

He nods. "Good, slower."

I blow out the breath.

He works his fingers into my hair. "Ruby, I'm not going to let anything happen to you. Trust me to do what's right by you. Do you think you can do that?"

My heartbeat starts to slow to a normal speed. "But…"

He shakes his head and says in a soothing voice, "I'm not going to put you in a situation you're not ready for."

"I'm not ready for this, I don't want to be around them."

"You're not ready to be around your friends who love and adore you?"

"Why do you have to put it like that?" I clutch at his shirt, and when I speak my voice is shaky. The truth stumbles across my lips but I force myself to speak it. "I don't want to embarrass you."

His expression softens. "You won't. I know you don't understand this, because you've put yourself under all this pressure, but they don't expect anything from you."

"They don't?"

His thumb brushes the line of my jaw. "They don't. Nothing has changed for you, like before, they aren't going to hide it, but no one expects your participation unless I say so." He meets my gaze and his expression is deadly serious. "And I don't say so."

There are implications to his words I don't want to think about but right now all I want to do is latch on to the fact that they make me feel better. Calmer. I bite my trembling lip. "You don't?"

He shakes his head. "I don't."

I calm, and all my crazy thoughts settle. I'm still anxious, but better. "Okay."

He kisses me. "Trust me."

"I do." Because, it's true. Chad is the most consistent man I've ever met. I put my head on his shoulder and soak in his warmth. "I feel bad."

His arms come around me and his hot palms slide over my back. "Why?"

"I want to be fun."

"You're fun."

I scoff. "I might as well be an eighteenth-century virgin."

He laughs. "That's a different kind of fun."

I wrinkle my nose. "It's annoying."

He kisses the top of my head. "I'm exactly where I want to be."

I do trust that. He's proven nothing different to me. I don't understand why, but I am thankful. I sigh, close my eyes, and admit, "Does it help I think about sex constantly?"

His hand slips down the curve of my hip to rest on my bare

thigh. "Does it help that thigh-high tights give me depraved ideas?"

I lift my head. "They do?"

His fingers tighten on my thigh. "Fuck yes. Especially on you, all that black against your pale skin. Very hot."

My nerves skitter away, leaving behind a lightness in its place. For the first time I try something daring, something different and forward. "I thought about how you'd look between my legs when I put them on."

All the times I have told him about my orgasms have made me bolder, more at ease.

His grasp on me tightens, and his eyes darken with what I now recognize as desire. "And what else have you been thinking?"

I tell him the truth. "I can't stop thinking about you and me…" I suck in a breath and blow it out. "I crave—something—but I can't figure out what it is."

A muscle in his jaw clenches and his cheekbones seem to appear starker, casting him in a dangerous light. His head dips as his fingers climb up my thigh. "You want to be taken. Possessed. Claimed."

That's exactly it. "Yes."

His mouth hovers closer. "Fucked."

My body instantly turns hotter. I nod. It's what I want, even though the thought of being a failure terrifies me.

"Are you wet?"

"Yes." The word is breathless. He hasn't touched me below the waist since the night of the engagement party no matter how much I've pleaded, rubbed myself against him.

"I think it's time I find out for myself."

I can barely breathe. Barely speak. I nod. Tilt my hips in offering.

His hand works between our bodies, sliding into my panties. I shift, parting my legs to allow him access. When his fingers slide over flesh that's been aching for him for weeks, a wave of pleasure crests across my skin. He circles my clit and I groan, my head falling back against the wall.

I don't think I've ever felt anything so good in my life.

He presses closer, leaning his arm alongside my head, and when he speaks, his voice is low in my ear. "I'm going to play with this hot little pussy tonight."

Oh god. I'm going to combust. I push into his hand.

His fingers slide on either side of my clit, squeezing, but not tight. Sensation rockets through me and I want something. It's on the tip of my tongue. I don't know what it is, but it's hot and demanding and insistent. My hands clutch his shirt, and I hold on, as something unknown and unrelenting beats at me.

He nips at my jaw. "And when I fuck you, I am going to ruin you."

I don't know what that means but I like it.

His fingers slide inside me and he grinds the heel of his palm into the hard bundle of nerves screaming for relief. I don't know what he does, but he creates this circular motion that is the best thing I've ever felt.

My hips rock.

"That's right, ride my hand." He laughs, low in my ear. "Show me how much you want it."

I gasp and moan, rising to meet his ruthless fingers. I didn't even know it was possible to be touched like this, but it's so, so good. I forget everything and everybody but him.

And suddenly he stops. He lifts his head. Both of us breathing hard, we stare at each other. He slips from my panties.

I feel cold. I don't want him to go. I grip him tighter. "Please don't stop."

"We'll continue this later." His voice is harsh, hoarse, and sends tingles over my skin. He cups between my legs. "This pussy is mine."

"Please." I press into his hand. I need…something.

He delivers a hard kiss. "I will. I promise."

He knows what I need, even if I don't, and I love that about him. He straightens and his hands fall away. I instantly miss him, pacified only when he takes my hand and brings it to his lips. "Ruby."

I tilt my head up to meet his penetrating gaze.

He cups my jaw. "For the rest of the night, I want you to think about how you were so wet you didn't care there were people around."

The rush of the restaurant comes over me, throwing me headlong into reality. I look around. It wasn't crowded, but it wasn't deserted either. "I didn't."

He tightens his grip. "You certainly didn't."

Chad

Ruby is the kind of chaos that sneaks up over you and kicks you in the ass when you least expect it. Because the truth is, I'd forgotten my surroundings as much as she had. And what really kills me is that I had her exactly where I'd wanted her.

She'd been hot, needy and ready. I'd had her there before, but she'd still been thinking, down there in that corridor she'd been mindless. Which is exactly where I needed her to be. She hadn't tensed. She'd arched to meet me. If I'd kept going, there's no question she would have come. I'd felt the tightening of her cunt on my fingers, saw the inevitable in her glassy, unfocused gaze.

And, like a fucking idiot, I had to put her there in a crowded restaurant that didn't afford me any privacy. I'm not above making a girl lose her mind in public, but that's not what I wanted for Ruby the first time. The first time I wanted her to scream and squirm. I didn't want her to have to be careful.

Of course, she could have slipped into that state because she hadn't had any pressure on her. Relaxed in the knowledge I didn't expect her to have an orgasm standing outside the woman's restroom. I suppose I'd find out soon enough, because I'd broken the seal and there was no turning back now.

I suspect downstairs, with her pressed against a wall, was a one-shot deal tonight.

That she'd start thinking. Worrying.

But that's okay; I'm prepared for that. I don't expect tonight.

We slide back into our chairs and the rest of the table looks at us with heavy speculation. I've purposefully not said much about my relationship with Ruby, and from what I understand Ruby has done the same.

Michael smirks and cocks a brow at Ruby, who pretty much downs her drink in the thirty seconds we've been sitting here. I look at this girl who's preoccupied almost all my thoughts for weeks. Her cheeks have a healthy flush and her lips are swollen.

She doesn't realize it, but her transformation into the woman she's supposed to be has already started. She walks with a little more sway in her step, with a little more boldness in her gaze. When she'd opened the door tonight I'd had to count to ten to keep from attacking her the way I wanted to. She looks hot as hell, dressed in black, her ivory thighs flirting under the hem of her skirt. It's not the outfit that has changed, because I've seen her in stuff like that before, but more the way she wears it. She's not as guarded. She's easier in her skin.

Which is exactly what I want for her. More than sex, I want her to be free.

It's a good thing I'm patient, that I have a lot of control, because she exercises every ounce of it.

We fool around, but she's right, there is something very virginal about our interactions and the tension between us is off the charts.

I want to tear into her. She wants me to tear into her. Tonight is the closest I've come.

Layla smiles at Ruby. "Everything okay?"

Ruby nods. "Everything's great."

I put my hand on the back of her chair and rub my crooked finger over her neck. "Do you want another drink?"

She looks at me, blinks with those clear blue eyes of hers that fairly glow from beneath her dark, almost black hair. Then she says sweetly, "Yes, please."

She has no clue how she sounds. She fucking kills me.

Layla's expression widens and Jillian grins at Ruby.

Ruby looks back and forth between them. "What?"

"Ouch!" Layla jerks and glares at Michael. "What was that for?"

Michael's eyes narrow. "What did you just say?"

"You pinched me!" Layla put her hand under the table. "Really hard."

"And you know why." He grips the back of her neck and squeezes. "I suggest you don't take it further."

I can see the calculation in her eyes, the spinning wheels to see how much she can get away with. As a dominant, that's one of my favorite looks, and it's a pleasure to see it on Layla's face. She's come so far from that girl I went out with that night when she could barely make it through dinner without crying. Where her skin was pale, her eyes shadowed with grief and loss, her body gaunt. Even back then she'd been a beautiful girl, like a ghost, drifting among the living, but she's come alive with Michael's help.

I am almost positive both Layla and Jillian have been told to leave Ruby and me alone, not to ask questions, not to put us on the spot. And I appreciate it, because Ruby is skittish enough without being forced to answer questions she's not ready to address.

I brush my thumb over the curve of her neck and she flutters her lashes at me, shy and adorable.

Brandon straightens, and Ruby once again goes on high alert. He's the one she's most afraid of, the most unknown to her. He grins. "What game should we play?"

"Everyone can come back to our place after dinner," Jillian says, her expression turning sly. "We could play strip Cards Against Humanity."

I put my hand on Ruby's thigh. "I have plans that don't involve an audience after dinner."

Under my palm, she relaxes fractionally.

"And I don't intend on watching my sister strip," Michael says, grinning at Leo. "Why do I have to keep mentioning these things?"

Jillian scoffs. "Please, I never lose."

Michael's head tilts to the side, then he nods. "True. But still no."

Brandon goes to speak but before he does, I say, "Ruby and I have had a long week, all we'll be doing is eating."

Brandon nods. "Fair enough."

The conversation moves on and Ruby relaxes under my touch. Five minutes later food starts to arrive. The group switches focus to the plates in front of us, diverted away from kinky games as Gwen comes to check on us.

In the commotion, Ruby leans over and whispers in my ear, "Thank you."

"You're welcome." Slowly but surely Ruby is coming to trust I have her best interests at heart. To know she's safe with me.

One more step closer to becoming mine.

13.

Ruby

So, yeah, after all that heat, here we are, watching TV.

I bite my lip and cast a sideways glance at him sitting there, all relaxed. Like he doesn't have a care in the world. Like I'm not sitting here anxious for when he's going to touch me. All through dinner I could only think about how he'd been down in that alcove. How much I'd wanted him.

But more than that, how I could trust him. To my surprise, nobody had batted an eye when Chad said to count us out of their kinky games. In fact, the topic had moved on and I hadn't had to worry about it for the rest of the night. Just like he'd promised, he'd told them I was off limits, and they'd listened. Being with Chad has highlighted truly how horrible my taste in men has been all these years. How I've kept myself safe, and emotionally isolated, by dating boys instead of men.

I suck in a breath, trying to focus on the movie instead of the man next to me. I'm stretched out on his couch, my feet in his lap, his hand on my knee, still covered in my thick black tights.

I felt good tonight, still awkward, but better. I know Chad's patience, his steadfast assurance is part of that, and I don't know how I feel about it. It goes against all my principles.

Did I really need a man to make me come alive? How sad is that?

His perspective makes me see myself in a new light. Has made me realize how stuck my life has been. How my desire to live unconventionally, and without the boundaries of conventions, has actually become my cage of choice.

He peers at me, his expression intent on me. Nobody has ever looked at me the way he does. Like he can see right into me. Like he understands me. Layla once said that people underestimate the value of being understood. I hadn't known what she meant then.

I do now.

He smiles. "I can feel you thinking."

The return tilt of my lips is automatic, as I am unable to deny him anything. "It's hard to turn off my brain."

He nods, smoothing his palm down my calf. "I know it is. Want to tell me about it?"

To my surprise, I find I do, even though the admission embarrasses me. I look away; back at the flickering screen I'm not watching. "At dinner, you took care of—" I can't think of the word to use. "The situation."

"I told you I would." Another stroke down my leg. He's different this way too. Unlike most men, he doesn't shy away from deep conversation, and when we talk, he always touches me. "My priority is taking care of what's best for you."

I like it. And it terrifies me. Chad now knows me better than anyone in my entire life, including Layla. I clear my throat. "You didn't seem bothered by it."

"Why would I be bothered?"

I shrug one shoulder and continue to study the screen. "That you were stuck with the unadventurous girl."

He chuckles and shakes his head. "Ruby, where does this competition come from?"

I frown at the word. "I'm not competitive."

"What do you call it?"

The words that come to my head alarm me. They're about approval. *His* approval. I don't like them, they sound like my mother. I swallow. "I just feel bad for you."

He studies my face. I've learned enough about him to know he's read something in my expression. That something put his instincts on high alert. I steel myself, waiting for whatever he says.

His gaze narrows. "I don't think that's it."

I shrug again.

"Tell me why."

I want him to be proud of me, but I can't say that. Can't admit I want something so backward. "I want to be fun."

"How are you defining fun?"

I don't like the path this conversation is heading. Or how it makes me sound. Or feel. "I don't want to hold you back."

Again he studies me in silence, and I can tell by his expression he knows something about me that I don't. Which is par for the course.

"You're not holding me back." His tone is soft and soothing. "You have to remember Ruby, Layla and Jillian have been with Michael and Leo for a long time. They are at different places in their relationships than we are."

Of course, he seems to know what I'm circling around and refuses to say. And he's right, I had forgotten. My brow furrows.

He squeezes my ankle. "You're Layla's best friend. Think back to when she first started seeing Michael. Do you honestly believe he'd have put her in a public scene two weeks in?"

I remember those days, where everything for Layla was a constant fight. A constant struggle. Back then she could barely get through the day. But I've dismissed all that, choosing to focus on how she is now. A vibrant, empowered female that awes me. I suck in a harsh breath and my eyes fill with swift and sudden tears.

Chad's fingers sweep back and forth along my calf, but he

makes no mention of my emotional distress.

I blink furiously, trying to quell the betraying rush of sadness. When I think I have myself under control, I squeak, "I guess I think she has a good excuse and I don't."

"Ruby." My name so soft on his lips.

I look at him.

"You don't need an excuse."

Then why do I feel like I do? I nod. "Okay."

"If you need to cry, let yourself cry." He takes my wrist and tugs. "I've got you."

No. I don't want to cry. I want to go back to the girl I was a couple of hours ago. I shake my head. "I'm okay."

He pulls harder, and I don't resist, tumbling against his chest. "I've got you anyway."

Some of the pressure against my ribs eases as I stare up at him, amazed. "Who are you?"

He smiles. "You know who I am."

I shake my head. "You're too perfect."

"I'm not even close to perfect." He cups my jaw and traces his thumb over my lower lip. "You just think that because you've never had anyone understand you before."

"I haven't." I swallow against the tightness in my throat. "I don't think I even understand me."

"I know. But you will, in time."

I settle in his lap, curling into him, because he feels so goddamn good I can't help myself. And I'm scared. I'm starting to need him. And as good as this is, I'm not Chad's forever girl. For forever, he needs someone else, someone better, that will be the woman he deserves. "Thank you."

"For what. I didn't do anything special."

"Yes, you did." I can give him this much. He deserves this much. I meet his gaze. "You put me first, and in my whole life nobody has ever done that, not even my parents."

His gaze darkens. "Who did they put first?"

"God." That one word says everything. And nothing.

"I see."

I bite my lip. "I don't want to give you the wrong

116

impression. They are lovely people, and good parents. And they mean well."

"I'm sure they do."

"They love me. They just don't get me."

He rubs a finger down the curve my jaw. "I get it. I understand. You can love your parents and not like some of the things they did."

"I know." I don't want to talk about them. But I don't know what to talk about. I only wish I could stop thinking, stop the millions of questions swirling in my head, including the ever pressing, why are we doing this? I've never cared much about the future, preferring to live in the now. But that's increasingly difficult with Chad.

I'm not willing to admit it to anyone, I can barely admit it to myself, but I've never felt about anyone the way I've felt about Chad. He matters to me. He's starting to feel like home, like the person I want to call when I'm upset, or have had a good day. I want to do stuff for him. Please him. Make him happy. I'm going to be devastated when it ends. When he goes back to the type of girl he's meant for.

I stiffen. If I were smart, I'd end it. Save myself.

"What?" He's too smart, too in tune.

My heart starts to hammer against my ribs. There is no future. There is only heartbreak. In the end, I'll only disappoint him. I open my mouth to say the words to sever the bond that's forming between us, but what I say shocks me. My voice trembles. "I have to go home next month for a reunion. Will you come with me?"

The invitation causes a riot of panic to stampede through me. What am I thinking? I was about to end it and instead I ask him to meet my family? Besides, you don't ask a guy to go meet your parents after so soon. I immediately backpedal. "Wait. That's too soon. Sorry. That's a lifetime from now."

"Ruby."

"I wasn't thinking. I didn't mean to pressure you."

"Ruby." His arms around me tighten.

"Forget I said that. It was silly."

"Ruby." My name on his lips is loud enough to still my babbling.

I look up at him.

He smiles. "I'd love to go with you."

I shake my head. "You don't have to. It's too soon."

"No it's not." He grips my jaw. "I'm going."

Everything inside me that's been bouncing around like jumping beans all night settles as I finally accept the truth of my situation.

I want him to go.

I don't want to save myself the heartbreak.

I want to be with him more than I want to protect myself.

It's terrifying and risky and not smart—but it's true. He is absolutely what I want.

I nod. "Okay. You don't feel obligated?"

"No." He kisses me and his hands roam over my ribs. "Have you ever brought anyone home?"

I shake my head. "Never."

His hand cups my breast while his thumb strokes over my nipple. "I'll be the first."

"Yes." My back bows in invitation, I want a deeper touch. Now that I've accepted I want him imprinted onto my skin.

His hand skims down my stomach and works under my top. His palm is hot, leaving a trail of heat behind. "I like being your firsts."

I suck in a breath. "I like it too." Because I do—if I can do one thing for him it's give him everything I've never given to anyone else.

He meets my gaze. "Do you want my fingers on your cunt?"

My hips twitch involuntarily in anticipation. "Yes."

"Good." His hand skims back down my body to rest on my bare thigh. "That's a pretty sight."

I watch as his tanned hand settles against my pale skin. My skirt is so high you can see my black panties. He's right it is pretty.

He grips my leg and slides up, his fingers brushing where

I've been so desperate for him. "I'm going to tease you, but I'm not going to try and make you come, okay?"

Muscles I didn't know had tensed ease.

He smiles. "That's right, you relax and let me take care of things. And, Ruby?"

"Yes." My voice is already breathless.

"Whatever you do, don't think about orgasms."

14.

Don't think about orgasms. Don't think about orgasms.

I swallow hard and watch as Chad's hand slides up my thigh in slow motion. My breath catches as his fingers brush over the silk of my panties. Panties I'd worn with him in mind, both scared and hopeful tonight would be the night he touched me.

Now it's happening and I can't turn off my brain.

"Breathe, Ruby." Chad's voice shocks me back.

My gaze flies to his face. He's watching me in that intent way he has. As though he's a mind reader. As though he can see every thought in my head.

I exhale, trying to slow my rapid heart.

His hand stops, resting on my mound.

"You're okay." His words are sure and steady.

Embarrassment washes over me and I nod. I hate this about myself. My fucked-up notions about sex are exactly the opposite of what I want them to be. Of who I want to be. I ⟩ be empowered. Confident. Alive and pulsing with ⟩. I want to own it.

I'm none of those things. No matter how hard I try.

It's why I started faking in the first place.

Pretending makes things so much easier, but Chad knows my secrets, most of them anyway, the important ones. There is no pretending with him.

As liberating as that is, as much as it's a weight lifted off my chest, all I want right now is to be someone else. I want my body to communicate to him how it thrums with lust for him, how it pulses with need, hammers with desire. What is wrong with me that I can't make that happen?

His hand retreats to my lower leg. "We'll try this another night."

I shake my head, and put his palm back where I've been desperate for him to be for weeks. "Please, no."

"You're too tense. Too on edge."

"I know." I tilt my hips. "But please don't stop."

With the lightest of touches he rubs a slow, teasing path down my panties. "Are you doing what I told you?"

I bite my lip, trying to remember. "What?"

"Are you not thinking about orgasms?"

"I can't help it."

"Stop." His finger trails light circles down, moving once again to my thighs. "What are you afraid of?"

I want to protest that I'm not afraid, but it's so clearly untrue, I can't speak the lie. "I don't know."

He continues his little circles, high on my inner thigh. "What's the worst-case scenario? Tell me."

I know him now, he'll ask me all night until he gets the truth. I swallow past my tight throat. "That I'll be cold and unresponsive."

He meets my gaze. "So what? Does it matter if I touch you and you're not wet?"

I nod. "It matters to me."

"Why?"

I look down at my lap. "I don't want to fail you."

"There's nothing I can say to assure you, but I'll try." He cups my jaw and forces my attention to him. "You're worrying

JENNIFER DAWSON

for nothing. You're already wet. And even if you weren't I wouldn't take it as a personal slight against my ego."

I blink at him. "You wouldn't?"

Again, his expression turns exacting and scrutinizing. "No. My ego can take it."

"I want to believe." Anxiety is a buzz through my veins. Vibrating over my skin.

"I know you do." He releases his grip and his hand slides down my chest, over my stomach and traces the edge of my panties. "Let's find out if I'm right, shall we?"

I shake my head. There's no way and I'll be humiliated.

"Yes." His fingers slip down my underwear and I clamp my legs together. "Open."

Almost as though guided by some sort of weird instinct, my thighs part even as my brain tells me to stop.

"Good girl." He circles my clit and, despite my distress, lust flutters low in my belly. He glides over my folds and I twitch involuntarily. He retreats; and I hold my breath as he raises his hand and paints my lower lip with the wetness slicking his finger. "Just as I thought."

I frown. How was that possible?

His lips curve. "Someday I'll explain it to you."

My frown only deepens and he laughs, flashing me a smile that makes my heart skip a beat. "Some girls can be nervous and aroused. It's not always mutually exclusive."

"It's never happened before."

His fingers slide between my legs and brush featherlight over my soft center. "What can I say? I'm a genius."

Now it's my turn to laugh.

His expression twists into exaggerated menace. "Are you saying I'm not?"

My mood lightens and I can't help but grin. "I don't know, we've only been to second base."

"What do you call this?" He traces circles over my folds, not really touching me with purpose, more playing. Teasing.

My body gives a pulse of desire. "Two and a half."

He cocks a brow. "Are you trying to force my hand?"

122

"Who me?" I flutter my lashes. "Never."

"Not you." He leans down and flicks his tongue over my lower lip. "I'm going to play with your pussy while we watch TV. All I'm going to do is play; I have no expectation you'll come. In fact, I am one hundred percent sure you won't so it's not even on my radar. I just want to touch you. Don't pay any attention to me, okay?"

"Are you insane?"

"Probably." He juts his head toward the flat screen. "Watch."

"But—"

"No talking. We're watching TV and cuddling. Completely innocent."

I bite my lip at the millions of questions in my head that all circle back to one. I clear my throat. "And if I don't? Watch TV that is?"

Something flashes in his expression and his eyes narrow on me with suspicion. "Then I'll stop. Anytime I feel you're trying, I'll stop."

I blink, tilting my head to think about his statement. "Trying?"

He nods. "Trying to come. Trying to force it. Getting into your head. Talking to distract me."

I laugh. "That's a long list."

"You have two jobs here. Watch TV and relax." His fingers play lightly over my skin. "That's the extent of your responsibility."

"I can do that." I don't know how he does it but he always manages to ease me.

"That's because you're a good girl." He gives me a hot, searing kiss that leaves me breathless. "Now watch."

I turn my head toward the TV and he begins.

I wait for him to go in for the kill, because that's what most guys do, but this is Chad.

So, of course, he doesn't do that at all. Instead, his fingers slide down my leg to the edge of where my tights meet my thigh. He traces a path over the seam, between my legs, touching fabric and skin, light and gentle.

My gaze may be on the flickering television but I couldn't tell you what we're watching, or even what's on the screen, because all my attention is focused on the stroke of his hand over my flesh and the anticipation buzzing inside me.

My heart flutters, my belly dips.

He continues his slow dance over my skin.

I shift.

"Comfortable?" His tone is mild and unconcerned.

I shrug.

"Hmmm... Maybe we should readjust?"

My head swivels to look at him and he grins. I'd never considered boyish sexy before but there's something about Chad that works. He's a study in contrasts. He's the angel and devil all rolled together. Everything a proper young man should be, until it comes to sex. I never knew a man could be so good, while his mouth and hands were so very wicked.

And I love the way he talks. I've never had a man talk to me the way he does. He makes everything sound hot, and delicious, like something I want, not something I need to cringe away from. Most men with his good looks and considerable sexual skills are usually jerks, but he's not like that at all. I didn't know men could be so considerate, could listen so intently. Could take so much time. He's the most fascinating man I've ever met and I want him so badly. Somehow, I need to find a way to give him everything.

"Straddle me for a minute."

His words startle me out of my whirlwind thoughts. I don't think about not complying. I move, sliding my body on top of him, my thighs cradling his lean hips. I look down. His open palms are high on my thighs, and in that second everything about us looks exactly right. Exactly the way it's supposed to be. The need, the urge, swells inside me like a wave, threatening to crash over me and pull me under its powerful current.

He squeezes. "Stay with me, Ruby."

I blink to find blue eyes peering into me, pinning me to the spot. For the first time in my life I don't want to play it close to the vest, don't want to pretend. I'm not wishing I could disappear or have some out-of-body experience. I want to be right here. With him. I trust him like I've never trusted another soul.

Looking into his penetrating gaze, the most miraculous thing happens, my heart opens, and something that had been a tight ball inside me breaks apart and shatters into a million pieces.

I touch his jaw and whisper in a shaky voice, "I want to give you everything."

Most men would have a panic attack at that statement, but Chad nods and says simply, "Don't worry, you will."

"I'm not afraid." I don't quite know what I'm trying to communicate, or how to articulate what's roiling around inside me. It's the best I can come up with.

"Good." His hands roam over my hips to rest at my waist. "Lift your arms over your head."

I do and he whisks my top off, dropping it to the floor. I expect my bra to follow, but instead he cups me and rubs his thumbs over my satin-covered nipples.

My breath immediately catches in my throat.

His gaze flickers. "I love that sound you make. That needy little gasp." His thumbs continue their leisurely circles. "It drives me crazy."

"It does?" The surprise is clear in my voice.

"Everything about you drives me crazy."

I bite my lip. I've been so anxious and worried and scared I can't imagine driving him crazy. "Really?"

"Really." He slides his fingers inside my bra and pulls the cups down, exposing my breasts, plumping them up and thrusting them out. He lightly pinches them before tugging, and a bolt of desire shoots through me.

It's going to be tonight. Suddenly I know all my worry has been for nothing. Ridiculous actually. The idea that Chad Fellows won't be able to make me have an orgasm is preposterous.

I want it. Want to sink into it. Into him.

He meets my gaze. "Has anyone ever told you that you've got the most fantastic breasts on the planet."

And it happens. What I've been searching for, what I've been missing, clicks into place. I'm not afraid. I don't know why or how it's happened, but I'm not.

I am free. Empowered. Confident.

Light in a way I've never been, I smile.

His gaze narrows, before peering at me closely, and I see the exact moment he recognizes the change in me. The air shifts, crackles and becomes alive with an electricity that's never been there before.

"Is that a yes?" His voice lowers, becomes more dangerous.

Instead of worrying me, I find it thrilling. I lick my lips. "Maybe once or twice."

He tugs at my nipple again, pulling and rolling them between his fingers. I put my hands on his knees. My back arches, my breasts thrust out in offering. Because it is an offer.

Gazes still locked together, all my shyness drains away, taken off for parts unknown and I love it. Love everything about the way I feel without it.

His lips twist and instead of his normal, reassuring smile, it's pure evil. It draws out his features, highlights his cheekbones so they slash across his face with sharpness and intent. It transforms him, and sitting there in black, he looks beautiful, slightly cruel, calling to some hidden, secret part of me.

But I don't cower before it. It makes me feel…powerful.

He pinches this time, harder—not painful, but with force—and I gasp as sensation travels from my breasts all the way deep in my core, making me clench and ache. Everything he's done before this moment has been a tease.

Things just got serious.

And I'm ready.

"Someone likes that." His voice is low and deep. He repeats his actions. Once. Twice. Again.

My head falls back as my fingers dig into his knees. I rock

my body, sliding against his hard cock.

I need him to fuck me. I don't care about orgasms. It doesn't matter. All that matters is he fills me up.

Makes me his.

One hand grips my hip. I bear down as he surges up. His fingers dig into the curve of my ass and I can feel the muscles flex and tighten under his touch. Then his other hand clasps me and he yanks me forward, grinding me against his erection.

Everything is on fire.

Everything that's been simmering below the surface comes to a rapid boil.

My thighs tighten around him.

And the friction. God, the friction. I never want it to end.

His hands tight on me, he says, "Give me that mouth."

Dazed, I lift my head, and then he's kissing me, delivering on the promises he'd made the first night he touched me.

He's hard and ruthless. Claiming. Commanding. Possessive.

And best of all he's not holding back. There is no deference.

His head slants, deepening the contact between us.

Our tongues tangle.

Our breaths turn hot and panting.

He growls low in his throat. The sound primal and guttural and it sends shivers racing down my spine and exploding over my skin.

He shifts. Tumbles us to the couch, trapping me under him.

The kiss turns hotter, wetter. More insistent and demanding.

He pulls away and looks down at me, shaking his head. "Fuck, that is a goddamn gorgeous sight."

I'm mindless. I lift my hips. "Please."

He kisses me again before whispering in my ear, "The way you say please makes my cock hard."

I bow, working my fingers under his shirt, stroking over his back. "Please keep talking."

He circles his hips, rocking against where I need him most, his breath hot in my ear. "Am I going to find your cunt wet?"

I clamp my legs around his waist. "Yes."

"That's right." My skirt is bunched at my hips and he slides his hands up my leg, squeezing the soft flesh there. "Because you're a good girl."

The words inflame me. "I need…something."

His fingers slide across my stomach. "I know what you need."

"What? Please tell me." I arch, silently begging him to go on.

He slips inside my panties. "You need to be fucked."

He goes lower. "Claimed."

Lower. "Ruined."

He circles my clit and I gasp at the slickness, at his words.

His teeth scrape my neck. "Ripped apart and put back together again."

"Yes." I arch my hips into his hand. That sounds exactly right. Exactly what I've been searching for. Needing. Wanting.

His lips play over my jaw as he teases me with soft feathery touches. "For a girl that's not supposed to be thinking about orgasms you're awfully wet."

I still and open my eyes, my vision sharp and focused. "Chad."

He lifts his head. "Ruby."

I trace a path over the line of his jaw. "I'm not thinking about orgasms."

Because I'm not.

His gaze flashes, his eyes darken. He circles my clit, over and over, not with direct pressure, just making me want it. "What are you thinking about?"

I tell him the absolute truth. I've said variations of these words before—trite and meaningless—with the intent to hurry the guy along, to distract him from my lack of involvement. This is the first time I've meant them. Understood them. This is the first time they've had meaning. "How much I want your cock inside me. How much I need to feel it." I swallow hard. *These* words I have never said to anyone. "I want to belong to you, to give you something I've never given anyone."

It's his turn to still, his fingers resting where I want him most. His blue eyes darken to sapphire, become fathomless. Captivating me so I lose myself. He slides out of my panties, up my stomach and over my breasts to cup my jaw. He kisses me, soft and sweet, before lifting his head and looking into my eyes. "Ruby, you do belong to me. You are absolutely mine."

I lick my lower lip. "I've never belonged to anyone before."

"Good." He traces a path down my collarbones and over my breast, stopping to tug at my nipple. "I'm not letting you go."

My hips arch and I suck in a breath.

He continues, driving me crazy, making me hot and restless and consumed with desire. "Your mind's accepting what your body has known all along."

"What?" The word is nothing more than a harsh pant.

He nips my bottom lip, running his tongue over the flesh he has trapped there before releasing me. "I own you."

I feel the words all the way in my bones. "Yes."

He leaves my breast and makes a path down my stomach and into my panties, only to touch lightly with no real pressure.

I arch my hips. "Will you do what you did at the restaurant?" It feels like I've traveled a lifetime since then.

"What did I do?" His words are gruff.

"I don't know." I gesture. "With your hand."

"Like this?" He makes a V with his fingers and squeezes, and it sends electricity rising through me.

I cry out, pressing into the couch and twisting at the sensation.

"Or like this?" He shifts, thrusts two fingers inside me, and grinds the heel of his hand against my clit.

"Yes!" My voice is a short, sharp burst.

"Which one?" His tone is amused.

"Both." I close my eyes, sinking into the couch as another keening bolt of pleasure spears through me. "Oh, god, please don't stop."

He plunges in and out, palm rubbing my clit, and it's so good.

JENNIFER DAWSON

So, so good.

My hips jerk and gyrate, catching the rhythm of his movements.

"That's right, ride my fingers like a good little girl."

Lust crashes through me—I don't know why his words cause such an inferno and right now I don't care—I just give in to it.

He shifts again, pulling out to rub my clit in that exquisite squeezing motion.

My harsh breathing fills the air. For the first time I don't think. Don't worry. Don't have an out-of-body experience. I'm right here. In this room. With Chad.

Who's so fucking talented he should be illegal.

I'm so close. I'm terrified he'll stop so I ask again. "Please don't stop. Please."

"I won't, Ruby." He plunges inside me again and sets a dirty rhythm that drives me out of my mind. "You just let go whenever you're ready and I've got you."

I clutch his shirt, fisting it and curling my hands into a tight fist. My head thrashes as I almost catch the orgasm, my muscles tighten and I chase it, but then it's gone.

He switches back to focusing all his attention on the hard, needy bud between my legs. "Don't try, girl. Don't even think. Relax."

I coil taut as another bolt of sensation lashes through me. I'm sweating. I'm so close. So, so close.

He stops, but before I can demand he continue, he pulls back and swats me, full on my mound. "Stop trying."

I freeze as the full impact of what he's done washes over me at the same instant pleasure explodes through me. My lids fly open and I meet his gaze.

His jaw is hard and a muscle works. He shakes his head. "I'm sorry, instinct took over."

I blink. "Instinct?"

"Yes." He swallows, his expression darkening. "Sometimes pain helps with focus."

"It didn't hurt."

130

He tilts his head. "No?"

"It did…but…" I flush, then do the most depraved act since that night we talked on the phone and I'd licked myself. I open my thighs and lift. "Do it again."

His expression turns hungry and feral, but he doesn't deliver. Instead, he raises a brow. "Is that how you ask?"

I arch more. I don't know what's happening between us, but desire and need has amplified, pulsing the air. "Will you please do it again, Chad?"

His fingers circle my clit. "Do what?"

I bite my lip. Not sure what words to use. I mean, I know the words, I just don't know how to form them on my lips and say them.

His eyes are bright, but unrelenting. "Ask me, specifically, Ruby."

This should be cooling my blood, but it's having the opposite effect. Lust is pounding through me like a stampede. My core literally clamps down in response to the words. I don't understand it, but I don't want to question. Because I'm on the precipice of something profound and I don't want to lose it. I lick my lips. "Please hit me like that again."

He pulls back and his fingers snap against me. "Like that?"

The impact radiates out like a rock plunking into the water, creating a rippling effect that crests through my body. I moan. "Yes, like that."

He does it again.

I close my eyes. And sink into the exquisite, wicked sensation. He's right; it does focus me. All other thoughts trickle from my mind, leaving my sole concentration on the strike of his hand. It's not hard. It's like a thud. A rhythmic, mindless thing I can lose myself in.

"More?" he says, hot in my ear.

I open my legs wider. Later I'll be embarrassed but I don't have time for that now. Not with something so important happening. "Please."

"Harder?"

"Can you?"

"Yes."

In answer, I arch higher. At some point my foot has moved to the floor, providing me leverage.

"Stay like that. Just like that." He starts again, this time with more stinging force.

I scream. Actually scream with the pleasure. I start rocking my hips to meet his strokes.

It's the best thing I've ever felt.

It hurts, kind of, but I don't know. It's too good to hurt. It's completely depraved, completely wanton and abandoned. Some distant part of my mind wants to insert itself, to stop what's happening as too much, but then he hits me again, and it dissolves into thin air. I don't even process the word before I say it. I just whisper it in a voice I don't even recognize. "Harder. Please."

He shifts, changing his angle, and then strikes.

I feel it everywhere. From the tips of my toes to the top of my head. My fingers tingle with it. It's in the tight pull of my nipples. The fullness of my lips. The rapid rise and fall of my chest, and shake of my thighs. I gasp out his name. "Chad."

His breathing is as fast as my own. "Let it happen, Ruby. You're right there. Just let it happen."

"I—"

He hits me harder. "Shhh… Don't think about it." Again he strikes, and then squeezes my clit. "You're so wet. Soaking my hand."

He's right, I'm right there. Ready to come. The words tumble through my mind. "I—" I trail off as he hits me again, the words scattering in a million directions.

He doesn't let up. Doesn't stop. "That's right, it's completely fucking depraved." Another thud. "And hot. So damn hot." A stinging slap. "All I can think about is how hot your cunt is going to be when I fuck you."

My hips move relentlessly, seeking the contact of his hand.

"Let go, and come for me."

And with that, on the next strike, I do. I freeze, my hips raised; all my muscles tense as the most powerful orgasm of my life screams through me, crashing over me. He smacks me one more time then ruthlessly works my clit as wave after wave washes over me in blinding, soul-drenching ecstasy.

Chad

I lose my fucking mind as I watch her come apart. She's exactly how I wanted her—mindless, unthinking, greedy in her own pleasure. She works her clit into my hand, demanding and gorgeous.

I didn't plan on fucking her tonight but I know that's no longer an option. I need it. She needs it. I don't question it, but I know it's right. What needs to happen. She needs to feel my ownership of her body, as much as I do. Even though she's not processing what's happening between us.

I don't want her to come down, so I kiss her. Unleash all my considerable lust on her.

I roll on top of her and she's still grinding her cunt against me, trying to chase the pleasure that had stormed through her. I'd seen the change in her, and had known that after all these weeks she'd come for me, but the execution. Christ. I never expected that.

It was the hottest, most beautiful thing I'd ever seen.

I roll her nipple, harder than I've dared before in all the hours I'd touched her. She moans needy in my mouth, pressing harder. I tug and twist, firmer and more insistent. Her body writhes and she goes crazy against me.

I stop being careful with her. Because, I realize my mistake now. She'd needed the coaxing at first, because that's the only way she'd ever trust me—if she felt no pressure at all. She needed to relax and be given the freedom to stop pretending.

But I see what really drives her now. How she needs to be pushed.

I move down her body, suck her nipple into my mouth and bite down. I'll leave a mark in my wake, a memory for tomorrow.

She cries out and bucks against me.

I'm going to lose it on her.

When I'd smacked her the first time I'd been riding pure instinct but the second she'd frozen I'd been sure I'd ruined everything. When she spread her legs and asked for more I thought I'd died and gone to heaven.

I sink my teeth into her flesh and tug.

She calls out my name, twining her hands in my hair, and pushes me closer.

Something has broken between us and there are absolutely no walls. No going back.

I've pushed past all her reserve and am seeing the Ruby that lives underneath. The one *nobody* has ever seen but me. It makes me greedy for more, demanding and ruthless.

I lift my head and slide up her body. "I'm going to fuck you now."

She drags her needy pussy against my stomach, slicking my flesh. "Yes."

I grip her chin. "Open your eyes."

Her lashes flutter open and all I see there is dazed, heady lust.

"I'm not going to take my time."

She sucks in a breath.

"I'm not going to go easy on you."

She's making desperate little circles of her hips, working her clit against me.

I nip her bottom lip. "I'm going to use you for my own pleasure and when I'm done, there's not anything you won't do for me."

She shudders, drags her nails down my back, and arches her neck in offering. "Yes. Anything."

And that's it. I'm done.

I rear up, think about ripping her skirt down her legs, but change my mind. I love the way she looks right now. Breasts spilling over her bra, skirt bunched around her waist, thigh highs against pale skin. Chest heaving, mouth swollen, she stares up at me with those brilliant fucking eyes and looks completely undone, completely debauched.

If I custom designed a fantasy, she'd look exactly like this.

I strip my shirt over my head, unbuckle my belt, and shove down my pants and underwear. Her eyes grow wide at the sight of my cock, and with all the times we fooled around I've forgotten she's never really seen me. I'm larger than normal, thicker. I'll stretch her and she'll be tight as hell around me.

I reach into the shallow drawer of my coffee table and grab a condom. She's still staring at my cock, and I see some semblance of rationality sneaking over her, so acting on instinct again I slap her breast, then her nipple.

Her attention jerks to me, and she sucks in a breath.

I raise a brow. "Should I do that again too?"

She gulps, and nods.

"Say the words, Ruby." Even riding high, I'm being careful to get her consent because she still doesn't really understand what's playing out between us. All she knows is she likes it, it makes her hungry, and she doesn't want to stop. I'm giving her no chance to think but I still insist on her agreement.

She licks her lips. "Please hit me again."

I rest between her legs and put the heel of my hand over her clit and smack her breast.

She arches her neck. "Oh god."

I set a dirty rhythm, alternating between slapping her tits and grinding against her clit until she's forgotten all about the size of my cock and if I'll fit in favor of her pleasure.

When I have her mindless, I hold her by the neck, and working her cunt I ask, "Are you ready to be fucked?"

Her throat muscles work under my grasp. "Yes."

I let her go, tear open the condom and roll it on. All I want is to slam into her but that's not possible. I'll need to be slow. I spread her wide and slide my cock up and down the length of her wetness and along her clit.

Her whole back bows off the couch. She's so slippery I glide right over her. Her knees come up to clasp my hips, as she moans and urges me forward. On my next pass I push into her, filling her just a little bit. Shallow strokes. I grit my teeth. She's so damn tight. I've been controlled for weeks and every primal urge is demanding to be unleashed, but I can't. Not quite yet.

When her body resists, I pull back.

She clutches at my arms. "No."

"Sshhhh… Just let me do all the work." I stroke my erection between her slick folds.

Over and over.

Until she's panting under me, desperate and wanting.

I begin again. Pushing into her. Farther now. Testing. Teasing.

Her nails dig into my back. Gouging my skin. Marking me.

I capture her mouth, matching the rhythm of my cock sliding in and out.

I hit resistance.

I pull back out.

"Oh, god, no." Her voice is a heady, mindless wail.

I fucking love it. I've been pushing her toward this for weeks and now that she's here, I'm addicted.

I rub her clit with my cock.

She begs.

Pleads.

Her nipples abrade my chest.

The air is hot, humid, almost sticky.

Sweat blooms across her chest, along my spine.

I push in again. Farther. Deeper.

Her body tenses around me, but instead of resistance, she's pulling me in. Closer.

I thrust hard and fill her.

She's. So. Damn. Tight.

I still, wanting to give her body time to adjust, but she jerks under me. "Please don't stop. I… I… Please."

Her muscles ripple down the length of my shaft and I lose the rest of my sanity.

I brace myself next to her head and lean down. I pull out and plunge back in. I whisper in her ear, "Mine."

She keens under me.

I thrust. "All fucking mine."

She moans, surges up.

Our hips slam together, and we both suck in our breaths at the shock of it.

"Again." My voice is demanding now.

I have never, in my entire life, felt like this about a girl.

I can't take her hard enough. Deep enough.

I look down at her face, her open lips and panting. Her cheeks are flushed. Her lashes flutter open and her glassy eyes meet my gaze.

Something hot and alive passes between us. Connecting us.

Base, feral urges storm through me and I stop resisting. Stop thinking. I follow my own advice, and let it all go, hoping she follows. "You ready?"

She nods. Gasps out, "Yes."

And I unleash on her, moving with purpose and intent.

Driving into her.

Her body tightens around me and I know she's close.

The couch strains under the weight of us, the pounding thrusts.

Her neck arches. "Oh god."

"That's right, you're going to come for me." I grip her neck. I'm fucking her so hard and it's still not enough. "And only for me."

She stiffens, clenches around me, and then starts working her hips in greedy abandon as the orgasm rips through her, tearing my own orgasm from me with such sudden ferocity, a rush of panic races across my skin. Then it's gone, and I close my eyes to ride out the most mind-numbing, powerful pleasure I've ever experienced.

I thrust into her, over and over again, until I've wrung every last ripple and swell from her.

I collapse like a sweating, panting beast on top of her as I come to grips with the most intense fuck of my life.

All the while trying not to think about how this would change me.

15.

Ruby

The first hints of the summer to come warm my face as a morning breeze washes over my skin. It's early. Too early. But I woke up and found I couldn't sleep, so I carefully pulled myself from Chad's arms, slipped on one of his shirts, and made my way downstairs.

I made coffee, and took two cups and the pot to the roof deck.

Now I'm sitting in his plush armchair, watching the sun rise high over the city alone while he sleeps. I'm more peaceful than I've ever been.

Every time I think of last night—which is about every five seconds—I blush. Furiously.

By some sort of silent, mutual agreement we hadn't discussed what happened and while on the surface we'd merely "had sex" we both knew it had changed things between us.

At some point during the night we'd made our way to bed and he'd taken me over and over again. I'd come every time without fail. I'd had more orgasms last night than I had in the entire year before I met him. I don't understand how or why. Maybe he's that skilled. Or maybe he managed to tap into that secret part of me I've never admitted before.

Whatever the reasons, until last night, I had no idea a man could screw like that, or come that much. I finally understood the expression fucked properly. Finally understood all the screaming I'd heard from Layla all those years ago. Finally understood what all the fuss was about. I'd been insane, absolutely crazy and completely abandoned. Nothing at all like myself.

My god—I couldn't even think about what I'd let him do to me. What I wanted him to do to me. I flush again.

Surely sex like that is evil. Unnatural somehow.

I frown, disturbed by the thought. I don't want to ruin it by thinking. Even as my rational mind pushes the idea away as ridiculous, that other part of me that had the Bible drilled into my head for as long as I can remember, doesn't want to let go.

My stomach jumps as I remember the thud and sting of Chad's hand on my skin. I have bruises this morning. They cover my breasts. My inner thighs. The imprint of his fingers are still on my hips. I looked in the mirror and told myself to be horrified. But I wasn't.

Somehow, I was proud. How messed up is that?

It made no sense. I need it to make sense. Chad can explain it to me. I press my fingers to my lips and blink away the tightness in my throat, peering out at a million-dollar view of the skyline.

What did last night make me? I'm a prude—that's what I have always been and assumed I would always be—but last night. I don't know, I can't deny all these weeks with Chad has given me hope as he made me burn. I'd started to suspect that if anyone could make me come it was him, but in my head I'd pictured it more like relaxing. Like I'd loosen up a bit. I hadn't expected to become completely undone. It was like a switch had flipped in my head and not only had I been desperate for what he'd done to me, I'd wanted so much more. Dirty, forbidden shocking thoughts I can't even think in the light of day.

How had he done that to me?

Chad's hand runs over my shoulder and tangles in my hair, I jerk, looking up at him.

Then promptly flush what I'm sure is scarlet.

In gray sweatpants and no shirt, he smiles, and it's boyish and charming with no trace of the cruel wickedness from last night. "You okay?"

I resist the urge to say, *it's still you*. Surprised somehow he hadn't changed into the devil since I'd left him. I nod. But my throat tightens and I look away.

He frowns and crouches down, forcing my gaze to him. He runs a finger over my cheek. "Are you overwhelmed?"

I nod. I am. Why should I start pretending with him now?

"It's a lot to process, I know." His expression twists. "I got carried away and probably took you a little too far past your comfort zone."

A little too far? Does that mean there's more? Because an awakened part of me demands more and that makes me afraid.

I shake my head and my lips curve down. "I don't want you to feel sorry." I clear my throat. I need at least to take ownership. It feels like a step forward, no matter how tiny. There wasn't one thing he'd done to me that I hadn't liked, hadn't craved. That hadn't felt like something I'd always needed and never had before. "I liked it."

He curls his hand around my neck, squeezes, then stands, grabs a chair and sits down so we're facing each other, our knees are touching. "I know you did, but it's okay to be overwhelmed."

I blink at him, the questions fluttering like a tiny bird in my chest. I turn and pour him coffee, handing it back to him before taking my own. He holds the mug in one strong hand while the other rests on my knee. I stare at his hands, thinking of the things he'd done to me last night, and more heat crawls a path over my skin. I meet his gaze. "How'd you do it?"

His mouth tilts. "Do what? Make you come?"

I nod, and hold his eyes even while the embarrassment wages war inside me. I need to understand his power over me.

He takes a sip of coffee before shrugging. "It wasn't that difficult. It's not like you couldn't have an orgasm, you knew how, you were just too in your head to have one with another person."

Something niggles in the corners of my mind, hovering just out of reach. "How did you get me out of my head? No one else ever has."

"Well, in fairness. I'm probably the only man who's ever been *in* your head, which puts me at a distinct advantage." He scrubs a hand over his jaw; his five o'clock shadow is thick now, making him look rugged and far too good looking. "It was a combination of things."

"Which are?" Somehow I need to know. It feels important and significant.

"I like you in my shirt." Almost absentmindedly, he runs a hand over my thigh. "Chemistry, obviously. I can't remember ever dating anyone I have this much chemistry with. Can you?"

"No." It's not even close. I've wanted, crushed on, and been infatuated many, many times. I've always loved the beginning, when getting real wasn't part of the package. That's the fun part. The part I can handle and fake my way through. But it's nothing like that with Chad who's a magnetic pull I can't resist. Calling, urging, demanding I pay attention. "What else?"

He slips his fingers between my thighs and I shiver before the rush of heat warms me. "Since this started, I made sure you associated me with orgasms. Reminding you over and over again that your desire to come was because of me. That I was the man you were coming for. But more important the *why*."

"Why?" My heartbeat kicks hard against my ribs.

His hands climb farther up my leg. He nods. "Wasn't there a part of you that wanted to resist, especially when you knew I'd know or make you talk about it?"

"Yes, all the time." I'd come home and promise myself I wouldn't almost as my fingers were slipping into my panties.

"That you wanted to resist and couldn't help yourself is *the why*."

I want to ask more, to find out how he knows this, but I suspect I already know why he's so intuitive, and I don't want to ask a question that will force me to confront his nature. I'm not ready for that. Am not sure I'll ever be ready. I tilt my head. "What else?"

For a few moments he studies me before he answers. "All this time we've been fooling around I've been paying attention. When something turned you on I did it more, when it didn't I dropped it. Once I learned what flipped your switch I kept twisting the knife."

I bite my lip and tuck a lock of hair behind my ear. "But I don't even know what flips my switch."

He grins, leans forward and kisses me softly on the mouth before pulling away. "I know. I'm teaching you."

"You are." I just can't think about what I'm learning. My lips tingle where he touched me and I want more. "What doesn't turn me on?"

He laughs. "Compliments. Soft kisses and restraints."

I blink. Startled. How closely had he been paying attention? "I like compliments."

He shrugs. "Maybe in theory, but they make you extremely uncomfortable, and they sure as hell don't make you hot."

I swallow hard. "You've never restrained me."

"I know because it doesn't do anything for you. I've held you down by your wrists a few times but you haven't seemed to notice. Although you do like it when I grab you by the throat." He reaches up and traces a path over my neck. "But that's more about possession, isn't it?"

It is. I love that surge of belonging. Something I've experienced so few times in my life. "What else?"

I'm both terrified and excited he'll bring up what I clearly loved last night but am compelled to continue. He peers at me, gaze narrowed, thoughtful. "You like it when I talk dirty to you."

He leans closer.

I hold my breath.

With one hand he flicks open the buttons on his shirt, baring my breasts. His attention shifts over them, taking in the bruises on my skin. He trails a finger over my nipple. "You tell me, Ruby. Did you like being marked by me?"

I gasp, the sensation a painful, jarring pleasure. "Yes."

He cups my breast and lifts it to his mouth. My thighs slide over his and I am wide open and exposed. He licks, laving over my too sensitive skin. He lifts his head while his finger tugs at my nipple. "Are you swollen and sore?"

"Yes." And it just makes it all the more delicious.

His pressure on my breast increases and it inflames me. "But as sore as you are, all you want is to fuck, right? So you can feel that thing you can't quite put your finger on but feels like a drug."

I nod. That's exactly right.

He grips my thighs and pulls me so I straddle him. My wet, aching center is flush against the soft cotton of his sweatpants and erection. He palms my ass. "It's the same for me."

This shocks me, works me up, and empowers me. "Really?"

I know he doesn't say things just to say them, but it's still hard to believe.

"Yes." His fingers grip my soft flesh. "Do you think I'm always like that? Just insatiably fucking over and over again?"

I bite my lip. "Um…kind of."

He laughs. "Not even close. Your cunt is addictive."

I jerk against him involuntarily.

He laughs again and that dark evilness is back. He squeezes, and slightly pulls the cheeks of my ass apart, allowing cool air to brush over normally private skin. "Have you ever been fucked in the ass?"

I suck in my breath and shake my head.

He meets my gaze as his fingers dip farther, closer to that part of me nobody has ever touched. "I'm going to fuck you there."

Even while my mind rejects the statement my body responds, heating and swelling, and pulling tight. I clear my throat. "I don't think I'd like that."

"Oh, I disagree. I think you're not only going to like it, that you'll learn to crave it." The tip of one finger brushes over puckered skin.

My core tightens. "Why do you think that?"

He moves his hand so his thumb circles my clit at the same time his finger circles over skin I had no idea was sensitive. The sensations war against each other, competing. I gasp and clutch his shoulders, not sure if I want to surge forward or back.

His eyes grow dark, his features intense. "I've noticed something else about you."

"What's that?" My nails dig into his bare chest as his movements pick up speed.

"I think you like things a little raw. A little taboo." He bites my neck, his teeth scraping over my skin. "It must be the repressed Catholic girl in you."

"I'm not...Catholic." My breath quickens. My breasts tingle. A low, needy groan escapes from my throat.

He laughs, dark and sexual, while his fingers are relentless. "You know what I mean."

My thoughts scatter. I don't know how he does this. I'm on fire.

I lean forward so our chests touch, skin to skin. I start to greedily, hungrily move, circling my hips so I first increase the pressure on my clit before I increase the pressure on my backside, all while abrading my nipples against his chest.

And, oh god, the friction, everywhere at once is so good. I don't want it to end. I want to go on like this forever.

He growls, low in my ear, "*This*, right here, is who you are. Now be a good girl and come all over my fingers while you think about me fucking this tight little ass of yours."

He pushes the barest tip of his finger inside me, squeezes my clit and I come in an explosion. I cry out, riding waves of near blinding ecstasy until I collapse in a panting heap on top of him.

Oh. My. God. What is happening to me?

He kisses my temple. "Ruby?"

I moan against him, trying to form a coherent response.

He laughs and drags another pulsing contraction from my drained body. "I'm meeting my parents and brothers for dinner tonight. I want you to come with me."

A burst of panic tries to break through, but I'm so damn boneless I can't move. I manage to gasp out, "You...did this...on purpose."

He tilts my chin and kisses me. "Climb up on my cock and we can talk about it."

So I do.

Needless to say, I'm meeting Chad's parents for dinner tonight.

16.

Chad

Ruby and I are at one of the buildings I'm working on. I'm trying to get some things done so my partner and I can list it. We've been here all morning, working away, and I'm surprised at how natural it's starting to feel with her by my side.

I look over at her. She's sitting cross-legged on the floor, her hair in a ponytail, her face scrunched up in concentration. It's warm today, the air hot, signaling summer is on the way. She has on torn jeans and a tight, black tank top that gives her that rocker, rebel vibe.

She's nothing like the women I normally date. The last girl I dated was a blonde. She was soft and curvy, with a bright, bubbly personality. A cute little submissive girl, who was compliant, loved shopping and didn't have a complicated thought in her head. I never would have brought her with me to sit in an abandoned building, and I'd never have introduced her to my family.

Watching Ruby, I can't figure out why that had remotely

interested me.

Her brow furrows and she huffs, drawing my attention to her full breasts. Under the scoop of the neckline, I can see the barest hint of a bruise. A bruise I put there. I've never been particularly sadistic, I don't get off on inflicting pain, but last night—my cock stirs—last night I'd been addicted to marking her pale ivory skin. Ruby hadn't really been in pain though, she'd moved past that so everything had been pure pleasure.

And what I'd said to her this morning was right, last night had been about possession.

Impossibly, I want her again.

Since we've been here Ruby has either helped me, or worked on her computer. When we'd first arrived, I'd put her on the island counter and taken her but that was hours ago. I find I'm impatient to get inside her. I hadn't realized it before but somewhere along the way sex had grown kind of boring. Even kinky sex hadn't really captured my attention. My seemingly bottomless lust for Ruby only highlighted how apathetic and lazy I'd grown.

I toss my rag to the counter and walk over to her.

She lifts her head, flushes before beaming at me.

My heart skips a beat. I raise a brow. "What were you just thinking about?"

She bites her full bottom lip. "Nothing."

My guess is she's either thinking about getting slapped or fucked in the ass. I'll be honest, she's managed to surprise me. Her being submissive I've known from the beginning, but I didn't expect her to be *this* kind of submissive.

A darkness lurks within Ruby that gets off on doing things she finds shocking. Ruby didn't like getting her breasts and pussy smacked because she's a masochist, she liked it because in her mind there was something wrong about liking it. The more twisted she sees the act, the hotter she gets.

That's her kink.

My challenge will be in taking it slow. Of pushing her enough she loses her mind but doesn't panic.

Her lashes flutter. "You're looking at me like you're

plotting."

I laugh. "Ruby, when it comes to you, I'm always plotting."

A red flush crawls across her chest. "Why don't I like the sound of that?"

"I beg to differ." I crouch down and rub a finger over her hard nipple. "I think you love the sound of that."

She does that little intake of breath that drives me crazy.

At some point we're going to have to talk about the fact that she's submissive and learning to accept herself for who she really is will only bring her happiness and freedom. She's not ready yet, but I see it lurking in her gaze, and I know at some point she'll have to let it out. Her nature will only stand being repressed for so long. Especially now that I've opened the floodgates and she no longer has orgasms to stress over.

I have no idea how it will go when we get there, but I'm guessing not well. From what I understand, Ruby's mom was a talented violinist that gave up everything the world had to offer to take care of her father's needs and become a perfect minister's wife.

In Ruby's eyes, any hierarchy is oppressive and stifling. I can prove her wrong…but only if she lets me. And that will be entirely up to her.

I glance down at her computer and see she has a graphic program open and the image there catches my eye. I shift, sit down against the wall, next to where she's sitting and take in the picture on her screen. The background is a gritty smudged black, with words in an intricate font. I peer closer—inside the words is an image of a woman, starkly beautiful and haunting.

I rest my head against the wall. "What are you working on?"

She mimics my posture, pulling her laptop up on her thighs, and swirling the pointer over the screen. "It's not quite done yet. Do you like it?"

I turn my head to study Ruby. Does she not see how unbelievable it is? Her expression is narrowed, her vision roaming over the screen, looking for flaws. "It's amazing. Is this for work?"

Ruby works for an ad agency and informed me they are beyond boring. I thought she told me the current campaign she's working on was for toothpaste. She laughs. "No, it's for fun." She shrugs. "A favor for my friend, Gene."

To my surprise jealousy stabs me right in the chest. I shake my head. What the fuck? My mother raised me better. She always said jealousy was a sign of the weak and I tend to agree with her. In a neutral tone, I ask, "Who's Gene?"

"A musician friend I sometimes hang out with. He's the guitarist."

I grit my teeth. Ruby's weakness. I not only play zero instruments I border on tone deaf and can't carry a tune to save my soul. My musical talents are in the negatives. I ignore the craziness in my head and ask, "What's the favor?"

"Their indie band is putting out their first album and they asked me to design it." She swirls the pointer over the female image in the words. "She reminds me of their first single but I don't think I have her quite right."

"She looks perfect to me."

She laughs. "Layla says I'm a closet perfectionist, and when it comes to this kind of stuff, I am. I'll make adjustments probably only I can see until I finally get the sense that it's right."

"I get that, I'll fix code for things nobody notices but me and could technically let slide. But they'll bug me until I take care of them."

"Exactly."

Sometimes these little similarities between us takes me off guard. I raise a brow. "And you do this as a favor?"

"Yeah. I'm happy to get a chance to do something creative for a change."

"Does favor mean free?"

She shrugs. "It's not a big deal."

I'm not at all surprised. These fucking guys are getting high-quality, professional work for nothing. "How many hours have you spent on this?"

"I don't know. Maybe twenty or so?"

I'd bet she's underestimating. "And you don't think you should get paid for that?"

"They're friends. I'm not going to charge them."

"Ruby, that cover is fucking brilliant."

"You're biased." She waves her hand over the screen. "It's nothing original. Nothing that hasn't been done before."

I narrow my eyes on her. "Why do you do that?"

"Do what?"

"Insist what you do isn't valuable."

She stiffens. "They asked me for a favor and I said yes, it's not a big deal. I wanted to do it."

She's deliberately missing my point. I want to push, but stop myself because I can tell she doesn't want to hear it. To me it's an example of her undervaluing herself, of minimizing her talents. I don't even think she's aware she does it but I've been paying attention. She minimizes any praise, diverting almost immediately if someone calls attention to her.

I take a breath and remind myself to be patient. She's going through changes and it's important not to throw too much at her. She doesn't realize this yet but not having her—*I'm frigid and can't have orgasms mantra*—as a security blanket to cling to is bound to cause emotional upheaval.

I can't add to it right now. So I tuck it away for another time and say simply, "They are lucky to have you."

"Thanks." Her expression relaxes and she stretches her neck, tilting her head to the side and rolling, before pressing her shoulders back, which thrusts out her breasts. "They're playing a show the night before the reunion, do you want to go check them out?"

I would certainly like to check out this Gene guy. "That sounds fun."

"Maybe we could see if everyone wants to go."

I love that she's suggesting this, and how she's including herself in that circle instead of apart. It makes me hopeful. "Should I make the call, or do you want to?"

"I'll do it." She frowns and looks down.

"What?"

She clears her throat and pays close attention to her keyboard.

I jostle her shoulder with mine. "Ruby?"

A shrug. "What does this mean?"

I'm lost. "What does what mean?"

"Are we like…what… A couple?"

A smile twitches at my lips. "Are you seeing other people?"

"No!" Her head jerks up and she looks at me, appalled. "Are you?"

I laugh. "No. You're the only woman I want."

Her features relax and she licks her lips. "So?"

"Have I not repeatedly told you that you belong to me?"

Another pretty flush across her skin. "During sex."

I grip her jaw and force her to meet my gaze. Her dark, thick lashes flutter. "You are mine. You belong to me and I do not share. Ever."

Her breath catches.

I release her jaw and brush my mouth over her lips. "So, yes, we are a couple."

"Okay." The word is a rasp.

I tangle my fingers in her hair. "I assume you're good with that."

She nods.

"Come over here and we'll make it official."

She does, and I sink into her heat and hungry mouth, and forget about doing anything but showing her what her body craves, but her mind's not ready for.

17.

"Layla, oh my god, help me." I'm standing in the middle of my bedroom, as desperation and panic eat away at me.

Layla grins like the proverbial Cheshire cat.

I screech, "Stop laughing! You're a horrible best friend."

I called in an emergency girlfriend session, because I have no idea what to wear to dinner with a bunch of doctors, but all she can do is snicker at my distress.

When another giggle spurts forth, I cross my arms over my chest and huff. "You are the worst."

Layla attempts to affix a serious expression on her face. She's wearing jeans and a T-shirt, her face free of makeup, her hair in a messy bun. Apparently Michael and she'd been cleaning out their closet when I called, and Layla was more than happy to abandon the task and help me. She looks so relaxed.

I used to be relaxed. I want to be relaxed again.

"Okay, how about this?" She holds out a halter dress with

152

an empire waist and pencil skirt. I wear it sometimes when I sing.

I shake my head. "Too sexy."

We must have gone through all my clothes by now.

"Where are you going again?"

"Harvest."

"Oh, fancy."

"Focus, Layla." I managed to avoid thinking about what I agreed to, until Chad dropped me off an hour ago, and now I'm in a panic.

She laughs again and turns back to my closet. She shifts through items before holding out a nineteen fifties shirtwaist dress. "This isn't sexy."

"It was a Halloween costume." I start pacing around the room. "This is a disaster. Why am I doing this? I don't like people. I don't like parents. I need to cancel. This is too much."

Layla grabs my arm, stilling me, before leaning in and peering into my face. Suddenly she gasps. "Oh my god."

My heart speeds up. "What?"

"You and Chad. It's serious." She releases her grip and points to me. "You care what his parents think."

I drag a hand through my hair. "I do. I really, really do, Laylay."

All her amusement fades away and she gets that serious, take-no-prisoners look on her face. "Grab what you need and we'll head to my house. I have lots of meeting-the-parents dresses to choose from."

I experience a flood of relief. Then race like mad around my apartment, throwing stuff in my bag, unsure of what I might need.

Layla rolls her eyes. "He should be shot, giving you no notice to prepare."

I toss makeup into a bag and say absently, "I think he did it on purpose."

She scoffs. "So typical of them."

The hairs on the back of my neck rise, and I turn my

attention to her. "What does that mean?"

She narrows her blue eyes, and shakes her head. "Nothing." She juts her head toward my door. "Let's go."

Twenty minutes later we're standing in Layla's bedroom, and she's kicked Michael out of the room. She hands me a tan dress. "Try this one."

"I hate that."

She rolls her eyes. "It's pretty, but conservative."

"I want to look good, but like me, not you."

She turns back and finds a black dress. A wraparound number, I've seen her wear before, she doesn't have my cleavage though. I frown. "I don't know."

"Just try it."

"Fine." I put my hands on my waist and go to pull off my top and at the last second, remember what my chest, thighs and hips look like. I freeze.

"What's wrong?"

"Nothing." I dart a glance at the bathroom. This is my best friend. We were roommates. Stripping into my bra and underwear is not supposed to be a big deal. I frantically try and come up with an excuse. I can say I have to use the bathroom, but what about the next dress? And the next? Her gaze catches mine and I must look guilty because her expression turns speculative.

She tilts her head. "Did you have sex last night?"

I flush scarlet. I could deny it but she's already on to me. "Um… Kind of."

Her brows rise. "Kind of?"

I swallow. I had the best night of my life and I don't know how to explain it to her. Ironically, she's the one person who would understand, but I'm not ready to talk. I shrug.

She grins. "How was it?"

I sink down onto her massive bed. I prop my elbows on my knees and drop my head into my open palms. "Mind-blowing."

I can't even communicate how mind-blowing.

She laughs. "Is that a bad thing?"

"I don't know." I look up at her. "It was so, so good, Layla.

Like better than anything times a thousand."

"I can't believe you didn't tell me right away."

"What was I suppose to say?"

She shrugs. "I had mind-blowing sex with Chad last night."

If only it were that simple. Because while the statement is true, it leaves out so much. "Well, now you know."

"And now you want to change in the bathroom?" She doesn't elaborate but I know she understands why.

I just blink at her. A mixture of startled relief and embarrassed shame. But underneath, desire burns as I remember what he did to me. How much I liked it. No matter how wrong it was.

She clears her throat. "Will this dress work?"

It won't. Layla's cleavage spilled from the top, mine will overflow it. "Maybe something less low cut."

She turns back to the closet and starts to rifle through her clothes again and I breathe a sigh of relief that she's not going to press. She rummages in there for a good five minutes, muttering and making disgusted noises, making me laugh. Finally she emerges with a white dress that still has the tags on. It's simple—a capped-sleeved, classic-cut dress that probably hits Layla's thighs and will come to my knees. It looks like nothing. She hands it to me. "Try this. I didn't try it on at the store so I'm not sure how it runs but it will look fabulous with your black hair." She picks up a pair of nude heels at least four inches high, and hands them to me. "These will work."

"Are you sure? It's new?"

"I'm sure. It's not a big deal. I impulse bought it."

"Thanks." I don't argue, even though I'm not sure about the dress. I don't have high hopes. Without looking at her I go to the bathroom and shut the door, stripping down to my bra and underwear, thankful I had the foresight to wear beige. I see now the dress is made from a stretchy fabric. I put the dress over my head, slip on the shoes and turn to the full-length mirror.

I start a bit at my reflection. The dress scoops low, but not so low you can see the marks on my skin. My breasts strain at the fabric and it fits like a glove. The dress looks custom made for me. I look like a grown up. Sophisticated, somehow. I'm not sure if I love it or I hate it. It's gorgeous. I feel like an imposter. And every other dress I put on will pale in comparison.

I take a deep breath and step out of the bathroom.

Layla's expression widens at the sight of me. "Keep the dress, it was clearly meant for you. I'll never be able to wear it now."

I shake my head. "God, no! Are you kidding? I'm not taking your clothes."

"Consider it an early birthday present."

"I can't!"

"I don't think you understand how that dress looks on you. Hang on, I'll show you." All the sudden she cranes her neck and yells, "Michael, can you come here?"

I hiss, "What are you doing?"

She waves a hand. "Trust me."

He pounds down the hall, and when he swings open the door, Layla gestures to me. "Tell her."

Michael takes one look at me and stops in his tracks. "Is that what you're going to wear?"

I put my hand on my stomach and shift on the balls of my feet. I clear my throat. "It was an option."

Layla pokes him in the arm. "Don't make her doubt the power. Tell her."

He gives me a long, slow once over. At six-five, he's not only scarily gorgeous, he's intimidating. "You look ridiculously hot."

I roll my eyes. "You have to say that."

"No, I do not. Let me put it another way." Michael grins, his unusual hazel eyes mischievous. "You'd better prepare to get fucked where you stand, so try not to blush during the story Chad gives to his parents about why you're late. You have a shit poker face, so keep cool. If you don't, one look at you in that dress will give you away."

Face heating fifty degrees; I stare at him in horror. "Is that supposed to make me feel better?"

Michael shrugs. "I hope Chad's not feeling particularly possessive, because if he is, you'd better watch out."

Oh my god, am I really standing here having this conversation with my best friend's fiancé? I scowl. "Would you stop that? Be serious."

"I am dead serious, girl." His tone, it does something deep in my belly.

My gaze meets his, and his…it's…knowing. He called me girl—as I've heard him and Leo do countless times. As Chad sometimes calls me when we are at our most crazed.

I swallow hard and glance at the floor. "Maybe I should pick the tan one."

He shakes his head. "No. Wear the dress. If you don't, I'll be forced to text Chad and have him pick for you. And I already know what he'll choose. So save us the trouble." Then he turns, gives Layla a hard kiss, and leaves.

She smirks. "See?"

I can only gape after Layla's fiancé, taken aback. "Did Michael just blackmail me?"

She laughs. "How else can we be sure you make the right choice?"

I turn to study my reflection. On the surface, the dress is perfectly respectable. It doesn't even show a ton of skin, but I can't deny there's something about it. Paired with my body type and coloring I'll be hard pressed to find something better. "Are you sure about this? His parents."

"Trust me. That's why it's so perfect."

My brow furrows. I'm not remotely a fashionista. My only dresses are the ones I wear to sing, other than that I like jeans, skirts and tees. "I don't follow."

"The perfection of a dress like this is that it *is* respectable. There's nothing inappropriate about its cut, or what it reveals. It's you inside it that transforms it." She gets a sly grin on her face, and really it's almost terrifying in its deviousness. "And you, my dearest, bestest friend, are going to learn the fun of having a very proper, respectable dinner with an evil man whose one and only thought will be how to make you pay for making him suffer."

The oddest, strangest thing happens at Layla's statement. I don't experience panic or worry, as I would expect. In fact, what rushes over me is an emotion I have very little experience with, although I've faked it many, many times.

Power.

Chad

Curiosity strums through my blood as I walk down Ruby's hallway. Michael texted me earlier, saying I needed to make sure Ruby was wearing the white dress.

When I questioned him, all he'd said was I wouldn't be sorry, and that I'd understand as soon as I saw her.

So, I'm guessing she's rocking a white dress, and I'm always game for that. Although why her clothes are important enough to warrant a text—from a guy—well, that remains to be seen. As Michael isn't prone to exaggeration I'm expecting something pretty good and I'm brimming with anticipation.

I knock on the door, tapping my fingers against the doorframe.

The door flies open and Ruby is standing in front of me.

She's wearing a white dress.

And I get it.

Everything about Michael's text makes perfect sense.

I take in the length of her.

Un-fucking-believable.

The dress is a stark contrast to her dark hair, which is a tumble of shiny waves around her shoulders. Her eyes, lined with some sort of smoky shadow are impossibly blue. Her lips look to be bare, but they are full and slightly swollen, the natural shade only enhancing her appearance.

And that dress—that fucking dress—brings her all together in one stunning package.

All I can think about is devouring her. My grip tightens on the wood.

"Hi." Her voice is breathless, her eyes excited.

I'm still trying to get my tongue to work properly. I shake my head.

She smiles, and there's something there that wasn't before. Slyness. Cunning. "Is everything okay?"

My gaze narrows. She knows the effect she's having on me.

When I speak, my voice is more growl than anything else. "We're going to be late."

And then I lay claim to her like this is the last fuck I'll ever get on this earth.

I push her inside, slamming the door shut with my foot as I eat at her mouth. Devouring her with a hunger that borders on obsessive.

Her hands clutch at my shoulders as she stumbles back. I swing her around and slam her against the wall—the first available surface I find—as my tongue plunges into her mouth. She lets out a sound like the wind's been knocked out of her, before our mouths crash together. I fist her hair, angling her head to my satisfaction. For ultimate penetration.

Her hips jerk against me and I kick her legs apart. Inserting my thigh roughly to grind between her legs. It's like some switch has flipped in my head and released the primal beast that lives inside me. In this moment I'm not interested in anything civilized.

My only interest is possession.

I pull her hair, tearing her mouth from me, to ask in a savage tone, "Are you on the Pill?"

She nods and tries to capture my mouth.

"I'm going to take you bare." Just the thought of it frays the last remaining thread I have on sanity.

She moans.

I push her against the wall. "Is that a yes?"

She pants out, "Yes."

"This is going to be quick and dirty. Understand?"

She nods, tugging my shirt out from my pants; her fingers

159

slide over my stomach. "Please."

I groan. She's going to be the death of me. I capture her mouth. My kiss is brutal. Ruthless and demanding. Full of aggression and primal hunger, and she just stands there, taking it. Giving it back while she rides my thigh, working herself up as she surrenders to my will.

I lift the skirt of her dress so it bunches at her waist, slip my fingers into her panties and play over her wet flesh. And god is she wet. I strip her panties, put them in my pocket, and fumble at my belt, never breaking the contact of our clinging, desperate mouths. I've spent hours kissing Ruby. *Hours.* I know exactly what she likes, how she likes it, and I give it to her, but hold nothing back.

Every ounce of dominance I keep in check comes pouring out and she responds, exactly like the good little girl she is, and goes crazy. I slide my pants down my hips, free my cock, and work my way into her tight heat.

Every sense I have is focused on impaling her.

She makes that needy little gasp, tilts up to meet me.

I push farther into her, pulling out and pushing in. Deeper.

I lift her knee and hook her leg on my hip.

Our mouths part, unable to maintain contact as we pant our way together.

When I'm finally seated inside her, I pull out and slam back into her. Her head thunks against the wall, her neck arches. I want to sink my teeth into all that offered flesh—because it is an offering—but I don't, because I don't want to mark her in such a visible way. Instead, I slide my hand around her throat and squeeze.

She cries out and rocks into me.

Under my palm I feel her muscles working, her pulse pounding, and it feeds that part of me that wants to claim her in the harshest and most brutal way possible.

I grow impatient. Even with her pinned against the wall I'm not deep enough.

I growl, pull out of her, yank her by the shoulders and push her to the floor.

She lifts up and I stare down at her for a fraction of a second—taking in the sight of her, helpless and wanton on the floor, her body bowed in invitation. I've never seen anything in my life as beautiful as Ruby lying there, completely undone, needy and desperate.

I fall to my knees and fucking impale her, so hard she slides across the floor. I grip her hips to keep her in place. Right where I want her. I slam into her again and again and again. I unleash on her, driving into her relentlessly. Her body tightens, but she doesn't go over the edge, and my body is demanding release.

I take one hand from her hip; grip her throat and growl into her ear, "You're going to spend dinner with my family with my come dripping down your thighs."

And that's all it takes.

She cries out. Convulses around me, and it throws me right over the edge. I spill into her with a blinding force that shakes my entire body, my entire being right to the core. Intense pleasure sears through me as I spurt hot inside her. I don't stop until I wring out every last bit of her orgasm and we collapse into a panting heap.

I'm trying to catch my breath when she giggles. A very un-Ruby-like sound.

I lift my head. "What's so funny?"

"Nothing." She laughs again.

I squeeze her hip. "You're going to tell me." I mean to make the words demanding, but I'm too mindless. My cock is inside her, her pussy still tight, like she doesn't want to let me go.

Her lips twitch. "Michael was right."

"Yeah, he was."

Her brow furrows. "What do you mean?"

I grin, and prop my elbows on either side of her. "He texted me a very odd message saying I needed to make sure you wore a white dress."

"He did?"

"Of course I didn't understand until I saw you. Then it all

made sense." I cock my brow. "How exactly did he see you in this dress?"

"It's Layla's."

"I beg to differ."

She smiles. "That's what she said. I didn't have anything appropriate to wear so we went to her house."

"I see. And what was Michael right about?"

"Your response." She bites her lip. "He said I have a terrible poker face and I should try not to blush when you explain why we're late."

I laugh.

"Do I have a terrible poker face?"

I kiss her sweet mouth. "Yes. It's one of my favorite things about you."

"You're so weird."

I glance at my watch. "We have to go."

She sighs. "I hope this isn't a disaster."

"Don't worry, they'll love you."

"Time will tell."

We manage to heave ourselves off the floor and spend the next couple minutes putting ourselves back together again. She looks around, turning in a circle before getting down on her hands and knees and peering under her couch. I bite back my groan at the sight of her ass high in the air, and try not to think about the fact that I'll be fucking it soon. How it's going to pulse down my cock when she comes. And she's going to come. By the time I take her there she's going to crave it like she's a fucking heroin addict.

Because I know her secret now. The dirtier and more forbidden I make the act, the more she'll want it. The hotter it will make her.

I put my hands in my pockets and my right one touches the scrap of silk she'd been wearing. "Are you looking for your panties?"

She cranes her neck to look up at me. "Yes."

"They're in my pocket, and that's where they're staying."

She straightens and sits back on her haunches, basically

kneeling before me. On impulse I step forward so I'm towering over her and look down.

She sucks in a breath. "I need them."

"No you don't."

She bites her lip, peering up at me. She opens her mouth and closes it. Shakes her head.

I brush her hair from her cheek. "I believe I told you what was going to happen at dinner."

"I didn't think you were serious."

I laugh. "Dead serious. I want you to feel my come sliding over your legs, slippery between your thighs. I want you to feel it when you walk, when you sit, while you talk."

"But…" She glances around the room. "That's…"

I don't make her say it. She already knows and that's enough. I nod. "It is."

I grip her hair and force her chin up, arching her neck at a position that emphasizes my dominance and her vulnerability.

She quivers, her pupils dilating.

"I know how wet it makes you." I let the statement hang in the air, suspended between us. Thick with meaning. Letting it change her, me, and our relationship without a single word.

When I've made my point, I release her, hold out my hand, and help her to her feet. She blows out a shaky breath and pulls down the hem of her skirt before straightening. "Do I at least look respectable?"

No she does not, but in the best possible way. And not in a way that affects her meeting my family or that my parents will be thinking about when they meet her. Although I'm sure my brothers will take notice. They'd have to be dead not to. "You look perfect."

She nods, grabs a purse then starts toward the door.

Just as she's about to open it an urge takes over. An instinct I would have ignored last week I now follow, twisting the knife deeper. I push the door closed with the palm of my hand. "One more thing."

She goes to turn but I shake my head. I grip her neck and push forward, while I take her hip in my free hand and urge her back. On instinct her palms come to rest on the door. I tap her thigh. "Open."

When she doesn't hesitate, my cock grows hard again.

I lift the hem of her dress, from behind I reach between her legs, where my come has combined with her wetness and draw it up to the crease of her ass.

She gasps. "Oh god."

I laugh. Repeat my actions until her puckered skin is slick and quivering. I circle my middle finger where she's most sensitive and when she's pushing back into my hand I lean down and whisper in her ear, "I wouldn't want you to forget I'll be fucking your ass when you're talking to my parents over salad."

18.

Ruby

I literally have no idea how I'm holding it together as I clutch Chad's hand and walk across the restaurant to where a group of people are seated around a large table. There's an older man and woman, both attractive who are clearly his parents. Even from across the room I see the resemblance between Chad and his dad.

I also see two guys.

All four of them are staring at me.

I squeeze Chad's hand tighter and he squeezes back. "Just breathe, girl. You're going to be fine."

My emotions are a mess. My body is a mess. Instead of the appropriate meeting-the-parents things I should stress about, all I can think is that I must smell like sex. How can I not? My thighs are slippery wet. I've been fucked within an inch of my life. And he did that...that...that...thing to my ass that screwed with my head and made me want it.

That doesn't even take into account the cab ride over. He played with me the whole way, while carrying on a completely innocent conversation with the driver, who had to know what Chad was doing because I couldn't stop gasping and shifting and moaning. The driver kept looking at me in the mirror but Chad just kept on talking.

To my horror and shock, I almost came.

It was the only time he spoke to me. Right when I was on the very edge and one hard press of his fingers would push me over, he lightens his touch, turned and whispered in my ear, "No coming for you." Then went back to talking about the Cubs third baseman or something like that.

I honestly don't remember. Are third basemen a topic of

conversation?

I'd spent the rest of the ride over in some sort of suspended state of tingling mess one step away from orgasm. Instead of the situation shocking me and pulling me back to sanity, I just kept getting hotter and hotter until I wasn't thinking about anything else. On the other hand, Chad acted like it was completely normal to have a needy, half-crazed, desperate woman writhing next to him while he carried on an innocuous conversation.

All of this swirls in my head, consuming me and suddenly I'm at the table, standing in front of them. They all rise to greet us and Chad releases his hold on my hand and slips his palm to my waist. "Hey, sorry we're late. Mom, Dad, I'd like you to meet, Ruby. Ruby, these are my parents, David and Alice, and my brothers, Cameron and Christopher." He kind of pushes me forward and like I'm watching someone else from a distance I'm holding out my hand.

I smile. "It's a pleasure to meet you." Thank god my voice is completely calm.

His mom grasps my palm and beams at me. "My, my you certainly are lovely."

"Thank you." *Your son is the devil and he won't stop torturing me.*

His father takes me in, nods at Chad, I think in approval. "Well done."

Chad laughs and shakes his head, giving my hip a little squeeze.

Cameron, Chad's oldest brother is dressed in a pair of gray pants and a white button-down, not unlike things I've seen Chad wear. They look remarkably alike, except Cameron's eyes are a dark brown. A smile on his face, his gaze flickers discretely, and in a second he's roamed my entire body before he meets my eyes and says to me in a voice as smooth as whiskey, "It's a pleasure to meet you, Ruby."

He's not what I expected. I always think of doctors as older, stately and comfortable. And, well, I kind of picture doctors as bald—probably because my pediatrician growing up was bald. Cameron Fellow's is none of those things. In fact, he's hot; if a doctor walked into an exam room looking like that, I'd run. He has the same penetrating stare Chad does, and I'd bet my last dollar he's a player. I nod. "Thank you, you too."

The youngest brother, Christopher grins at me, all charming and affable. Chad told me he's twenty-seven and in his residency. He's cute, with messy butterscotch-colored hair and light brown eyes, he favors his mom. He gives me a boyish grin, chuckles and gestures to the table. "Hey, Ruby. No pressure here at all, is there?"

I laugh, and some of my tension abates. "Nope. None at all."

We sit down. I put my napkin on my lap, and suddenly it occurs to me wearing a white dress is completely stupid. What if I spill something?

There's some chitchat around the table, and a waiter comes over. Chad's dad orders two bottles of wine—red wine—before everyone settles. I cast a glance to the ceiling. *Please dear God, don't let me get wine on this dress.*

Chad's mom is very put together and sophisticated, with her sleek chin-length bob the same color as her youngest son's. Chad shares her blue eyes. She's wearing a business suit, classically cut, that fits her trim figure like it was made for her. She's the kind of woman I'd expect to be cold and remote, but when she smiles at me her face is warm and open. "We're happy you could join us, Ruby. Chad never brings anyone to dinner."

I attempt to ignore the flash of pleasure that statement brings me. "Thank you for having me."

"Chad tells us you're a singer?" David Fellows asks, steepling his hands.

I shake my head. "Hardly. I sing a couple times a week at a place by my apartment. For my regular job I'm a graphic designer at a small ad agency."

"Interesting." He nods, he has the same dark eyes as Cameron and they are quite penetrating. I wonder if he wishes I was a doctor.

"Our whole family is musically challenged," Alice says. To my surprise, her expression turns a bit amused and pouty. "I've always been jealous of people who can sing. Did you train in the musical arts?"

I laugh. "No, nothing like that. I discovered my love of singing in the good old-fashioned church choir." It was the only time I enjoyed the endless hours of church I was forced to attend growing up. The only time I ever felt peaceful under the watchful eye of God.

Chad's arm is on the back of my chair and I can feel his eyes on me. The questions there.

David nods. "A churchgoing girl."

I say simply, "My father is a minister."

Chad knows this is an uncomfortable subject for me so, of course, he steps in. "Ruby's family lives in southern Indiana."

"Very good," David says, as though I passed a test.

I bite my lip. I want to pass their test. It's something I've never cared about. Rocker boys don't bring home girls to their parents, it ruins their mystique. If you asked me six months ago, I'd swear I wanted no part of this, but here I am, wearing a dress that's not mine, meeting an employed, conservative, nice guy's parents. And I care.

I shoot a sidelong glance in Chad's direction. The truth dawns on me. Chad's not actually conservative. That's the story I keep trying to sell myself in hopes of keeping him at a distance, but it's not true. I mean, sure on the surface he's the all-American guy next door I assumed him to be the first time I met him, but he's nothing like any man I've ever met.

He is both angel and devil. Good and evil. Saint and sinner.

Alice's voice rips me from my thoughts. "And why were you late, young man?"

I tense, and I will my body not to flush. Chad puts his hand on the back of my chair, and his fingers brush over my shoulder. "I had an inspector come late."

Alice's face clears. "Ah, understandable." She picks up her menu. "What shall we start with this evening?"

That's everyone's cue to pick up their menus. I relax and

adjust in my seat, biting my lip at the slick of my skin when I move. I let out a tiny gasp, recover, only to catch Chad's oldest brother's gaze. I try not to blush when he winks at me, before saying to Chad, "I do hate when that happens."

Chad's hand skims intimately, suggestively over the curve of my neck. On the surface, it's an innocent touch, but Cameron's smirk makes it seem sexual.

I cross my legs, once again calling attention to my current state. Heat flares through me. Oh god, no.

Chad's thumb presses against my pounding pulse and he says in a low voice, "Do you blame me?"

Cameron's gaze flickers to my mouth, which now feels impossibly swollen. "No, I don't."

"Some things can't be helped, as you well know." Chad's tone is wicked.

I grip my menu as my nipples pucker impossibly tight.

"I do." Cameron tips his head. "I hope the visit was satisfying."

Chad's still rubbing over my neck in slow, methodical circles. "Very."

Cameron meets my eyes again. "Good."

What in God's name is going on? They are deviants. I glance around the table, but none of the rest of the family seems to notice this exchange.

I shift restlessly in my chair and the press of my thighs rubs against my needy flesh, reminding me all over again of my craziness in the cab. My stomach jumps, heats.

Chad's fingers curl around my neck and Cameron's attention tracks the movement.

Without saying it, Chad has clearly communicated the exact reason we are late. And Cameron isn't hiding his appreciation. A month ago this would have horrified me, but because Chad's done…something to my brain, lust rushes through my body at warp speed.

He's *corrupted* me.

I give him a little glare, silently ordering him to behave.

Instead he gives my throat a squeeze, leans over, and

whispers in my ear, "He knows I fucked you."

I suck in my breath and my gaze flies to Cameron, who's watching us instead of paying attention to the menu like everyone else. He smiles, and runs his fingers the length of the wineglass.

I look down at my menu and dig my heel into Chad's foot under the table.

He laughs and moves his foot out of reach, but still speaks into my ear. "Every time I put my hands on you under the table you're going to wonder if he knows what I'm doing. And the answer is, yes, he will."

"This is perverse," I say in a barely audible hiss.

"Yeah, it is."

He's so…so… Wicked. I scowl and whisper, "Why are you doing this to me?"

"You know why."

Understanding rushes over me like a freight train and everything seems to click into place. Suddenly, I remember Layla's words this afternoon, and her true meaning finally sinks in. A million seemingly unrelated threads coalesce and soul-deep knowledge practically explodes through me. It sinks into my bones, makes my heart pound, and my palms sweat. I understand, for perhaps the very first time in my entire life. Chad's words from this afternoon come back to me, *this, right here, is who you really are.*

This isn't something he's *doing* to me at all.

There's one reason and one reason only why he's doing it.

Because I like it.

Chad

We're riding in the back of a cab from dinner with my family to Brandon's club and I'm trying to give Ruby some time to process instead of attacking her the way I want to. When I'd teased her in front of Cameron I'd seen something shift in her eyes. It had been written in the widening of her expression, the intake of her breath, the tightening of her muscles under my hands. Only because of our surroundings I hadn't been able to ask her what it was, and that, combined with the fact that we were at dinner with my parents and I wanted her to be able to form a coherent sentence, I took it easy on her.

But every time I slid my fingers up her thighs she'd been wet. Very wet.

Right now she looked out the window, seeming lost in thought.

I squeezed her knee. "You survived."

"I did." She shifts a little. "Your family is nice."

"They are." I slide my hand up her leg. "When you went to the bathroom my mom gave you a huge seal of approval. They loved you."

"I'm glad. I liked them too."

"Do you want to talk about whatever is on your mind?" I prompt her. She's reflective. Not angry or upset, but thoughtful.

She clears her throat. "Do you think I'm changing for you?"

Individuality. Lack of conformity is important to Ruby. Having grown up in such a rigid household where there was only one narrow line to follow made an impression. I make it a practice to answer Ruby directly, but I find I want to push a little bit and go with my gut. "Do you think you're changing for me?"

"Yes." Her fingers tighten on her purse.

She is, the question is if she's becoming more of who she really is. "Is that a bad thing?"

Even in the darkness of the car her brow furrows. "It doesn't feel bad."

"Isn't that the important thing?"

"I don't know." She looks out the window and the lights pass over her face. "My mom gave up everything to be with my dad. She lived in New York when she met him. He was there for a conference and he saw her play. She gave it up to go live in that small town and be his wife. The day I left home for college I swore I'd never go back. Swore I'd never change for a man. But I feel myself changing for you."

I contemplate how to handle this, unsure what direction I should take. I'm saved from an immediate answer when the cab pulls up to Brandon's club. There's a line down the block. I pay the driver, grab her hand and we climb out, but instead of going to the doorman where our names on the list, I pull her in the opposite direction.

She frowns. "Where are we going?"

"I want to finish our conversation before we go in." We walk a half a block down and I tuck her into an alcove before turning to face her.

I slide my hand over her neck and run my thumb down the line of her jaw. I tilt my head. "Have you ever asked your mom how she felt about it?"

Her expression tightens before she shakes her head. "No, I never did."

"So you don't really know how she felt about that time in her life."

She shakes her head again. "She'd never admit to making a sacrifice."

"That's what you're assuming."

She lowers her eyes. "True."

"You know, I'm changing for you too." And I realize it's true. It's not as drastic, because I know who I am in a way Ruby hasn't ever given herself the luxury to discover and I'm not shifting my perception of self, but it's still true.

She laughs. "You are not."

"Not true."

"How?"

"Before we started I was consumed with work, but I've stopped putting in twelve-hour days and working all weekend. It's not that I don't care about work anymore, because I do, but I've relaxed about it. I come from a family whose careers are their lives; it's part of who they are. Even though I wasn't ever going to be a doctor, work has been my one and only priority for as long as I can remember. Before you, I sized up every woman I met in terms of how much time she would take away from my job, from my buildings and from me. It's why when I called you the day after Valentine's Day to make sure you were all right, I didn't press, even though I knew there was something between us. You were going to take time I didn't have or want to give you, so I let it go. I didn't realize it but I didn't want to make room for someone. Didn't want someone in my life."

She peers at me, her expression filled with surprise. "What made you change your mind?"

"You did." I lean down to brush my mouth over hers. "You looked at me with those big, needy blue eyes and I couldn't resist."

"Oh." A smile trembles at her lips.

"The question you need to ask yourself is if the ways you're changing are a sacrifice."

"They're not." Her brow knits. "But they still feel like a betrayal, you know?"

I do, but I want her to say the words to me, so she'll be forced to think them through. "Give me an example."

She bites her lower lip then smooths her hand over her stomach. "This dress. I like the way it makes me feel. I like the way you look at me in it."

When she falters, I encourage her. "Go on."

"It's nothing I would have ever picked for myself. It seems too... I don't know...mainstream. Like I'm dressing in my mom's clothes."

I understand what she means, but what makes the dress so spectacular is that on her it doesn't look mainstream, but that's not the point here.

She laughs and shakes her head. "It's a grown-up dress and even though I'm thirty years old, I don't want to become—" she makes air quotes, "—an adult. Pretty stupid, huh?"

I smile. "Did you ever think that maybe you don't have to choose? That you don't have to be one or the other? That it's possible to be both? Holding on to ideas that no longer fit you is just as stifling as trying to be someone you're not, it's only a different kind of box. Both hold you back from who you really are."

Slowly, she nods. "That's true. I never looked at it that way."

"Your job is to figure out how to satisfy both the girl and the woman." I kiss her again. "My job is to support you in that."

"Okay." She grips my wrist and rises to her tiptoes and captures my mouth before breathing into me. "Thank you, Chad."

Fuck. She is sweet. "You're welcome. Ready?"

I take her hand and we start to leave our private little spot on the street, but she stops. "Chad?"

I turn back to her. "What's wrong?"

"Nothing." Her fingers tighten on mine. "I want to say something."

By the tremble in her voice I hear her nervousness. I put my hand on her hip to steady her. "Please do."

She licks her lips and sucks in a little breath. "What you did with your brother was very twisted."

"It was." There's no denying it. But it was a safe risk I didn't push too far. Everyone had been paying attention to their menus and Cameron and I understand each other. My oldest brother isn't into the scene, but he enjoys making a pretty girl squirm as much as I do. There was no way he didn't know why we were late.

She meets my eyes. "Did you do it because you thought I'd like it?"

It's the first time she's asked a question that gives me any indication she's starting to realize, or get curious, about the unspoken dynamic that's playing out between us. I answer her directly and honestly. "Yes, I did."

"So you think I'm twisted?" Her gaze is searching.

I nod. "I don't *think* you are. I *know* you are."

"Even though I have all these sex hang-ups?"

"Yes." I narrow my eyes and take the first step into leading her where she wants to go but is still afraid of. "I think you have sex hang-ups for precisely that reason."

"I don't follow."

I make my statement much more specific. "You have hang-ups because you've spent your entire sexual life denying exactly how twisted you are."

Emotions play over her expression—and the equivalent of a storm cloud passes over her face—before she settles. Then she straightens, squares her shoulders and looks me dead in the eye. "I liked it."

"I know." My cock grows hard as I watch her own it. I raise a brow. "Anything else?"

The cords in her neck work as she swallows. "During dinner, I kept getting distracted."

"Why?"

"I wanted more."

I close the distance between us, but instead of sliding my hand through her hair I grip it and yank, so her chin juts up. "That can be arranged."

She makes that needy little gasp.

My heart gives a hard thump and something hot and foreign races through me like lightning.

Fuck. I think I'm in love with her.

19.

It's been two weeks since the night Ruby met my parents and I've watched her come alive. Everything about her has become more vibrant. She's lost that closed-off, worried look. Every day she becomes more empowered, more confident, more the woman she wants to be.

She's still Ruby. Still my little rocker princess. But it's like the rough edges have smoothed away. She's experimenting more, laughing more, and as I watch her doing her makeup from my bed, where I'm still sprawled naked under a sheet, she practically glows.

Instead of getting ready in my master bathroom she's standing at my dresser mirror because I told her I wanted to watch her. She's wearing nothing but a black bra and—I smile—batman boy shorts. I've discovered that Ruby has a fetish for superhero underwear and it's the most adorable thing I've ever seen.

I put my hand behind my head. "Cute panties."

She glances at me and grins. "Why do I not like the sound of that?"

Because she's a smart girl.

We continue to avoid having the discussion about dominance and submission, even though that's exactly what we've fallen into. I've been waiting, but she hasn't brought it up again since that night on the street, and I'm content not to push the matter. Other than forcing her to accept all facets of her nature, I'm not sure there's a need.

Sex with Ruby is goddamn mind blowing. Taking her has become almost an obsession. She's eager, compliant, blushes at the drop of a hat, and is increasingly easy to turn completely perverse. Now that she's not only accepted but embraced this part of herself, her limits have expanded exponentially. She still hates it—in the way all submissive girls both hate and love the twisting of the knife in equal measure—but she's stopped questioning and surrenders when I push her.

I let my eyes roam over her body before meeting her gaze in the mirror. One brow is raised and she's wearing a smirk. She's fully anticipating I make her take off her panties, because that's what I usually do. I let her think that because it suits my purposes. "Do you really think I'm going to let you wear them?"

This has become old hat to her by now, and there's no more wariness left in her eyes. There's only excitement and lust. She finishes with her mascara, tosses it to the dresser before she turns, and puts her hand on her hip. All cocky and confident. "Yes, it's only fair."

"And why is it fair?"

"You made me take off my panties last night." She huffs. "At the table."

Yesterday after work, we went to dinner, and she came at the table with every course. After I pushed her in between the buildings, bent her over, put her hands on the wall, and fucked her while people passed us on the street not three feet away.

My cock stirs. I shift, and the sheet dips low on my hips. Her hungry gaze tracks the motion. "You forgot how I made you leave them on the booth for the waiter to see."

She flushes, probably remembering when the waiter's

expression had widened when he saw them.

She flings out her hand. "You made him drop his bread basket."

He did, the poor guy had flushed scarlet, fumbled his words then spilled the contents all over the place. "You did that all on your own, girl. I didn't have anything to do with it."

"Ha!" Her hip cocks farther out, clearly feeling quite certain of herself.

I give her another once over. "What does that have to do with tonight?"

We're going to see her friend's band and I have plans.

"It would be nice to keep my underwear on every once in a while."

God I love it when she plays right into my hands. I shrug. "All right then. Go ahead and keep them on."

Of course, her expression instantly falls, because she really doesn't want that. She doesn't want to walk out of the house without being toyed with. Not that I'm about to let that happen. I'll save that game for another day.

Her brow furrows and her shoulders square. "Fine. It's settled then."

"Yep. All settled."

She turns back around to fiddle with her hair, ignoring me completely, and I watch her, amused. Unable to help herself, her eyes meet mine in the mirror. She smirks. "I guess there's no reason to wear a skirt then."

I smirk back at her. "Are you saying you only wear skirts so that I'll play with that greedy pussy of yours?"

She sucks in a little breath and pushes her hips against the dresser. "Never crossed my mind."

"Uh-huh." I tilt my chin at her. "Why don't you hook your leg on the corner of the dresser so you can relieve the pressure on your clit properly?"

She rolls her eyes. "You're impossible."

"Like the idea doesn't make you wet." I laugh, and it's low and evil in that way that makes her hotter. "Tell me you aren't thinking about how dirty it would be to grind your cunt against the surface while we both watched you in the mirror."

The muscles in her legs tighten and she pushes her hips closer to the dresser. "I'm not."

"Liar."

She licks her lips and looks at me with a mixture of fear and lust.

Perfect.

This is exactly the kind of thing that gets her. I have to admit, I've never been with a girl like Ruby, and I love it.

Because I never wanted to get involved, I'd always picked girls that didn't want anything too deep, that were content with the trappings of dominance without the intent. Like playacting. Before Ruby I hadn't realized how long it had been since I'd really dominated someone. Where I worked at it. Even if I dated the woman for a while I'd kept it light and fun and easy. I wouldn't really push. I was lazy. Doing the bare minimum to keep us both satisfied without establishing the bond that made domination and submission worth it.

With Ruby, I work. Constantly thinking of new ways to torture her. The only thing we are really missing is established rules, but the truth is, I've never been much of a rule guy. The only one I ever cared much about was orgasms and I've been controlling Ruby's pretty much since Valentine's.

She picks up lip-gloss and slicks it over her mouth, her gaze on me. This Ruby is seductive. This Ruby practically begs to be put in her place.

I hood my lids. "What if I said this would be your only chance to come tonight?"

She takes a stuttering breath. "Is that what you're saying?" She's trying to mask it, but she can't hide her desire.

I test her constantly—pushing forward then stepping back—teasing her with the possibilities, the threats, to see her reactions. Sometimes I deliver, sometimes I don't.

If I went over to her, she'd be wet. She might protest, she might resist at first, her pretty cheeks might flush with embarrassment, but if I want it, she'll be riding that dresser.

Tonight, I don't deliver, because it doesn't suit my plans,

which include her coming many, many times. "Not today, but another day the answer will be yes."

She lets out a sigh of what I assume is relief and puts down the tube of makeup she's been holding.

"I have other plans."

Her gaze flies to me, her expression full of questions.

"Open the top drawer on the left."

She does and a gasp escapes her lips.

I laugh. "That's the only reason you're keeping those panties on."

Ruby

I stare into the drawer and swallow hard. A mixture of fear, lust, panic, and excitement all rush through my blood at Mach speed. He's been teasing me, but somehow I hadn't expected this.

I blink. "What's this?" Somehow I'm hoping it's not what I think it is. I've never seen one before in person, but I'm pretty sure I know what it is. But...what exactly is he going to do with it? And what does that have to do with the state of my panties?

Through the mirror I meet his eyes. Of course he's watching me. Gaging my reaction.

A couple of months ago I would have hated this idea. Every day, what I'm capable of, and who I'm becoming is changing because of Chad. If a girlfriend said those words to me, I'd roll my eyes over them and silently judge her for changing for a man.

I didn't get it before, because I always picked guys that were bad for me. Guys that brought me down instead of lifting me up. Guys that let me coast because they wanted to coast too. But Chad is my greatest champion. With him I'm taking risks I never have before and as a result I'm starting to learn who I really am. I've never had acceptance before. I might be changing, but I've never experienced such unconditional support in my life. I love it.

I'm pretty sure I love him.

I'm no longer questioning.

In the mirror he crooks his finger, beckoning me to him. "Bring it here."

His hair is messy; his eyes hot, the sheet low on his hips. I can't believe there was a time I dismissed him as cute but too straightlaced. Clearly I'm an idiot.

I return my attention to the contents of the drawer and run my finger over what's nestled there. I shiver. "What are you going to do with it?"

"You know perfectly well what I'm going to do. Bring the plug here, Ruby."

My throat goes dry. It is exactly what I thought. What I feared. And hoped. I've learned all these things can now go together, and instead of competing, only enhance my arousal.

I blow out a breath and pick it up. It's shaped like a lazy L. It's black, and while it's bigger than Chad's finger, which he uses relentlessly to torment me, it's not huge. Low in my belly it's like lighter fluid is added onto the already raging inferno that is almost a constant ache. Anal sex is not something that ever crossed my mind until two weeks ago. Now, I'm obsessed with it. I'm afraid, but I want it to the point that it preoccupies me.

Of course, that's Chad's fault.

I've learned that's one of his tricks. It's the exact tactic he used to get me to come in the first place. He implants the idea over and over and over again until it's all I think about.

He pushes a finger inside my ass the second before I come.

He calls me at work to tell me he's thinking about how it's going to feel when he slides his cock in my ass the first time.

He rubs his erection along the crease of my ass, teasing me with the tip before gliding away.

The list goes on and on.

I can't lie; it feels good. Like, ridiculously good. Once Ashley told me she'd had anal sex with Trevor and she'd been all giddy and gooey about it. I'd thought she was lying.

I was wrong. It's a forbidden, addictive type of pleasure I can't quite explain.

I owe her an apology.

I turn away from the mirror and look at him, holding the silicone in my hand. "Is this new?"

He laughs. "Of course."

"When did you buy it?"

"Last week." He crooks his finger again. "I've been saving it for tonight."

I bite my lip as the lust leaps in my belly. "What are you going to do with it?"

"You're going to wear it all night." His gaze turns sly and evil. "All night while we talk to our friends, while you walk, dance, and fuck you're going to wear it."

I shake my head. "You can't expect me to walk around with this thing all night."

"But I do."

I want to protest, because I don't really want to wear it, but I can't explain it. I don't even understand it. But there's become a disconnect between my brain and my pussy. It's so confusing. I don't even know how to articulate this constant contradiction between what my brain tells me and my lust demands. I give protest a try. "I don't want to."

He raises a brow. "So I'm not going to find you wet?"

I lower my gaze and sigh. Therein lies the rub. I shrug.

"Let's find out. Come here."

I do, and embarrassingly, I have to work to keep my gait slow instead of sprinting to him like an eager puppy. When I'm at the bed he nods. "Get on all fours."

The statement has desire crashing through me. I climb onto the mattress and assume the position he commanded.

He sits up and palms my hip. "Good girl."

I try not to start panting.

The sheet slips from his body as he rises to a kneeling position at my side. I glimpse his cock, hard and enticing. I lick my lips, recalling the feel of him sliding over my tongue, full in my mouth.

He places one hand on the curve of my back and slides the other down my panties, skimming over the curve of my ass before he strokes along the slick folds. "You don't have a great argument here, girl."

I moan, pushing back into his hand and hiss, "I hate you."

He laughs, all wicked. "I can see that."

I lean down so my head rests on the mattress and close my eyes, losing myself. Without letting up from his light feathery touches, he pulls my underwear down to my knees. Then he moves. The drawer opens and closes. He taps my thigh. "Spread them farther."

I widen my stance. The elastic of my panties cut into my skin in the most delicious way.

Oh god. He's so good. He makes everything about sex fantastic, even when it feels dirty and wrong. He moves, coming up behind me. Then his face is pressed between my legs and he's licking my pussy in the most depraved way.

I let out a startled yelp and start pushing back as his tongue pushes inside me. From behind, this is nothing but a tease. He licks and sucks and probes but doesn't deliver. He just makes me want and need.

"Chad." His name is a gasp. I grip the bed sheets. "Fuck."

I want to turn demanding but I know better. If I do, he'll find other ways to torture me. So I bite my lip and stay quiet, silently urging him.

More. More. More.

Then his mouth is gone. He straightens. I hear rustling and other noises before his fingers settle on the puckered skin of my backside. Slick with lubricant, he circles and teases my opening until I'm a quivering mess.

I have no idea how I've turned into this girl. Her ass high in the air, panting and crazy and moaning like she's in heat, desperation coating her inner thighs. I have no idea how I've transformed from a woman who couldn't even have an orgasm with a man to this needy creature.

Right now, the why doesn't matter. I simply am. And it

feels like home. Like freedom. Exactly where I need to be.

"Please…" My voice is a broken rasp.

"Please what?" His tone is strong and sure.

I admit what I want, cave in to the desire he's cultivated in me, I don't care anymore. "Please, fuck my ass. I'm begging you."

He shifts on the bed until he's at my side instead of behind me, pushes his middle finger inside. I jolt and quiver and cry out.

He slowly pulls out and inserts another and the pressure grows. It's not painful, but it's a stretch. A fraction too much. But it only increases my desire. He grips my chin, cranes my neck toward him and kisses me.

He starts to move, slow, steady and deep. Against my lips he whispers, "I will. As soon as you're ready."

My breath is harsh. Tinged with all the lust and longing I feel. "I'm ready."

"Almost." He kisses me again. "Trust me."

Then his fingers leave my ass and the cool silicone brushes my overheated skin.

I groan as he pushes it inside. Instead of seating the base, he circles it, over and over and it creates the most delicious ache.

"Feels good, doesn't it?"

"Yes." The word is nothing more than a gasp.

He pushes it the rest of the way in then he taps it, hard.

I cry out, jerking forward as sensation vibrates through me.

He laughs. And does it again. And again. Until my vision dims and I'm throwing my hips back to meet his hand.

He fucks me with the plug, alternating between small circles and thrusting. Until I'm a mindless, needy mess.

It stops, and my panties are sliding up my legs. "Time to go."

He's an evil, evil man.

20.

I shoot Chad a death glare.

From across the room where he's talking to Leo and Michael, he winks in response.

I blow out a breath, and increase my scowl. How is a girl supposed to focus with a plug up her ass? How?

Jillian laughs, pulling me away from Chad's magnetic presence.

I turn to see both Jillian and Layla watching me with expectant expressions on their faces.

"Yes?" I'm still close lipped about Chad and me, although my friends obviously know we're dating. That we are a couple. I don't say much about the other...stuff. Maybe because I'm not ready to confront the one thing that remains unspoken. It's coming, I can feel it crackling in the air, but I'm not ready to choose.

"Anything you'd like to tell us?" Jillian's voice is ripe with amusement.

My boyfriend is an evil sexual torturer. I suspect you can relate, but can't work up the courage to talk about it yet. I shake my head.

"Nope."

"Are you sure?" Layla's blue eyes search my face. She's in tight jeans tonight and a black spaghetti-strapped halter-top.

"I'm sure."

Chad doesn't seem inclined to press me on the matter. Doesn't seem interested in pushing me the way I've seen Michael and Leo push even though I know he's got it in him.

Despite how far I've come, I don't think I want that. I don't want to have to ask for a drink, or to dance, or what to wear like I've seen Jillian and Layla do.

My mind drifts to getting ready. Chad did ask me to wear a skirt. But he asked. He didn't demand. I complied. I bite my lip.

Layla's expression twists in exasperation, and she huffs, but doesn't say anything.

Jillian, dressed in an off-the-shoulder, black slouchy dress, presses her lips together.

They look at each other, and something seems to pass between them before their shoulders slump, and they shift their attention back to me.

"Okay," Jillian says, the word light. "You know you can talk to us, right?"

"Of course." A part of me wants to talk to both of them so badly, I just can't figure out the right words to say.

"Are you sure?" Layla puts her hand on my arm. "You can tell us anything. You know that, right?"

"I know." I shrug. "You know everything. I'm with Chad now, what more is there to say?"

A thousand things. Something niggles at the corners of my mind. Is he going to get bored soon? If I don't give him what he needs, eventually he'll have no choice but to walk away, won't he?

"Are you happy?" Layla asks, then darts a glance at the men.

"Don't I seem happy?" Is it not written all over me? I'm in love for the first time in my whole life. It consumes me. Isn't it as obvious as it feels?

She smiles. "I've never seen you happier."

Jillian grins at me. "Or hotter."

I laugh. "So what are you worried about? You like Chad, remember?"

"I love him." Layla tucks a lock of hair behind her ear, glares at I presume Michael, much the same way I glared at Chad before. "You normally tell me a lot more details."

I do. And it's not that I don't want to spill, I just…can't. I do my best to reassure her. "I guess because he's an actual adult there's not much drama."

Only passion. Lust. And debauchery.

Jillian straightens and her expression turns innocent. "They're coming this way."

We all turn to look at them but I barely even notice Michael and Leo. Chad's wearing jeans and a charcoal pullover that's tight across his chest and broad shoulders.

I've been telling myself I think I'm in love with him but that's a lie. I know I am.

For all my past infatuations with angsty rocker boys I've never actually said those words to anyone. I smile at Chad and his gaze roams down my body. I'm wearing a micro mini ripped denim skirt, a white tank that shows a strip of belly, and black, calf-high combat boots.

I look like me. But different somehow. Instead of feeling like I don't match Chad I think we look exactly right. We've blended together somehow. Like I belong to him and him to me.

He sidles up to me, and puts his arm around my waist, his fingers playing along the strip of bare skin. "What are you girls up to?"

"Nothing." We all say together and perfectly in sync.

Three sets of male eyes narrow.

"Layla?" Michael asks, resting a hand on her hip.

"Nothing." She beams at him and he looks at her with grave suspicion.

Leo grins, putting an arm around Jillian's shoulders, pulling her close to kiss her temple. "Are you going to tell us?"

I hold my breath, hoping they won't give up that we were talking about Chad. I mean, sure I adore the guy, but I'm not about to give him that kind of ego stroke.

Jillian smacks a kiss on Leo's lips. "Nope."

He studies her face, looking for I'm not sure what, before he shrugs. "Fair enough."

I breathe a sigh of relief.

One band ends and they take their bows before the lights turn off.

Layla nudges me. "Is Gene next?"

"Yeah."

A few minutes later the lights go on. The stage has a big screen the bands can project images onto and do cool light shows while they play. This is one of the places music execs come to check out the indie scene so the bar has great production for their shows. Gene and his band have been trying to get a gig here for over a year, so this is a huge night for him, and I'm super excited for him.

I love the music scene. With all its vibrancy and life. There's nothing quite like music. It can help you transform, grieve, laugh. It can make you instantly recall a forgotten memory or fall in love. If I could find a career in music, I'd actually be excited about a career. But that's not meant to be.

I'm a good enough singer, better than most probably, but I do that for fun—it's my hobby—I don't have the talent or the relentless drive to sing professionally. I'm okay with that. I made peace with that a long time ago, and I don't love it the way I should to be really successful.

The screen flickers and the album cover I designed flickers on the screen. I smile at the image. It came out pretty good in the end. It was worth all the fussing I'd done. It looked great and most important, Gene and the guys had loved it.

I sense Chad watching me and I turn my face up to his. "What's wrong?"

"Nothing." He peers at me. "Aren't you going to say something?"

"About what?"

He tilts his head. "About your stunning accomplishment sitting front and center for five hundred people to see?"

I laugh and wave a hand. "Don't be silly. It's not about me. It's about the band."

He blows out a breath and shakes his head then turns his attention to the group. "Did you guys know Ruby designed the cover?"

I flush, turning hot with embarrassment.

Layla's expression widens. "Are you serious? Why didn't you say anything?"

I shrug. "It was a favor. It hardly seemed worth the mention."

I want to kill Chad but I don't want to make a scene.

Layla turns back to the screen. "Some favor. It's awesome."

"It's really good," Jillian says, looking at it with a critical eye of the art dealer she's becoming. "Do you do any digital art?"

I shake my head. "It's not art. Sometimes I design covers or logos for bands I like since they don't have a budget for anything."

Layla lets out a little scream. "You did that for free?"

I roll my eyes at her. "Not everything has to be about capitalism, Layla."

She waves a hand at Chad. "Would you please talk some sense into her?"

One brow raises and Chad turns his attention from me, to Layla. "Have you had this discussion before?"

Oh no.

Layla shrieks. "Yes! Although she's been going behind my back on this stuff."

"I am not," I yell before throwing my hands in the air. "It's no big deal. I did a favor for a friend. So what?"

Layla blows out a breath. "The big deal is you're talented and you continue to let people take advantage of that talent."

"I do not. Stop being dramatic." I cross my arms over my chest and turn back to the stage. With gritted teeth I stare at the image, all my previous happiness about the results gone.

Chad grips my arm and looks down at me, a frown on his

face. He turns to the rest of the group. "We'll be back."

Then he starts dragging me away. I glare at him. "What are you doing?"

He doesn't speak, just continues to walk in the direction of the front door until we're outside. He leads me down the sidewalk until we reach a spot that isn't littered with people. I jerk my arm away and point in the direction of the bar. "I don't want to miss him play."

"We have time before it starts." His expression isn't contrite or apologetic, it's angry. What does he have to be angry about? "You're upset. We need to talk it out."

"There's nothing to talk about." I don't want to fight with him about something so trivial. I just want to forget it and go back inside and watch the band and have a good time.

He raises a brow. "Why are you upset?"

"You know why."

"I want you to tell me anyway."

I blow out a breath. "Can't we have a good time? Why do you have to make this a thing?"

"We can have a good time after you tell me what upset you."

I let out a short scream. "Why did you have to go and say something to them?"

He crosses his arms over his chest. "Because my girlfriend did something pretty fucking awesome and I want to brag about it."

I shake my head. "Don't put it that way."

"How would you like me to put it?"

I put a hand on my chest. "Don't make me the unreasonable one."

"You *are* the unreasonable one."

I huff and drag my hands through my hair. "I don't get what the big deal is. So I made a stupid picture. So what?"

He raises his gaze to the sky as though he's just too exasperated for words. "Right here is the big deal. Why do you do that, Ruby?"

"Do what?"

He looks down, pinches the bridge of his nose, and shakes his head. "You know what really pisses me off? I actually believe you have no idea what I'm talking about."

"That's because I don't." I blow out a breath. "Look I get that you and Layla care about me and that makes you want to be my cheerleader. I get it and I appreciate the support. But I promise you it's not necessary. I don't need a sticker that says good job. I don't need a participation ribbon. I did the album because I thought it would be a fun, interesting challenge. Nothing more. Nothing less."

He steps forward, and like lightning he grips my chin and jerks my head up to meet his gaze.

I blink. I've never seen him angry before.

"That's what *you* don't get, Ruby. I'm not saying it to pat you on the head like a good little girl." He shakes me a little. "You're so goddamn talented and you're content to let it rot away because you're too fucking scared to try."

Defensive rage spikes in my blood, turning hot and jagged. "You saw one picture, Chad, don't you think it's a little premature to be talking about me like I'm some sort of genius. You don't know anything about art or graphic design. Trust me, I'm nothing special. You're making it into a huge deal and it's not."

He releases his hold on me. "Do you think I'm paying so little attention?"

I cross my arms protectively around myself. "I don't know what you mean."

"Do you think I don't notice what you're working on when we're sitting on the couch?" He narrows his gaze and leans forward. "Do you think I didn't Google your name and see the other covers you've done. And those are only the ones you've gotten credit for, because I'm positive you didn't insist your name be noted as the designer. I mean, why would you?"

He's right. I never ask. It hardly seems important. I choose to focus on his violation. My hands clench into fists. "How dare you Google me."

"I dare because I know how you are and you sure as hell

wouldn't show me. You'd blow me off and tell me it's nothing. I got curious and I looked."

"Well, so I did a few covers. Nobody cares about me, it's about the band."

"Sometimes I want to throttle you and your stubbornness." He shakes his head and a muscle jumps in his jaw. "Let me ask you this. And if your answer is no, I will drop it. Deal?"

I've been with him long enough to sense a trap and the hairs on the back of my neck raise. "What's the catch?"

"No catch. Just a simple yes-or-no question."

"Fine." The word is a huff.

"Have you had people contact you because they've seen the work you've done for other bands?"

The implication sinks in and my gaze slides away. Besides Gene's, the last three covers I did were because of other work. I shrug. "Yes."

"So is it possible I might have a point?"

"Maybe, but so what?" I look at him, my heart beating fast. "I don't understand why it matters." Because I don't. "What's wrong with having a creative outlet? I like doing it. I want to do it."

"Nothing is wrong with that." He steps close and puts his arms around my waist and pulls me to him. "All I want is for you to glimpse your value and believe it's worth something. I want you to see what I see. What Layla sees."

I lean back. "And charging money will somehow prove that to you?"

"It's not about that. Although you should be paid, because you put your whole fucking heart and soul into it, and deserve to be compensated for that effort." He leans down and kisses me. "But acknowledging you did something pretty cool is a start."

"I'll try."

"You do that."

With that, he seems to relax, but a sense of foreboding creeps over me, leaving me cold.

Afraid.

Chad

I'm nursing a beer, watching Ruby talk to her friend Gene while trying to control the irrational possession beating away at me. I don't like the way the guy's looking at her, smiling at her. I thought he lingered too long when he hugged her. I though his gaze was a little too hungry.

Of course, I'm ninety-nine percent sure this is all made up in my head and even if it's not, Ruby's a big girl. She can handle herself. I've always rolled my eyes at jealous boyfriends, and I'm sure as hell not about to become one of them, even though that's how I feel on the inside.

I'm too enlightened for that.

My mom raised me better. Girl power and all that.

Gene puts an arm around Ruby's waist and hugs her again.

I grit my teeth and signal the bartender for another beer.

Someone taps me on the shoulder and I turn to find Layla looking up at me. She smiles. "Hey."

"Hey." At least I'll have a distraction away from the guy talking to Ruby and how much I don't like it. I don't even understand the emotion. Except that it's wrong. That it says something about me.

Jealousy is weakness. It's a lack of confidence.

So that must mean I don't feel confident about Ruby even though, in theory, she's exactly where I want her.

Layla tilts her head to the side. "You know, I've been thinking."

The bartender hands me the beer and I sit down on the empty stool to focus on Layla. "Oh yeah? That's dangerous."

"Indeed." She sounds so much like Michael right then it can't help but make me smile.

"And what have you been thinking about?" I take a sip and ignore the compulsion to find out what Ruby is up to.

"How life is funny. When we met on that blind date so long

ago it was like I knew you, even though you were a stranger."

I nod. It's true. Even though it was pretty clear she was traumatized at the time, Layla and I had connected that night. Not sexually, but in that instant kinship kind of way. So much so that when I ran into her months after on a fluke it didn't surprise me in the least. "It was like that."

She waves a hand at Ruby. "Maybe she's why."

Given an excuse to drink her in I gaze at her, still talking to Gene, but now the other guys from the band are there too. It's hard to remember back to when I first met her and didn't give her more than a passing glance. It wasn't that I hadn't thought she was smart and interesting and pretty, but more that we came from different, incompatible universes. "Maybe."

She clears her throat. "Did you tell her not to talk to me about you?"

I raise a brow. "Do I really seem like the kind of guy that would do that?"

In fact, I wish Ruby would talk to Layla and Jillian. In my experience women need other women to talk to, to help calm the noise in their head. That Ruby chooses to remain silent about her relationship with me is worrisome.

"No." She shakes her head in the rhythm of the word. "But I don't understand why she won't talk to me. I'm her best friend. I have experience. I know her. Her fears. Her reservations. It has to be overwhelming, and I can help her with that, but she won't open up." She waves a hand in Michael's direction. "But he insists I have to let her come to me."

I'm not surprised Michael's said this; he's a very intuitive guy, almost scarily so. But the request didn't come from me. I shrug. "You'll have to listen to your fiancé, Layla. You know I can't help you with that."

A sly expression crosses over her features. The kind smart, submissive girls are prone to. "He said I couldn't talk to Ruby, he didn't say anything about *you*."

I laugh. She's found the loophole. "I wish I could help you, girl. But this is between Ruby and me. She'll talk to you when she's ready, but I'm not stopping her."

"I know, but I want to make sure she's okay, you know?"

"I know."

"At least I can rest assure that you're a good guy who will finally treat her the way she deserves."

"I do my very best."

"I know you do. I've never seen her so happy."

"I'm glad." And I am, my main priority is keeping Ruby happy.

Layla fingers the silver necklace she wears, a tiny lock around her throat signaling to anyone who knows about that kind of thing, that she's owned and spoken for. In our crowd it speaks as loudly as the ring on her finger.

I wonder if I'll ever put something like that around Ruby's neck.

And just like that it hits me like a two by four.

Why I'm jealous and possessive. Because there's a part of me that feels like she's not really mine. For weeks I've been telling myself I'm cool with the way things are between us. Because everything is so, so good. And it's true, in theory, I've been taking exactly what I want from her almost from the very beginning. I've been slow and careful and methodical. I make sure she craves everything I do to her, and god does she respond, but it's not settled.

I want more.

I don't want to ignore the elephant in the room.

And while I don't need a bunch of rules the way other dominant types might, I do need acknowledgment that I control her. That I'm the one running the show.

Like Layla, I want Ruby to finger the necklace at her throat and know it's there because of me. That she wears it because she chose to belong to me.

I need her acceptance. Her submission. Not by default, as it is now, but because she gave it to me of her own free will. Because it's what she wants and needs as much as I do.

I haven't pushed her, or forced her to talk about it, telling myself it was because she wasn't ready.

But that's bullshit.

I've been lying to myself. I haven't pushed because I'm afraid. Afraid all the time I've spent showing her how submissive she is, and how good it makes her feel, won't matter. That I'll lose her because of this.

She's ready; it's straining at the seams to get out, even if she doesn't see it that way. I've known since I touched her for the first time the confrontation wouldn't be easy. And at the start, I'd been right not to force it. But we're past that now.

It's me—and my fear—that's standing in the way.

That's not a good reason.

I can't keep pretending it doesn't exist. That it's not important to me.

Because it is.

She needs to understand that. If she can't, if she won't accept it, then I can't let either one of us go deeper.

I can't ignore it any longer. Good dominants don't let things slide. It's their responsibility to push. To help their submissive grow and become everything she's meant to be. And I can't do that if Ruby doesn't give me that power over her.

If she doesn't get down on her knees and officially turn it over to me.

I turn back to look at her. My stubborn rocker princess.

Deep in my gut I know the truth. As I've known it all along. I'm in love with a girl that only wants a part of me, and as much as I don't want it to matter, it fucking does.

21.

Ruby

Something is wrong.

We're back at Chad's, but he hasn't attacked me the way he normally does. Hasn't tried to consume me, or driven me crazy, or sexually tortured me. Instead, he's watched me. Intently and with purpose. As though he's waiting for something, only I don't know what it is.

On the ride back home he hadn't teased me at all. He hadn't touched me. He'd been silent.

I'm not used to his silence.

I'm afraid to ask what's wrong.

I'd removed the plug—such exquisite torment at the beginning of the night, now forgotten. I'm in the bathroom not sure I want to face whatever is waiting for me. Earlier, I'd thought all I'd had to be nervous about was Chad's big cock in my ass, but I know now I'm not going to get that lucky.

I'm wearing a black tank top and my batman panties and I want to put something else on but all my clothes are in the bedroom. I bite my lip. It's time to stop stalling.

I take a deep breath and go meet my fate.

When I open the bathroom door, he's waiting for me, as I suspected he would be.

He's sitting on the edge of the bed, his elbows on his knees, fingers laced, and that's not happiness on his face.

Unable to stand it a second longer, I clear my throat. "Are you still mad about before?"

He shakes his head. "No. That's not it, but we need to talk."

Panic rushes through me, turning my stomach, and making me sick. Oh my god, he's breaking up with me. Here I've been falling in love with him and he's breaking up with me.

Hot spikes of fear prickle across my skin. I cannot handle that talk, not from him. I walk over to where a pair of my jeans are draped on the chair and jerk them on over my feet. "It's not necessary. I'll get out of your hair."

I yank the denim over my hips.

"Where do you think you're going?" His words are low and deadly serious.

I zip up and turn to him. "You can spare me *the talk*."

His gaze narrows. "Sit down, Ruby."

"I don't want to do this." I shake my head. "Everyone in the world knows what—we need to talk—means, and I don't want to hear you make a bunch of excuses about ending it."

A muscle ticks in his jaw. "You think I'm ending it?"

"Aren't you? Isn't that what—" I make air quotes, "—the talk means?"

"In my case it means I want to talk to you." He sighs. "I don't know if it will end us or not."

My eyes tear and I blink them away. "Where is this coming from?"

"I'm in love with you." The words are even, almost flat sounding.

Stunned, I sink with a thud into the chair. "You're in love with me?"

He nods. "Aren't you in love with me?"

"Yes."

"Say the words to me. At least once."

I mean them with my whole heart but I stumble over the sentence anyway. "I…I love you."

"I love you too, Ruby." Unlike my own, his voice is rock steady.

This declaration should fill me with elation, but the dread continues to grow like a thorn bush, knotty and painful. I suck in my breath. "I've never said them before."

He smiles. "Me either."

I look down at the floor. "So why do I feel like crap?"

"Probably because of what the I love you means to me." His tone is serious.

Suddenly, I know deep down where this is going. My respite is over. He's not going to let me ignore what he is any longer. I don't want to ask the question but I do. Because it's the adult thing to do, and I've recently discovered being an adult is who I want to be now. I gulp down my fear. "What does it mean to you?"

I meet his gaze and he's studying me intently, fingers still laced tight between his knees. "I don't think I can keep ignoring the elephant in the room." He smiles, gently, almost with resignation. "I want to own you properly."

My heart starts to pound. "What does that mean?"

I'd known this was coming but everything was so good between us I didn't think it would be this soon. I thought I'd have more time. I need more time.

"It means I don't want to pretend the power dynamic between us doesn't exist. It means I want you to acknowledge that you're submissive and I'm dominant. That I have control over you."

My chin starts to tremble. Somehow it seems unfair to me. I've always been upfront about my feelings on that subject. "You've known since the beginning how I feel about that. I don't like it. I don't want that kind of relationship."

"I've known from the beginning what you've told yourself, but that's not the truth."

"Because you don't want it to be." A tear slips down my cheek and I swipe it away. "That's not the same thing."

He laughs, and it's dry and filled with sadness. "What exactly do you think is going on between us, Ruby?"

"We're in a relationship. But you don't control me." He doesn't. He just pushes me a little. And not even hard.

He raises a brow. "Don't I?"

"No!"

"What do you call it?"

Everything inside me wants to back away from this conversation but I force myself to continue even though I want to run away. "You don't make me do anything I don't want to do."

"So when we started seeing each other you wanted to get fucked in the ass, is that it?"

I frown. "Don't twist that around." I point at him. "You made me like that."

A muscle in his jaw jumps. "And how exactly did you think I went about that?"

"Not by dominating me."

"You don't even know what the word means."

"I do too. I've seen it with Layla and Jillian and I'm not going to ask you permission to go to the bathroom."

He rolls his eyes. "You see what you want to see because you don't want to admit you get off on it."

"I don't get off on it." I don't. "I don't want some guy telling me what to do. Why is that so hard to understand? Just because you like it and all of you think it's so awesome doesn't make me wrong."

"You're absolutely right. But here's the problem with that, Ruby. You love me telling you what to do."

I gasp and straighten in my seat. "I do not!"

He taps his temple. "Really think about it. Think back and ask yourself this—when was the last time you had an orgasm that wasn't directed by me? Even from that first night at the engagement party? I told you to come for me and you did. The night of dinner, I told you to call me and you did. From the beginning I have controlled every single aspect of your sexuality and you have loved it. You just won't admit it because you think that domination and submission is about being a 1950s housewife."

Our relationship rushes over me and everything twists and tangles, his words force me to see it in a whole new light. The knowledge overwhelms me.

In a soft voice, he says, "Ruby, the stuff you like, the stuff that gets you off like nothing else, those are the kinds of things submissive girls like. How do you think I've managed to tap into all your hidden twists and kinks so well? Why do you think I'm so good at working you up?"

I start to tremble all over. Is it true? I think of that first night. How I liked when he slapped my breasts and pussy. How I came at work because he called me and told me to. How he's been making me crave for him to take me in the most forbidden way possible. The way he plays with me while talking to people. How I'd come in the cab. How he's made me go from practically anorgasmic to needy and hungry.

Does that make me submissive? But I don't want to be submissive. I want to be empowered and independent.

"Do you think it's a coincidence I'm the one guy you came with?" His voice is soft now.

"So you're saying anyone could have done that?"

He shakes his head. "No, not anyone. Maybe not even most guys or most dominants. But because I have intimate knowledge on how a submissive's brain works I had a head start on knowing what would work with you and what wouldn't."

I can't take it anymore. It's too much. "I don't... I can't... I need to think."

He's silent for a very long time before he nods. "I understand."

My head snaps up. "What, you're not going to push me? Make demands?"

Please say yes, please say yes. A chant. A plea. And yes, I know how fucked up I'm being.

201

He narrows his eyes and his lips twist sardonically. "Try not to think too much about how much you want me to push you right now and maybe you'll be able to keep deluding yourself."

I bolt up and start grabbing belongings, stuffing them into a bag of mine that had been tossed into the corner of the room previously. I shake my head. "I need space."

"Understood."

Don't you even care? I want to scream the words at him, even knowing how unfair they are. Tears blur my vision and I brush them away. When I've filled my bag and given him plenty of time to stop me, I straighten, and without looking at him, say, "I don't think you should come with me to the reunion this weekend."

"Okay."

He's not going to try and talk me out of it. He's not going to stop me. I stare at the door. I'm going to leave and he's going to let it happen.

"You know," he says, his tone soft. "You don't have to leave."

My throat closes tight. "Are you going to stop me?"

"No, I'm not. Those choices always have and always will be yours to make."

I suck in a strangled breath and will myself not to cry. "I'll be in touch."

"I hope so."

And, with that, I flee.

22.

After hours of volatile, twisted thoughts I'd broken down and called Layla. She's sitting on my couch, handing me tissues as I cry uncontrollably, and she rubs my back.

I have no idea how long I've been at it but every time I think I'm done, a new batch of tears crop up and I start all over again. I hiccup, my chest heaving in uncontrollable, gasping sobs.

Layla hasn't asked me what happened, she's just let me have it out and the words tumble from my lips. "I-I... L-love... Him."

She runs a slow circle over my back. "I know you do. Kind of sucks, doesn't it?"

I half laugh, half wail, "Yes! H-h-help me."

More soothing sounds. "Do you want to start by telling me what happened?"

Shoulders shaking, I shred the tissue.

She hands me another.

I take it, twist it in my fingers, and manage to gulp out through forced puffs of air. "He...wants..." I wave my hand.

"You know."

"You'll have to be more specific." Her voice is soft.

It's a few more minutes before I can speak. "He wants what you and Michael have."

She tilts her head. "You mean it hasn't been?"

I shake my head.

"Really?" Her brow furrows. "Because I was sure."

"No!" I shake my head again more vehemently. "You know I don't like that."

She stares at me, her expression scrutinizing, before realization dawns. "That explains it."

"Explains what?"

She sighs. "I couldn't figure out why you weren't talking to me about what you were going through emotionally, but now I see."

"See what?"

She bites her lip. "Remember, that first date you had with Chad… I told you how he was. And, well, guys like that don't want to hide it."

"I told you it wasn't like that." I sniff.

"But it is." Layla looks away and then looks back again. "It's exactly like that."

"How can you say that? You don't even know!"

"I know because it's obvious."

"How can it be when we've never spoken about it?"

A smile curves the corners of her lips. "Let me ask you this, when's the last time you wore panties out?"

My cheeks instantly heat and I look down at the floor.

"My point is made."

And suddenly, just like that, I stop fighting it. Stop fighting myself. Stop fighting the truth of my relationship with Chad. Stop pretending all of this isn't me. I close my eyes and give up the ghost as my momma used to say. All the questions and confusion bubbles to the surface, but instead of denying it, instead of avoiding, I accept.

The tightness in my chest eases, my lashes flutter open, and I peer at Layla. "So…is that like a thing?"

"Yes, that's a thing. In my experience no panties is both pathological and universal among dominants." She laughs, soft and tinkling. "It's like they are offended by their very existence. Unless, of course, they can be used against you."

My mind fills with last night...the only reason I wore panties. When exactly had I stopped questioning him on the state of my underwear?

I find I can't remember. It seemed gradual. I gulp. Natural.

I clear my throat. "What else is a thing?"

She relaxes into the futon and tucks her feet under her. Even wearing yoga pants and a gray T-shirt, her hair in a ponytail, the furniture looks wrong on her. Something belonging in our past. My past.

I blink as it dawns on me. I want a new couch. I want a proper bed.

I want a life. Not a dorm room. The realizations coming so quickly they are threatening to overwhelm me. I blow out a deep breath.

She shrugs her shoulder. "Orgasms are definitely a thing."

"How?" Curious at how closely her reality mimics my own.

"I suppose only the degree depends. I only have observational experience, my experience and Jillian's to go by. Jillian's the only person I've ever talked to in any depth. John wanted control of them, but only during sex. Michael basically wants me to ask permission. Leo is the most hardcore. Jillian has to ask before she can even touch." She laughs, and her expression is radiant and flushed with pleasure. "And you can be sure he makes it hard for her to resist asking."

I shift, and cross my legs, letting all the questions I've been dying to ask come to the surface. "I don't really understand the difference between Michael and Leo."

A little pink stains her cheeks. "I can touch myself whenever I want to. I can work myself into a frenzy, but at the end of the day, if I want an orgasm, I need to ask for it. Jillian doesn't have that luxury. Anything to do with sex requires Leo's permission."

My brow furrows. Have I been asking permission without

realizing it? I didn't think so, but to Chad's point, I didn't remember the last time I'd had an orgasm that didn't involve his direction. I'd merely chosen not to think about it that way. "And you want that?"

"God yes." There's no conflict in her voice, no resentment or anger.

"Can you tell me why?"

"Because it's a privilege." She picks a piece of lint off her black pants. "It means he cares about you. He gives a shit. That he thinks you're worth the effort."

I shake my head, the confusion still not lifting. "But aren't you the one putting in all the effort?"

Layla laughs. "No, silly! You don't think being dominant is hard work? It requires patience, understanding, self-discipline, and delayed gratification. And, because we're little brats, consistency."

I think of all the weeks Chad spent on me—kissing me, touching me, understanding me, talking to me. How steady he'd been in the face of all my fears. His unrelenting patience as he listened to me insist I'd never orgasm. His understanding as I talked about my childhood, the pressure, the rebellion and the wrath of God. Selfishly, I'd been so wrapped up in my own head, fighting my own emotions so hard I hadn't thought about the work he had to put into that. Into me.

He'd been an anchor in my tumultuous storm.

She smiles. "I can see you thinking."

I bite my lower lip. "I never thought of it like that."

"It takes a while to figure it all out." She touches my arm. "But you have me and you have Jillian to walk you through it."

"And you really don't mind asking Michael if you can dance?"

Her expression goes completely blank. "What are you talking about?"

"On Valentine's, you and Jillian asked if you could dance."

She giggles. "Oh that…that was just for a special occasion. When you go to parties like that you become a bit more of an exaggerated version of yourself. Yes, there are some rules, but not tons—just enough to establish that he's the boss and I'm not. Just enough to remind me of his control and why it's so hot and why I want it."

"What are your rules?" I twist the tissue around my finger. "If you don't mind me asking."

"Not at all." She taps her finger on her chin. "Well, I already told you the orgasm one. Anytime we go out he gets final say on my outfit, underwear and any other accessories he's decided to torture me with that day."

My mind flashes to the black plug, the way it moved when I walked, the way it made me wet.

"I can see you have at least a passing knowledge of that one." She winks and her expression is ripe with amusement. "Where was I? Oh…okay. Any direct order has to be obeyed unless I have a damn good reason and lastly I have to answer any question about my feelings directly and honestly." She waves a hand. "And that's it."

That doesn't sound too terrible actually. And to Chad's point, how far off is it from what I've been experiencing with him? Yesterday, when he'd talked about me rubbing against the dresser, the thought had both excited and embarrassed me in equal measure. If he'd pressed, wouldn't I have done it? Liked it? I remember all the times I'd been with him where a moment would come and I'd lose myself, and the whole dirty wrongness took over.

I blow out a deep breath. "I have a lot to think about."

"You do." She smiles.

I tuck my hair behind my ear. "I need to tell you something."

"Anything."

It's time I admit to her what's been going on with me, even though she won't be happy. "I owe you an apology."

Her brows rise in surprise. "For what?"

I clear my throat. "I've been feeling jealous of you. I know it's petty and wrong of me but I've been out of sorts for a while and didn't want to talk to you because I felt stupid."

She glares and me a runs a hand through her ponytail.

JENNIFER DAWSON

"Why on earth would you feel jealous?"

I shrug. "I think I've just been clinging to the way things used to be. I didn't want to change, and you were going on changing without me. I'm completely awed about how you pulled your life together, you've been through so much, and I couldn't even manage to date a good guy. But I want you to know, I'm sorry. And I promise I won't put distance between us again."

"I wish I had known. I could have talked you out of being an idiot." Layla hugs me tight.

I squeeze back, feeling a weight lifting off my chest. "I'm better now. It's time to start making changes."

We part and settle back into our respective seats.

I sigh. "It's time to start making a life."

Layla's expression fills with hope. "With Chad?"

I want it. But I need to think too, to process our relationship without his intoxicating presence driving me so crazy. To let go of the past, my preconceived notions, and my judgments about what I should and shouldn't want and figure out what *I* want. "I want to run back to him but I need to be sure. He deserves that from me. I don't doubt how I feel about him, I'm just…scared. Unsure. If I go back, I'm committing to something I'm not sure I ever wanted. You know?"

She nods. "I'm not sure if this helps or hurts, but I invited you on Valentine's Day because I wanted you to see. I've felt for a long time that your questions were…telling."

My brow furrows. "I'm not sure I understand."

She shrugs. "Sometimes the things we fear the most are the things we need the most. When I first met Michael I rejected and fought our attraction more than I ever fought anything in my whole life. I wanted nothing to do with him and told him that over and over again."

"I'd forgotten." Because I had, I only see her as she is now, as they are now. I forgot about their tumultuous beginnings.

"He didn't believe me." She smiles, her gaze far off and distant as though she's remembering something fond. "And I don't believe you."

208

I don't know what to believe about myself anymore. I take a deep breath. "I'll think about it."

"Good. What are you going to do now?"

"I'm going to go home to visit my family, just without Chad as I'd planned."

"We'll miss you at the art show Saturday."

I tuck my hair behind my ear. "Make sure Chad goes, okay? So he can get out of the house."

"I'll try. But tell me some of your worries. Maybe I can help."

I sigh. My worries seem long and fraught with peril, so I focus on the least daunting. "Don't you ever feel stifled?"

She tilts her head and her ponytail swings. It's all shiny again, lush and healthy. Gone is that gaunt, haunted girl. She's the woman she used to be and more. So much more. "No. I feel free."

23.

Chad

"Come on, let's go." Michael and Leo are standing at my door wearing their cop expressions.

I'm in a shit mood and don't want to go anywhere. It's been twenty-four hours. I didn't think she'd last this long and I've begun to doubt my hold on her. I rake a hand through my hair. "I guess you heard."

Michael and Leo glance at each other then both nod at me.

Michael takes keys out of the pocket of his jeans. "Come on, we're going to Brandon's."

I cringe. The last thing I need is memories of the first night with Ruby that started us down this miserable fucking road. "I'm not in the mood for that place." I wave my hand. "It's too... Shiny."

Leo laughs. "Oh, we're not going there. We're going old school."

I roll my eyes. They want to go to Brandon's underground club. It's seedy and dark and filled with all sorts of depravity.

"I'm not going to a sex club. In fact, I'm not going anywhere. I don't need a girls' night out."

"Whatever," Leo says, then juts his chin over his shoulder. "Let's go."

I open my mouth to protest but Michael says, "We're getting drunk and we're not taking no for an answer."

"What are you going to do, spank me?" The words are filled with sarcasm.

Leo laughs. "If we have to."

"Like I'd let you."

Michael raises a brow. "Someone sounds like a bratty sub."

"Fuck you." The urge to chuckle is sneaking through my misery.

"We're not taking no for an answer." Leo crosses his arms over his chest.

I sigh. What's the harm? Do I really want to sit here all night wallowing? "Fine. But I'm not going to like it."

Michael and Leo stare at me, lips quirked.

"Fair enough," Michael says.

I'm about to spout off something equally petulant, but at the last minute I lose steam and my shoulders slump. "Is she gone?"

Michael nods. "She went home."

To the reunion. I'm supposed to be with her right now. Holding her hand. Making her laugh. Fucking her senseless. I'd planned all sorts of kinky shit that would feed right into her particular sense of perversity. But I'm not doing any of that. I swallow hard. "I don't think she's going to come around."

Stupid family and all that patriarchal bullshit she grew up with is fucking up my future. Her future.

"I don't know." Michael's keys jingle in his hands. "Layla has hope and she'd know."

"I'm not wrong about her." My voice is stubborn and defiant.

"Nobody thinks you're wrong," Leo says.

"We'll hash it out over liquor." Michael points at the car. "Let's go."

Hashing it out will solve nothing, but there's really nothing I can do except get drunk and pass out.

At least that way I can forget. For a while.

Until I feel for her in my sleep and find her gone.

Ruby

It's weird being home, staying in my childhood bedroom, under my parents' roof. The reunion is underway and the backyard is filled with every relative in my family tree. I'm on the grass, on a blanket playing with my blonde three-year-old niece.

She picks up a plastic teacup and saucer and hands it to me. "We're going to have a tea party."

I smile and take the offered cup. "How lovely. And what kind of tea will you be serving today."

She giggles, picks up her teapot, and tips it into my cup to pour her imaginary beverage. "It's purple."

"Well, of course it is, darling." My voice is exaggerated posh. I take a sip. "This is divine."

Lydia mimics my expression, holds out her pinky, and says in a miniature adult voice, "So lovely."

"She loves you." My sister, Alissa, sits down next me. She looks pretty in a yellow sundress, her face barely touched with makeup, her hair a light shade of brown.

"Crisscross applesauce, Momma," Lydia says, pointing to her mom's legs.

I laugh, glancing at her skirt. "Good luck with that."

I turn my face up to the sun. With my skin tone I have to wear SPF 5000 to avoid getting burned because I don't tan at all, but I love the warmth of it on my skin. Even though I look like a vampire.

I miss Chad. I wish he were here with me. Wish he sat here watching me, that fond, amused expression on his face. I'd never really thought a man would look at me like that. I'd always assumed I lacked the gene that inspired devotion. I was wrong. Am I willing to give that up because of some promise I'd made to myself?

"Aunt Ruby." Lydia's voice rips me from my thoughts and my eyes flip open. She hands me a plate. "Have some cake. I made it myself."

There's a small half-inch blob on my plate. I look questioning at my sister.

She winks. "Easy-Bake Oven."

"Ahhh…" I put the crumbly morsel with a hint of chocolate in my mouth and say in my best English accent, "Delicious, dear girl. Where can I find the recipe?"

Lydia giggles and jumps up, pointing. "Daddy's getting ready for the treasure hunt."

Then she takes off running, leaving me along with Alissa. I turn to her. "How's things?"

"Good," she says, tilting her head. "I'm glad you came. Mom would have been disappointed if you didn't."

I'm the black sheep in my family, but they still love me. I don't begrudge them their different life. And I don't think they begrudge me mine. It's not even their fault I warped it in my head. I look at my older sister, so different from me, and I realize I don't really know her. And, I think I want to change that. "What have you been doing with yourself?"

"Oh, you know, the kids take up a lot of time. I'm head of the PTA, and volunteer coordinator at the church. I keep busy." She smiles, and I see it falter at the edges, waiting for me to judge her. "I'm sure it sounds pretty boring to you."

I don't want to be that person anymore. I've always had an adversarial relationship with religion—feeling judged and found lacking—but really, was I any different? Dismissing others because they didn't want the same things as me. I shake my head. "No it doesn't. You're happy doing what you love best and that's something to be envied."

Because it is. Most of us aren't doing anything we love. I sure as hell hadn't been.

Alissa's face lights up. "Thank you."

"I mean it." I put my hand on her knee and squeeze. "You're a good sister and I'm lucky to have you."

She laughs. "All right, what's gotten into you?"

A million things. Chad. That adult that's been living inside me, waiting to get out, while I'd been busy resisting. I shrug. "I've been doing a lot of thinking lately and I want to be a better sister and daughter."

"I'd like that. Not that you haven't been a good sister, just that I hardly know anything about your life, and as I get older, family becomes more important to me."

I pick up a blade of grass and twist it around my finger, remembering growing up and making them into reeds as we marched around the yard. I glance at my sister. "I met someone."

Her eyes turn wary, but she works hard to keep her expression impassive. "Really?"

I laugh. "You'd like him. He's not my normal type at all."

"Hmmm…" She gives me a sly once over. "What's his name?"

"Chad. He's got a job and everything." I lean over and say in a conspiratorial whisper, "Don't tell Mom, but he's an IT manager and he owns property." I lower my voice even more. "He wears khakis." I don't mention he looks like sin in them.

My sister howls with laughter and slaps my knee. "Your dirty little secret is safe with me."

Later that evening I'm alone with my mom in the kitchen and the house is quiet. We're drinking coffee and I've eaten about twenty-five chocolate chip cookies.

I glance at my mom. My whole life people told me I looked like her, and even though her hair is salt-and-pepper now, her skin is still pale and beautiful. She has this otherworldly quality to her I've always felt I lacked. Maybe it's her peace—such a contrast to my restlessness—that makes it so.

I think about the conversation I had with Chad when he'd asked if I'd ever talked to her about the past. I'd said no then, but I intend to rectify that now. I decide to be honest. "I met someone."

"Of course you did, dear."

My brows rise. "You know?"

"A mother always knows." She folds her napkin in a neat little square. "And where is your young man?"

I bite my lip. "I needed to think."

She waves a hand. "You and your thinking. That was always your problem. Too much thinking."

"I love him, Mom."

"I'd hope so." She smiles at me. "That's always the best place to start."

"I'm afraid." I might as well admit it. One of the many things Chad has taught me is the value of not keeping everything so bottled up all the time, turning me into a pressure cooker.

"Of what?" She narrows his eyes. "Is he bad to you?"

"God no, he treats me like…I'm some sort of precious object." I frown. He does. Like I'm rare. Special. Like I belong. To him.

"Then what are you afraid of?" My mom's expression is curious, thoughtful.

"We're very different." Are we? Or is that what I keep telling myself to remain at a distance? To avoid getting too close? "There are things he wants I'm not sure I can give."

"Then you don't love him enough."

The statement is a direct hit to the solar plexus. Defensiveness is like a thorn in my side. "I do."

"No you don't. If it's important, you make it happen." How can she state this so simply? So easily? Like it's black-and-white instead of shades of gray.

I lay my palm on my heart. "Why do I have to be the one giving up though?"

Calm as can be, she takes a sip of coffee. "You don't, all I'm suggesting is that if you don't want to make the sacrifice, then he's probably not the man for you."

This stumps me. Scares me. And I realize the truth, right here, right now. More than anything I want Chad to be the one for me. I clear my throat and ask the questions I've always assumed I had the answers to. "Do you regret giving up your career to marry Dad?"

Her expression is blank, as though she didn't know what I was talking about. "What makes you think I gave it up?"

"Didn't you?" Under the table, I stretch out my legs. I'm in shorts and a tank top my dad deemed immodest, but he laughed when he said it so I didn't take him too seriously.

"You know the story of how we met."

"Yes, you were a talented violinist, and you gave it up when you met Dad."

"Where do you get these ideas, child?" She raises her eyes to the heavens. "God always gives you a challenge."

I'd be offended but she actually says that to all of us kids— just for different reasons.

I grin. "Well, if he didn't, think how bored you'd be."

She chuckles. "True. But to answer your question, I didn't give anything up." She gets a sly look on her face. "In fact, he was willing to give it up for me."

Now this is brand-new information. "Really?"

"Really." She winks at me. "When we met, I was a bit wild and rebellious, full of colorful ideas. As most young people believe about their time in history, it was the start of a revolution, and we were all ready to set the world on fire."

Fascinated I lean forward.

"Truth be told, with your father being a minister and all we created a more—" She clears her throat. "Watered-down version of how we met for polite company. The true story isn't the kind of thing you tell your kids, so that's the version we told you too. You're not as prissy as the rest of them, so if you'd like to hear the truth, I'll tell you."

I'm floored and I say in an impassioned voice, "I would *love* to hear the true story."

She points a finger at me. "You have to promise me that

you will never ever tell your father I told you. You also can't tell your brother and sister."

"I promise." I will die if I don't hear this story. I zip my lips and throw away the key.

She, glances at my dad watching the History channel in the family room, before leaning in to whisper, "Well, I was quite a looker in those days, and so was your father. Yes, I was playing in a very respectable venue at the time, but that's not really where we met. We met in this scandalous club. I was playing a mean violin to 'Devil went Down to Georgia' when I saw him, staring right at me. We had some sort of mad, instant, crazy chemistry, and I played four more songs just for him. Did you ever stop to wonder why we grew up in my hometown instead of his?"

I shake my head. "I just assumed it was because grandma and grandpa died before we were born."

"That's part of it. But your father was a bit of a troublemaker in his youth before he got the call." She glances toward the door where my dad sits and continues softly. "The story is that mothers locked their doors when he walked down the street."

"Daddy?" I can't keep the shock out of my voice. Yes, my father is a handsome man, but he's like a lamb. Docile and sweet. Harmless.

"Yep." She laughs.

My father instantly perks up, turning to call out, "What are you laughing about in there, woman?"

For the first time, I really listen, move past my judgments, and hear the affection in his tone. I'd always thought when he called my mom woman he'd used it as a way to put her in her place, but now I hear it for what it is—an endearment.

"Nothing, dear," she says, a sassy smile on her face.

He turns back to the television and my mom continues. "He'd already reformed his wild ways by then, and it's true he was already studying theology, and had plans to be a minister. But our proper courtship is a bit exaggerated." She snickers and her cheeks turn a pretty pink. "Unless you include sex in the storage room thirty minutes after we met proper."

In shock, my mouth drops open. "Mother!"

She gives me a pure, angelic innocent smile. "I love how each generation believes they alone discovered the one-night stand."

"I can't believe you." My tone is as flabbergasted as I feel. How is this even possible?

"I'm afraid to admit I'm including the time I played in that thirty minutes." She giggles again.

Again my father turns to face her. "What are you up to?"

I hope I'm not gaping at him like a fish out of water. I don't think one can appreciate the shock of finding out your parents were not who you thought they were. That you did not spring onto this planet through immaculate conception.

"I told you, nothing." She calmly takes a sip of her coffee.

"It's something," he says.

"Go back to your program and let me talk to my daughter."

He looks back and forth between us and I do my very best to look innocent, until he finally turns back to the television.

My mom straightens, all proper in her chair, cup in hand. "I'll spare you the gory details, but I'd never been with a man who knew where the clitoris was. That wasn't talked about then."

"God! Yuck!" My cheeks flame red and I cover my ears. "We don't talk about it with our moms now!"

"Don't take the Lord's name in vain, dear." She harrumphs. "All I'm trying to say is it was quite good."

Deliver me from this sharing. I both equally love and hate everything about this story. "I get the picture."

"Well, we agreed we had no future, I was off to Europe and he needed to go back to his studies. But we couldn't stay away so we spent the week in bed, trying desperately to get sick of each other."

My mother and my father. The two most pure, devout people on the planet had spent an entire week trying to essentially screw each other out of their systems. How has this happened? How can I ever look my dad in the eye again?

A shadow crosses over her face. "The day came and we were forced to say goodbye. His studies were over and I was set to go to London. It was the worst day of my life. In between all our…" She smiles. "Craziness, we talked for hours and hours. He'd gone from a stranger to the person who knew me better than anyone in the world. Thinking I'd never see him again was the most miserable time in my life. He stayed away for two whole weeks and showed up two nights before I was to leave for Europe. He said he couldn't live without me. That'd he'd follow me anywhere. That he loved me. I said yes and that night we planned for him to come with me. I was going to let him do it, give it all up for me. But the next day I went with him to church where he was a guest speaker and once I saw him, I couldn't let him do it. His calling to God was too important to sacrifice for me. I'd always loved music, but I never planned on doing it forever. I'd always dreamed of a family. I was talented, but I'd already gone as far as I was going to go. In the end, I loved him more, and he made me happier than playing violin in the orchestra. So we struck a bargain. I'd make an honest man of him, but I wanted to live in my hometown. I promised to be a good minister's wife, and upstanding pillar of the community, as long as he stayed wild where it counted. We've kept our promises and I have never regretted a single second with that man. I truly believe if we'd parted, I'd be out there, alone and unhappy, longing for my missing half."

I blink. My parents are a love story. Not a tragedy. I cover her hand. "Thank you for telling me."

"You're welcome." She smiles. "My motherly instincts thought you needed to hear it."

"I did." I ask the other question, but with a different understanding now. "You like taking care of him, don't you?"

She beams, and her whole face lights up, knocking ten years off her in an instant. "I know it's old-fashioned but I do. Over the years I've learned I'm a nurturer at heart."

I squeeze her fingers. "I wouldn't have it any other way."

"Good." She gets up and kisses me on the cheek. "Go to

bed and sleep tight, baby girl."

I nod and my throat goes tight. I meet her gaze. "I'm sorry, but I'm going to need to go home."

"I know." She hugs me. "You bring him home to us soon, okay?"

"I will." Chad might not be whom I envisioned, but he's mine and he makes me a better person, makes me happier, more complete.

I want my love story.

24.

Chad

I am fucking miserable.

I have no idea why I decided to come to Jillian's art show at the Lair, for the up-and-coming artist, Gaston Lamar, but all I want to do is go home. Of course, because Brandon and Jillian are evil geniuses this is a private party and everyone who was anyone wanted in.

I take a gulp of my scotch, swallow with a hiss, and glance around the room. I don't know much about art but even I have to admit the guy has talent. There is something haunting and beautiful about his art that makes you want to stare into it for hours and watch how it transforms.

Not that I give a shit about that right now.

I swallow the rest of my drink and then I grit my teeth. Ruby's not going to come back.

I can feel it in my bones.

I pinch the bridge of my nose. I have to be okay with that, because eventually I would have grown unhappy. Right or wrong, I need something from Ruby she doesn't want to give me and I can no longer take it on the sly. So even though I'm miserable and suffering, I suppose I can take some stupid fucking solace in doing the right thing.

And I'd kept myself busy. Since I went out with Michael and Leo I realized drunk is better. Tonight I'm well on my way.

Leo walks over to me, eyeing my drink, then me.

I nod. "Hey."

He points to my empty glass. "I got you another."

"Good."

He cracks a grin. "When I stupidly left Jillian, drunk seemed the easiest."

I tilt the glass to capture the last drop before rolling the ice in the glass and wondering when the waitress would come.

"Wanna tell me why you left Ruby when it's clearly not making you happy?" Leo rubs a palm over his jaw.

"I don't need a therapy session, thanks." Where's that fucking drink?

"Fair enough." Leo doesn't seem inclined to press.

With my empty glass I point to where Brandon and Jillian and the artist are talking to a couple in their early forties. "Why aren't you over with your girl?"

He shrugs. "They have it covered and that's not really my thing. Between Brandon and Jillian every piece will get sold and they don't need me as Jillian says—hovering and being scary. So I let them do their thing and stay out of the way."

I laugh, but there's no real humor in the sound. "Does it bother you? That they are so close?" I don't really know where the question comes from but I'm curious. Leo seems completely at ease with his fiancée's relationship with one of his best friends.

Leo shrugs. "At first, but you can't stop fate."

I frown. "They're fate?"

Leo waves in their direction. Brandon and Jillian are standing there, tall and beautiful, one blond, one dark, both in black, clearly captivating the hell out of the couple they are talking to. "Look at them. They are charming and effortless and have perfect rhythm. Together they could sell air. Brandon's also teaching Jillian everything she ever wanted to know about business. Why would I put a stop to something that is so clearly good for her?" He grins at me. "Besides, I'm a cop on a city salary, and Jillian's going to make us rich. It's kind of hard to be upset about it."

I nod and stare down at the melting ice in my glass.

"Brandon and Jillian were destined to be great friends and business partners. I'm destined to be her husband and share every aspect of her life. So I let him see her come sometimes as a consultation prize." Leo chuckles. Jillian has an exhibitionist streak that Leo continuously likes to mess with.

The waitress finally brings us another round. "Brandon said to make them doubles."

Grateful, I take the glass and down a third of it in one gulp, waiting for that moment my head will go numb. When she leaves, I frown and sigh. "You guys are lucky. I hope you appreciate it."

"I do. Every day." He's silent for a bit and we nurse our drinks for a couple minutes before he says, "You don't think it will work out?"

"Nope." I think I'm starting to feel fuzzy, blurry around the edges and I drink more to hurry it along.

"Why's that? You guys are clearly perfect for each other."

I scoff, "In some ways yes." I think of talking to her. Watching movies nobody but us wants to see. Sliding inside her, her tight wet heat enveloping me. I clear my throat and find the alcohol has made my tongue loose. "She doesn't want to be submissive."

Leo shrugs one shoulder. "What she wants and what she is are entirely different things."

I shake my head. "She's got a mental block. I've tried my best to work through it, but I can't keep pretending it's not there."

Leo takes a sip of his drink, catches Jillian's gaze and grins at her. Her whole face lights up and she beams back. Leo turns his attention back to me. "She's submissive, that much is clear.

And in the times I've seen you two interact it's obvious. Her mind might reject it but her body knows. Maybe you need to give her more time."

I blow out a breath. My buzz turning into depression. Maybe I made a mistake. "I want what you guys have. And maybe it's crazy but I can't keep living like it's not important to me."

"Maybe you won't have to."

At his words I furrow my brow and say an astute, "Huh?"

He points at the entrance.

I glance over and the wind gets knocked right out of me.

Leo whistles. "She is not messing around, is she?"

Ruby is standing at the front of the bar, scanning the crowd. She looks…stunning. Gorgeous in a black dress that's cut practically to the navel and is short on her thighs. Her black hair is sleek, curving just a hint at the bottom in a gentle wave, her lips are crimson, and even from across the room her eyes are electric. My grip tightens on my glass as about a hundred male eyes turn to watch her.

Her gaze finds mine and her focus locks in on me.

My tongue is thick and I can't speak.

She starts walking in my direction.

"Good luck with that dress." Leo's voice is amused as he kicks back against the wall, grinning.

Over by the bar, I see Layla and Michael, and they stop what they are doing to watch Ruby's walk across the room.

Everything drains away and all I see is her while the blood rushes in my ears. The time it takes to make her way through the place seems like the movies, when the distance grows instead of shortens, but finally she's standing in front of me.

She gives me a tentative little smile. "Hi."

I still can't seem to make my tongue work.

"You're looking quite fuckable, girl," Leo supplies, oh so helpfully.

I turn to glare at him but before I can even try and find my voice, Ruby grins at him. "Thanks."

She shifts her attention to me and smooths a hand down

the dress. "Do you like it? It's new."

I wave my finger at her cleavage. Ruby is stacked, but unlike a lot of girls built with her body, she doesn't normally put her breasts on display. "It's missing a front."

Yep, these are the first words I manage to say to her.

Leo chuckles. "And it's very appreciated."

"Would you leave?" My voice is slightly slurred and I realize I'm drunker than I thought.

"I don't think so." Leo winks at her. "I'm curious what the lovely Ruby has to say for herself."

Ruby puffs out her bottom lip and actually pouts at me. Pouts.

I blink, trying desperately to focus and failing miserably.

She puts her hands on her hips. "I thought you guys liked putting your property on display. I thought that was like—" she waves a hand, "—a thing."

I can only gape at her and when I fail to form a coherent sentence Leo steps in. "It is absolutely a 'thing'."

She raises a brow at me. "So I'm not wrong?"

"Um…no?" I end the word on a question. I'm so confused, so taken aback I'm at a complete loss.

Leo laughs.

She takes a breath that threatens the confines of her dress before she slowly exhales. She glances at Leo then back at me. "You were right."

"About what?" There, I've said two words.

"My mom is happy." She grins and cocks a hip. "And a bit of a slut."

"Huh?" What is she talking about? I have no earthly idea.

"Really, now?" Leo's beyond cool and collected and seems able to follow her train of thought. "Do tell."

She turns to Leo. "So you probably don't know this but my dad's a minister and my parents are very religious and traditional and I've never really liked it." She winks at him. "It's why I've never been too keen on male patriarchy."

Leo roars with laughter. "Quite a predicament you got yourself into there, girl."

"I know, right?"

Is her voice flirty? Because it sounds flirty. My brain is only capable of base emotion at the moment.

She continues. "Anyway. It turns out I had it all wrong. My parents…" She waves and lowers her voice. "You know."

"Fucked?" Leo chuckles, expression amused.

"Yuck!" She wrinkles her nose. "But yes, about thirty minutes after they laid eyes on each other, and he was willing to give everything up for her. So I was wrong." She rolls her eyes and shrugs. "I guess male patriarchy isn't all bad, *if* you're into that kind of thing."

They both turn to look at me, and I'm still trying to catch up to wherever she's at. When I don't say anything, Leo asks the question for me. "And are you into that kind of thing?"

She gives a little shrug. "Maybe a little."

Leo shakes his head, turns and punches me in the shoulder. "Are you going to pick up any of these things she's throwing your way?"

It finally shakes me from my stupor and the world jerks violently into crystal-clear focus. I straighten, put down my drink and grab her upper arm. "Let's go."

Ruby

Now this is more like it. I was starting to worry.

Chad is dragging me toward the back of the bar, not saying a word, the set of his jaw making me shiver. I wave to Layla, who gives me a thumbs-up sign before I'm yanked down a corridor.

The second I saw him I knew I couldn't live without him. I mean, I knew it for the last couple of days, but this made it sink in. Feel it deep down. Understand how integral he was to me, to my life. How much I need and want him.

Can I live without him? Sure. Do I want to? No, I do not.

Why on earth would I?

Like my mom, if I let him go, I'll spend the rest of my life lonely, looking for my other half. It doesn't matter that he's nothing like I envisioned, because he's better. So. Much. Better.

He pushes me into Brandon's office before he shuts the door with a slam.

I give him a wide-eyed innocent look. "Are you mad?"

The man could barely speak—which isn't too bad on the old ego—so I'm pretty sure he's not mad. But I'm finding this innocent damsel thing kind of fun.

He drags a hand through his hair. "I am trying to figure out what to do with you first."

I nod. "What are your options? Maybe I can help you out."

He stares at me. Unblinking. His expression endearing and confused. Finally he says, "You left."

"I did." I straighten my shoulders. "And it was the right thing to do. I needed to think, and I can't do that with you driving me crazy all the time. I needed to figure out what I wanted. Without your magic fogging my brain. But I'm sorry it hurt you."

He frowns. "You didn't think I could help you?"

"Of course you could help me." I take a step toward him. "But some things you need to figure out for yourself."

His gaze dips, cruising the length of my body.

The first thing I'd done when I got home was go shopping and when I saw this dress I knew it was perfect. It was exactly who I wanted to be. Who I really was. I look like a grown up—as I should, because I'm thirty, it's time to stop living like I'm a college kid. Time to get a life with a bed on a frame and something besides ramen noodles in my cupboard. I'm ready. But the dress still has a bit of an edge to it—which I like, because I still don't want a traditional life.

It's only what I define as traditional that has changed and expanded.

And let's face it, there's nothing traditional about kinky, dominant sex. Assuming that's what Chad's been secretly giving me all along.

A muscle jumps in his jaw. "And what did you figure out?"

"Gene called me while I was away. He said everyone loved the cover work and he wanted me to do some new stuff. I told him I'd love to, but that I would have to send over a price list for the services."

His expression goes wide with surprise and what I think is delight. "Good for you."

"I was nervous." I'd actually shaken a little, proving to myself how much I undervalued my work. How much I didn't want to make it a thing, even though it's important to me. "But he didn't even bat an eye."

"That's because you're worth it."

"So I have to come up with a price list and...stuff." I'm not sure where I'm going to go with this, but somewhere. I can almost touch it—this hazy vision floating through my head— of me, on my own, working for artists in the industry I love, completely independent and on my own terms. I can do it. I have contacts. I know lots of people. I have always believed I had no drive, but I'm pretty sure that's what's been burning a hole in my chest since I talked to Gene.

"I'm proud of you."

Pleasure fills my chest. "There's more."

"Tell me."

"I love you, I know I said it before I left, but I do, in an 'I need this person to be complete' way. I'm never happier than when I'm with you. You make me a better person." I swallow. I believe it, but I still have trouble speaking the words out loud. "I want to be yours. I like that you're all bossy and dominating. I've missed your guiding hand when I was gone. I told my family about you. I was happy to admit to my sister that you had a job, are musically challenged, and wear khakis. My mom is anxious to meet you."

His gaze is intent, his eyes dark.

When he doesn't speak, I continue. "I think I needed to step away to realize there's nothing dismissive or repressive about the way you treat me. That, if anything, being with you empowers me in a way I've never felt before. That I like the feeling." I swallow hard and bite my lip. "I'm assuming none of that will change if we make it official, right?"

"Correct." He clears his throat. "And it goes both ways. You do the same for me."

I smile. "Good. That's what I want."

"We want the same thing."

I step a bit closer and let my gaze dip to his mouth. That mouth I've missed and I want to claim me in the way only he can. "What would you like to see change?"

His gaze heats. "Nothing really. Except for you to acknowledge that when it comes to sex, I'm calling the shots and that you do what I say. We can change and revise as we go. As a couple."

My thighs clench. "And what about orgasms?"

A smile twitches at his lips. "What about them?"

A flush crawls up my neck. I'm learning to embrace and accept, but years of conditioning don't disappear overnight. "Layla mentioned that she can't have them without permission."

He puts his elbows on his knees and laces his fingers. "Is that what you'd like?"

I meet his gaze and answer completely honestly. "I want to know what you want. And then I want to do it."

"What I want?"

"Yes." I suck in a breath. "I want to give you something. To show my…" I falter on the word but keep going. "My submission. But I don't know what you want."

He crooks a finger. "Come here."

I do, and he clasps my hips and pulls me down. My dress stretches, bunches high on my thighs as I straddle him. He brushes his mouth over mine. "That's the sweetest thing you've ever said to me."

I slide against him, and his erection nestles against me and I finally feel like I'm home. Exactly where I am supposed to be. Where I belong. "I mean it. I want you to see. To work for it." I furrow my brow. "Does that make sense? I'm not sure where the idea comes from but it's been there for a while."

"That's how you're wired." He pulls me down and surges up to meet me halfway. "You want to please me."

"I do." My breath kicks up and I put my hands on his shoulders. "So tell me what you want and I'll do it."

His expression clouds, his brow knitting and I realize he's nervous. Scared I'll reject what he wants.

I kiss him, melding my mouth over his, and just before it turns hot and demanding I pull away. "Please tell me."

He nods. "All right, I've never been much of a rules guy, just choosing to wing it as I go along. Rules shouldn't be about the rules themselves, but should add value to the relationship and have meaning, and I think we're still figuring that out. But this is where I want to start."

"You have my undivided attention."

"No orgasms unless I say so."

I have no idea why this thrills me, but it does. It's been on my mind since the moment Layla brought it up. I grin. "Okay."

He narrows his eyes. "I know you want it."

"I do." I'm done pretending I don't.

"I want final decision on your outfits whenever we go out, you can give me choices to pick from."

I pretend to think it over. "That sounds reasonable."

His expression turns cautious. He clears his throat. "There's something I've been wanting but I'm not sure how you'll feel about it."

I trail a path over his jaw. "Try me."

He takes a deep breath and blows it out. "I want you to move in with me."

Surprise has my spine straightening. "You do?"

"I do." He meets my gaze. "I like you in my house. You feel like you belong there and I have hated sleeping without you."

I can see in his face he's waiting for me to reject the idea. I kiss him, soft on the lips. "I feel like you're getting the short end of the deal here."

"I get you. That's all I want."

"I'll move in with you."

"Thank you. We have a lot to talk about."

"We do."

He squeezes my ass. "But all I really want is to take you home and fuck you in the ass."

"Deal." I give no thought to protest. I've wanted it, craved it for so long it feels like a need. "I'm ready. And I'm yours."

"You are." He kisses me, long and deep before pulling me back. "First, I have to take you on this couch. It's a tradition and we're the only couple that hasn't taken advantage of it."

I laugh. "Tradition?"

"The arm is just begging to have your body draped over it." He juts his chin at the end of the rich, leather couch. "I'm going to take you, dig my fingers into your hips as I claim you, and then I'm going to make you scream."

I groan and sink into him, "Yes, please."

25.

The desperate, knife-edge of our lust had been satiated back at Brandon's, and now I'm standing at the edge of Chad's massive bed, trying to figure out if I'm more excited or nervous. I've learned since being with him that they are not mutually exclusive, but I'm not sure which is winning at the moment.

Chad puts his hands on my shoulders and kisses my temple. "Nervous?"

"Yes." I suck in a breath. I'd lost my panties somewhere along the way, as I'm prone to with Chad around, and I can feel the fullness between my legs, my slippery thighs, still wet from where he'd come inside me a couple hours ago. We'd stayed for a bit, long enough to appease our friends, to tease out the anticipation of the night to come.

He skims his hands down my bare arm, and goose bumps break across my skin in his wake. "This is when you start to learn about what submission is. How it's going to look for you."

"How?" I know I want this—what we've been playing at all

along—but now I don't know what it means since it's not hidden away, an off-topic subject we don't discuss.

His palms slide over the curve of my waist, the swell of my hips, before reaching the skin on my thighs. "This is about surrender. Your surrender to me. Giving me what I want, even if you don't like it."

He works his fingers under my dress and dips between my slippery folds. "How your cunt will betray you, because it answers to me, and what I want, not you."

My heart skips a beat and I sink against him as that throbbing need takes over, pounding through me.

He thrusts his fingers inside as his thumb sweeps over my clit. "You like the sound of that, don't you? Your pussy desperate to fulfill my every desire. No matter how twisted."

My breath speeds up—I came so hard over Brandon's couch I feared I'd never come again—but as always, I'm wrong. Chad knows exactly what to say to me, how to work me until I'm crazy. Unthinking. Nothing but a mess of need and desire and soul-sucking, demanding lust.

He pulls out and slaps me full over my swollen flesh. "Answer me."

And God, forgive me, it makes me that much hotter. "Yes."

He roughly grinds the heel of his palm over my pelvic bone, creating a sensation that makes me jolt and bow up to deepen the contact.

"I've never been sadistic." He laughs. Wicked and knowing. "But, Christ, if you don't bring that out in me. There's something about all this pale skin, that needy gasp, and the way you beg for more that makes me want to mark you. Make you feel me on every single inch of your skin the next day."

"Chad." It's my turn to lose my ability to speak. I reach up, twine my fingers through his hair. "Please."

"Please what?"

I'm on the very edge of coming, but somehow he's managing to stave off tipping over. My mind empties and I surrender to the storm he's creating inside me and let it carry me away. Peaceful somehow in its very chaos. "I...please." The words are a pant.

"What do you want?" His voice is gruff, low and deep, filled with all that dominance he's been repressing for my benefit all this time.

"Everything."

He stops.

I want to curse him, but press my lips together. Even before tonight I knew that was a bad idea.

He takes off my dress in one swoop, then presses his palm in the small of my back until I lean forward.

"Spread your legs."

I do without hesitation.

He strikes me, full on the ass, hard enough my vision blurs but I feel it, the gush of heat between my legs. The beast that lives inside me that wants more.

He does it again.

And again.

Harder, faster. It hurts but I'm pushing into him, silently asking for more.

More. More. More.

Abruptly he stops and leans down over my back, his pants rubbing along my fiery skin. He whispers in my ear, "You, and you alone, bring this out in me. I haven't even scratched the surface of what I want to do to you."

"Good." I pant out the word.

He laughs. "Somehow I'd expect nothing less from you, because deep down, Ruby, you are nothing but a greedy little slut, desperate to be used by me."

If he'd been touching me, I would have come.

That's how deeply the words shoot through my body and make me throb.

Of course, he's too smart for that, and his hands are nowhere near any place that tips me over the edge. I grip the comforter, squeezing tight. I shift forward, and suddenly become aware that I can press against the mattress to relieve the ache. I circle my hips, groaning when I find the spot, and without thinking, start grinding away.

"Look at you." His voice is evil and sinister, he grips my hips and jerks me away right as I'm about to go over the edge. "Did I say you could come yet?"

I gulp and gasp for air. He pushes me down on the bed, flips me over then looks down at me, shaking his head. Then he smiles, like a villain in a movie and it thrills something deep and unnamed inside me. "There's nothing pure left, Ruby. You're mine to do with as I please."

In answer, I just spread my legs and hope he'll take it as the surrender I'm intending.

He reaches down, slicks his fingers, pulls my wetness between the crease of my ass, his touch circling over my quivering flesh.

I blink up at him and my voice is full and husky when I speak. "What if I don't like it?"

He shrugs and continues his teasing. He leans down and circles my clit with his tongue.

I bow off the bed, letting out a cry. He raises his head. "You might or you might not, but either way you're going to come your fucking brains out."

I have no idea how that's possible, but Chad has never once not delivered what he's promised and I trust this is no different.

"Don't move." He straightens, walks over to the nightstand and brings out a bottle of lubricant before returning to me.

I stare at him and he smiles. His features gentling. "Trust me, okay."

"I do."

And then cold fingers are circling where I want and fear him most. He meets my gaze and pushes one finger inside. This is something he's been doing for weeks and my body accepts him without protest. "I love you."

"I love you too."

"There's something else I want." He slides two fingers in and with his other hand presses down over my pelvic bone.

To my shock, it sets off a violent wave of pleasure and my

head falls back and rolls, my neck arching as he continues. "Anything."

"Anything?" His voice is amused.

"Yes." I gasp. "Just don't stop."

Another finger slides inside me, and it's full. Impossibly tight and stretched. I'm not sure it feels great, but with him grinding the heel of his hand over my pelvic bone it creates a sensation that blurs my vision. He moves his fingers, at the same time he pushes down and I cry out.

"Play with your nipples." His voice is gruff.

I release my death grip on the comforter and stroke over the aching buds.

"Harder." His tone is all demand now.

I pluck them between my fingers, and combined with all the sensations rioting through my body, I get lost. I roll them, becoming more aggressive as he murmurs, "That's right, girl."

It doesn't take more than a minute before it becomes too much and I yell, "I'm going to come."

"No, you are not." He gentles his touch, slowing everything down. "Not until I'm inside you."

And then he's gone. My hands fall away.

He strips down until he's gloriously naked, takes the bottle, and liberally coats his hand. With hooded lids, he strokes his cock, eyes dark. Intense. His cheekbones in stark relief. He's never looked more gorgeous. More dangerous. And I thank the heavens that someone was smart enough to give him to me.

This man loves me.

Loves me like nobody ever has or ever will. Unconditionally and ruthlessly. Without apology.

He flicks his gaze down my body. "You ready?"

I lick my lips. "Yes."

He climbs onto the bed, adjusting me up and crouching on his haunches between my legs. I go to turn over but he stops me and shakes his head. "No. Face-to-face. So I can watch you."

My brow furrows. I didn't know it could be that way.

"Trust me." He presses my legs farther apart, and lines up,

the head of his cock nestling at my opening, both a promise and a threat. He keeps one hand on his cock and moves the other to my clit, using his thumb to stroke in slow circles.

I nod. Suck in a breath.

"Breathe, girl." He pushes the tiniest bit before he retreats. "I've got you."

I attempt to breathe, unsure what to expect, but trusting him.

He pushes again. Pauses, then retreats. Over and over. Again and again. Until it's nothing but a tease and I find myself straining to get him closer.

His touch between my legs is featherlight. Excruciating. I break out into a sweat.

"Chad." I arch when he retreats again. "Please."

"Soon." His teeth are gritted, the cords on his neck, coiled tight.

He surges forward, only to retreat. Picks up the bottle and trickles lube where we're joined, then starts again.

My muscles quiver. And somehow, even with everything impossibly slow, I'm about to come.

He leans over me, putting his hands on either side of my shoulders. "I'm going to push past your muscles and it's going to hurt, but then it will be over and I'll be in. And you'll be claimed." My core contracts at the word and he bites back a vicious curse. "I can't wait until you come on my cock."

Another clenching and his eyes grow darker than I've ever seen and he pushes completely inside.

It doesn't hurt as much as it's uncomfortable, like pressure, and I'm stretched far too tight. I suck in a breath and he whispers, "I know." But he doesn't stop. He just keeps going. Pushing past my discomfort. Just when I think I can't, he pushes, something releases and the pressure eases.

I slowly exhale and he brushes my hair off my cheek. "You okay?"

I nod. "I think so."

He slowly pulls out and pushes back in and my breath catches on a gasp. I'm not sure what I feel, but it's dark and forbidden, irresistible. He does it again.

"Look at me." His voice is gruff.

I snap my gaze to his.

"You are mine." He thrusts, and then grinds his pelvis over my clit.

"Yes."

"You belong to me."

I nod. My throat grows tight.

He begins to move in earnest, each time making sure he hits the bundle of nerves between my legs. Pushing me closer and closer to an orgasm I thought impossible to achieve.

Although I should know better than to doubt him. He's always right. Always.

His movements pick up speed, and the darkness grows, threatens to consume me.

"I love you, Ruby."

"I love you too." My words are a gasp.

I'm on the precipice of something extraordinary. It builds and coils. I flutter my lashes up at him. "Chad."

"You're a good girl." His thrusts become pounding, punishing, and I can't pretend I don't like it. How can I not? It has all the components that drive me mad with lust. There's something dirty and taboo about liking it. About being this kind of girl.

My nails clutch his back. Drag down his skin as my need increases. "Please."

"You can come." My body clenches. Strains. He leans down and whispers darkly, "But only because I own every fucking part of you."

The orgasm rolls over me, rocking through me, crashing in on me in a pounding blur where all thought ceases and all I can focus on is the pleasure raging through me. My body clenches around him, rippling down his cock and I can feel it—more acutely somehow—greedy and hungry and desperate.

He growls, slams inside me and comes, triggering another intense orgasm, right on top of the last and it goes on...and on...and on...until I collapse into a helpless heap and float mindless and blissful on the orgasm to end all orgasms.

I have no idea how long we drift like that before coming back to reality. I stir, and he raises his head.

He looks down at me, his hair flopping down over his forehead, making him look boyish and angelic instead of the devil he is. He grins. "You did it."

"I did." My eyes sting with tears I don't quite understand.

He kisses me—long and slow and soul deep—before he raises his head. "I'm proud of you."

I beam, my throat tight. And suddenly I get it.

Everything I've been struggling with comes into crystal-clear focus, sharp and defined. I finally understand what all this dominance and submission stuff is all about. The yin and yang. How he fits with me, and how I fit with him. The perfect, beautiful symmetry of it all.

I want to please him. I want to rock his world and give him everything. I want to surrender. He's mine. And I'm his.

That's who I am.

Get a taste of book 1 in the series—CRAVE

Eleven P.M.

Two months. Five days. Twenty-one hours.

It's my new record, although I have no sense of accomplishment. No, I'm resigned as I walk down the dark, deserted alley. The heels of my knee-high, black patent boots click against the cracked concrete in echo of my defeat. The distant sounds of the bass thuds in my ears in time to the heavy beat of my heart.

My own personal staccato of failure.

I'm not sure why it's always a surprise. Maybe because, at first, my conviction is so strong. By now my pattern is long and established—I vow, I crave, I give in.

Rinse. Repeat.

But, like any good addict, I always swear this time is the last.

Of course, I try. My therapist has given me "management tools" to get me through the hard times, and like a good patient, I follow her instructions to a tee—I meditate, do yoga, and write all my crappy feelings in the journal she insists I keep.

Only, it's backfired and become part of the ritual. When the cycle starts, it's a matter of time before I end up here.

I'm sure when John brought me to this underground club the first time, he'd never envisioned I'd be back on my own, wandering through the crowds, looking for my next fix. The club reminds me of him, and I wish I could go somewhere else so I wouldn't be confronted with my betrayal, but I don't have a choice. There aren't ads for places like this. Or maybe there are, and I don't know where to look.

Swift and sudden, anger clogs my throat, and for a split second I hate him for changing me so irrevocably, and leaving me so permanently. Fast on the heels of anger, the guilt wells, so powerful it brings a sting of tears to my eyes. In the pockets of my black trench coat, my nails dig crescents into my palms.

I push away the emotions. Exhaling harshly, my breath fogs the air as I spot a hint of the red door that signals both my refuge and my hell. I hear the muffled hum of music that will crescendo once I'm inside to pump through me like a heartbeat.

My pace quickens along with my pulse.

As much as I hate giving in, I can't deny my relief. Once I step through that door, I don't have to pretend. I don't have to be normal.

The tension, riding me all day, distracting me in meetings, making me wander off in the middle of conversations, ebbs. A twisted excitement slicks my thighs as the bare skin under my skirt tingles.

I haven't bothered with panties. It makes things easier, quicker. Less about getting off and more about taking care of business.

I have on my usual club fare: short, black pleated skirt that leaves a stretch of thigh before my stockings start. A sheer, white silk blouse unbuttoned low enough to show the lace of my red demi-bra. My lips are slicked with crimson and my dark chestnut hair is a tumble of shiny waves down my back.

My outfit is carefully orchestrated. I leave as little to chance as possible.

No leather or latex. I'm not into bondage. Chains and rope do nothing but leave me cold. Once upon a time I loved to be restrained by fingers wrapped tight around my wrists, digging into my skin, but now I can't handle even a hint of being bound.

I reveal plenty of smooth ivory skin, my clue to guys into body modification or knife play to stay away. I like fear, but not that kind. I want my bruises and scars hidden away, not worn like a badge of honor for the world to see.

My wrists and neck are free of jewelry so the Masters don't confuse me with a slave girl. I tried that scene once, thinking all their hard play and intense scenes would focus my restless energy and make me forget, but there is no longer anything submissive about me.

2.

The scream leaves my throat, echoing on the walls of my bedroom, as I start awake. I jerk to a sitting position, sucking in great lungfuls of air. Drenched in sweat, I press my palm to my pounding heart, the beat so rapid it feels as though it might burst from my chest.

I had the dream again. Not *a dream*—dreams are good and full of hope—no, a nightmare. The same nightmare I've had over and over for the last eighteen months. An endless, gut-wrenching loop that fills my sleep and leaves my days unsettled.

I miss good dreams. Miss waking up rejuvenated. But most of all, I miss feeling safe. I'd taken those things for granted and paid the price.

Lesson learned. Too late to change my fate, but learned none the less.

On shaky legs I climb out of bed and pad down the hallway of my one bedroom, Lakeview condo and into the kitchen, my mind still filled with violent images and blood trickling like a lazy river down a concrete crack in the pavement.

I go through my morning ritual, pulling a filter and coffee from the cabinets. Carefully measuring scoops of ground espresso into the basket as tears fill my eyes.

I blink rapidly, hoping to clear the blur, but it doesn't work, and wet tracks slide down my cheeks. But even through my fear, my ever-present grief and guilt, I can feel it. It sits heavy in my bones, familiar and undeniable.

The want.

The need.

The craving that grows stronger each and every day I resist. That the dream does nothing to abate the desire sickens me.

I know what Dr. Sorenson would say: I need to disassociate. That the events of the past and my emotions aren't connected, but she can't possibly understand. Throat clogged, I brush away the tears, and angrily stab the button to start the automatic drip.

My phone rings a short, electronic burst of sound, signaling an incoming text. I'm so grateful for the distraction from my turbulent thoughts I snatch up the device, clutching it tight as though it might run away from me.

I open the text. It's from my boss, Frank Moretti. *CFO is leaving to "pursue other opportunities". Need to meet 1st thing this AM to discuss.*

I sigh in relief. As the communications manager at one of Chicago's boutique software companies, this ensures a crazy day I desperately need. Frank will have me running around like a mad woman. I take a deep breath and wipe away the last of the tears on my face.

Salvation. I won't have time to think. Won't have time to ponder what I'm going to do tonight. I type out my agreement and hit send, hoping against hope I'll be too exhausted this evening to do anything but fall into bed, dreamless.

Too tired to give in to my drug of choice.

ABOUT THE AUTHOR

Jennifer Dawson grew up in the suburbs of Chicago and graduated from DePaul University with a degree in psychology. She met her husband at the public library while they were studying. To this day she still maintains she was NOT checking him out. Now, over twenty years later they're married living in a suburb right outside of Chicago with two awesome kids and a crazy dog.

Despite going through a light FM, poem writing phase in high school, Jennifer never grew up wanting to be a writer (she had more practical aspirations of being an international super spy). Then one day, suffering from boredom and disgruntled with a book she'd been reading, she decided to put pen to paper. The rest, as they say, is history.

These days Jennifer can be found sitting behind her computer writing her next novel, chasing after her kids, keeping an ever watchful eye on her ever growing to-do list, and NOT checking out her husband.

95120553R00152

Made in the USA
Columbia, SC
05 May 2018